POMPEII AT DUSK

Romantic Suspense Among the Ruins

Book 2

Deborah L. Cannon

© Copyright 2019 Deborah Cannon
© Cover design Copyright 2019 Aubrey Cannon

All rights reserved. No part of this publication may be reproduced, stored in a retrieval system, or transmitted, in any form or by any means, electronic, mechanical, photocopying, recording, or otherwise, without the written prior permission of the author, excepting brief quotes used in reviews.

This book is a work of fiction. Names, characters, businesses, organizations, places, events, and incidents either are the product of the author's imagination or are used fictitiously.

ISBN-13: 978-1090932143

Cover design by Aubrey Cannon

FRESCO NIGHTS SAGA

Fresco Nights

Pompeii at Dusk

Midnight in Palmyra

Baghdad before Dawn

What readers are saying about **Fresco Nights:**

"A well thought out mystery with a confident and intelligent main character. She proves on numerous occasions that she is resourceful enough to rescue herself AND the men in her life…very enjoyable to read simply for the character development alone. This is what happens when a truly skillful writer is at work." – James and Gina, Amazon.com review **4-stars**

"Absolutely amazing! Great story. While you can predict some of what is coming, there is enough to keep you guessing. Can't wait to read the next one." - Tammy, Goodreads review **5-stars**

"Excellent! The book was impossible to put down as one was drawn in by the end of the first page. Fresco Nights was recommended by the magazine ARCHAEOLOGY. I enjoyed it very much, would recommend it to everyone who enjoys history or archeology." – Lynn Porter, Goodreads review **5-stars**

To Carolyn Niethammer

CHAPTER
1

A Gorgon's head sat on my desk in the lab aboard the billionaire archaeologist's yacht. Luke claimed she was Medusa, one of three mythological sisters who had snakes for hair. It was quite a fascinating piece, a broken portion of fresco, almost perfect except for some discoloration on one cheek. Was this dried blood? Or was this just my imagination working overtime?

The piece was all the talk aboard the yacht. Where exactly had it come from? One thing was certain: it had not come from the excavation beneath the Church of Santa Maria Assunta where the team currently worked. Yes, Luke preferred his secrets. And, if he was going to keep his secrets then I had one, too. Contrary to what I had told him when he insisted I be his date, it took me *more* than fifteen minutes to change for a fancy dress ball. So sketching the Gorgon's head would have to wait.

I gave the precious fresco to Emily to test. She was our expert on the analysis of artifact residues. Luke wanted the stain identified. Why? I don't know, but he had his reasons. I carefully passed it from my cotton-gloved hands into hers.

"No problem, Lucy. I'll get the results back ASAP— Hey, have fun tonight."

I gave her a wistful smile, peeled off the gloves. "I wish."

"Well, if it helps. I don't think Luke really wants to go either."

I grinned, sent her a limp wave and went to the door. Executive members of the International Council of Museums were meeting in Naples this evening and Luke Trevanian was the guest of honor. He was nervous about the event. Did that account for his distractedness? Why *was* he so anxious? I could think of no reason—except that Arianna Chase, his ex-wife was attending, too.

I left the lab, and walked the few minutes to my room. I checked the time on my smartphone. I should have quit earlier. Really, for someone like me (flat hair and colorless cheeks) it took time to primp for a fancy party.

Every time I entered my room aboard Luke's fancy yacht I felt like I was in sort of a fantasy world. He had given me a suite which included a master bedroom with a king-sized bed, a sitting room and a marble and glass bathroom with a standup shower and a spa-sized soaking tub. The decor was white, grey and black with red pillows (my contribution) arranged stylishly over a thick duvet on the mattress. Sheer, voluminous curtains draped the lozenge-shaped windows that allowed angling sunlight to stream across glossy cherry wood floors. Outside I had my own private deck.

Luke had his own cabin and we only shared a bed when the mood struck. It was a favorite axiom of his that everyone needed his or her own private space. He never tired of reiterating that it gave a person a sense of control. Not that I wanted to be in his bed all the time. It was true. Too much of a good thing could become bad. And while doing the horizontal tango with Luke was great, as far as he was concerned, sleep and sex were separate things.

That idea was new for me. *Me*, museum illustrator Lucy Racine, who before Luke Trevanian had never dated anyone with such an obscene amount of money. So the eccentricity

was odd. But after the fun this room was *mine*.
I wrapped a fluffy white towel around my head as I left the shower, and mopped myself down with another. I escaped the bathroom, steam following into the bedroom. On the bed was my evening gown, a gorgeous shimmering black silk. Cut deep in a V at the neckline to a fitted waist, the fabric in back draped sexily low. On the floor below the bedside were matching black stilettos.
I looked nervously into the shiny mirror of the vanity. My skin was fresh and glamorously backlit by very clever lighting. My wet hair gleamed as I combed it out. I carefully applied my makeup. When my hair was almost dry, I styled it with the blow dryer into soft waves. Ordinarily I hated to fuss like this. I was a pretty casual person (like I said: flat hair and colorless cheeks). However, knowing that Arianna Chase was going to be at this shindig had me hyperventilating big time. I fussed my hair into cooperating before dropping the brush onto the vanity. I daubed on extra blush.

The silk dress slipped fluidly over my bare skin, and I went to the mirror to judge my transformation. Not bad. I had managed to convert myself from grubby artist to cocktail queen in forty minutes. On occasion I had dressed up for museum functions; I had never spent much on clothes. Luke had bought me this dress and now I realized because of the pricking under my arm that I had forgotten to remove the price tag.

"Careful, don't snag it," I muttered, twisting about. This dress cost more than three months of my rent.

Yeah, I still counted pennies. (Okay dollars. Pennies are worth zilch anymore.) Even though I am officially Luke Trevanian's girlfriend... Oh, God, how would Arianna feel about that? I mean being Luke's ex and all, and me being her employee, though I doubt she even knew it. Directors of museums generally had no idea who worked for them.

I flushed involuntarily. I had managed to zip up the dress without snagging the silk. Was I about to break into a sweat and ruin it? Why should I give a hoot what Arianna thought?

It was not like she could fire me. Wait a minute. She *could* fire me. Although on what grounds? That I was dating her ex? I glanced at my phone. I had ten minutes before I was supposed to meet Luke on the helipad and I was still wrestling with the tag in my armpit. We were taking a helicopter from his yacht—which was anchored offshore Positano—to the National Archaeological Museum in Naples.

I stepped over to the floor-length mirrors that covered both sliding doors of my luxurious closet to see if I could get a better view of the irritating tag. The movement of my leg in the sexy stiletto defined my calves nicely. My thoroughly moisturized thigh parted the dress where it slit, revealing a smooth, recently shaved leg.

A girl could get use to this. I sighed. Then I snapped myself out of my daydreaming. Oh crap, what was *with* this wretched tag? I dared not cut it. What if I cut my dress? That would be a fiasco. Not to mention three grand down the drain. Luke's three grand; he'd paid for it. But still money was money.... And I could never throw money down the drain, even if it was someone else's money. Or someone else's drain.

I gave up in frustration. Tearing the tag would be worse. I returned to the bathroom to find a pair of scissors. I was rattling the drawers and cabinetry underneath the marble countertop when I detected a presence behind me. I swung around and saw Luke's bodyguard standing in the open doorway.

"Hey, Lucy."

My heart gave a little flip. We stood and stared at each other. He was dressed in business attire. If it wasn't for the sexy French drawl I could have mistaken his silhouette for Luke.

"I knocked and no one answered," he apologized. "So I came in."

"I thought I locked the door."

"You did."

I smiled, decided not to bother asking how he'd gotten in, and turned back to the bathroom counter. It was his job to be able to pass through locked doors. "I'm sorry. I didn't hear you, Norman. I was looking for a pair of scissors."

His muscled arm came around one side of me, and he pulled a half-opened drawer out and poked a finger inside. "There they are."

"Thanks."

I took the small nail scissors, studied them for a split second, and then extended them to him. They looked incongruously miniscule in his big hand. "Will you please rescue me and cut this price tag off my dress? But please, *please* be careful."

"Sure," he said.

Norman took the scissors from me and I raised my arm. He was standing very close. I could smell his soap or shampoo or something. It was nice, subtle and very, very masculine. I got a grip on myself from the inside and forced my mind to ignore it. He gently slipped his hand underneath and caught the tag. His knuckles brushed my underarm. A thrill went down my side. I held my breath.

"There. Done. Anything else I can do for you?"

"No. Thanks. Is it time to go?"

"It is. Luke's waiting at the helipad."

***

Naples, compared to Positano, is a dump, despite being the third largest city in Italy. All of the ancient and beautiful architecture is there, but it has a neglected feel. Don't get me wrong; there's an air of rustic elegance about it, but it's one of faded splendor. There seems to be a pall of dust over the area, and a sense of lives having been lived in another time, a time of excitement and prosperity, a ghostly feel of centuries gone by which does not exist in upscale Positano, town of the rich and famous where we are currently based. It certainly does not measure up to the wealth and beauty of Rome. But while Rome is very much of the here and now, and exudes modern luxury and the success of a world capital, Naples is 'old world' and has a melancholy charm and magic all its own. Still, from the air and in the dusk it seemed mysterious and even a little dangerous, and that appealed to my sense of adventure. I'd even heard stories of how the city was a nexus for the black market, and that the mafia effectively ran it. So why was ICOM meeting here? All I could think was because it housed one of Italy's national treasures, the Museo Archeologico Nazionale, aka the National Archaeology Museum.

I felt safe enough as part of Luke Trevanian's entourage. The billionaire archaeologist surrounded us with opulence and personal protection. We regularly travelled from his luxury yacht via helicopter, boat or submarine. If we needed to leave the continent fast for any reason, there was always his Lear jet.

We touched down in a private courtyard behind the museum. We entered through a back door. The museum had grand domed ceilings with multiple arches into different connecting galleries. This place housed some of the most important pieces of art in Italy including valuable frescoes and mosaics from Pompeii. Luke drew my hand to his lips. Out of the corner of my eye I caught Norman watching. I felt a pang. Why did that bother me? It was his *job* to watch.

Luke kissed my hand. He was always nervous at these things. Odd, because his public persona was one of outright confidence, even arrogance. No one, he assured me, was aware of how much he hated the spotlight. He had only ever confided in *me*. "I hate how people's expectations put so much pressure on me," he complained. I found that hard to believe. What about Arianna? He had been married to Arianna Chase for ten years before the divorce, which by the way was far from finalized.

Our heels clicked down the marble hallway. A stout man with an entourage of his own came around the corner to greet us. It was the director of the archaeology museum. Several other guests accompanied him.

"So glad to see you," the director beamed. He was impeccably dressed in an exquisite black suit with crisp white shirt and black tie, which drew away from his lack of height. From the tip of his polished shoes to the top of his manicured head he looked the picture of wealth and breeding. Either they paid museum executives a lot of money or he had a night job on the side. I chuckled.

That remark never left my thoughts. I smiled graciously while Luke leaned forward and received the traditional Italian double kiss on the cheeks.

"*Ciao* Bruno," Luke said. "How are you? So nice to see you again." They yammered on in Italian, some words familiar to me, but most of the conversation unintelligible. I did get the feeling that they were catching up on old times. I fidgeted silently and twisted my hair, a long thick lock of which draped over my right shoulder. Then Luke suddenly remembered me. He drew his hand away from the director's arm where he had placed it in a gesture of affability, and laid it on mine. "Where are my manners? Bruno. Let me introduce my friend, Lucy Racine."

Why did I suddenly feel slighted? His *friend?* Is that all I was to him? "Lucy, meet the host of this magnificent palace, and a long-time acquaintance of mine, Signor Bruno D'Agostino." He spread out his hands, dropping mine, to take in the scene.

"*Buonasera, signorina.* Welcome to our fine establishment."

His eyes dropped to take in my gown. I think I met with his approval. Then he clapped a hand on Luke's shoulder and led him into the Atrium where the festivities were taking place. Luke had brought two bodyguards with him, and one now followed behind the dapper and very expensive tuxedo of his boss. Luke was a James Bond type, although his hair was never combed so neatly. That part of him was always rather beach-boyish. Even so, he looked striking no matter what he wore. In dress formal he was Hollywood handsome.

Feeling deflated, I remained standing in the corridor.

And then I noticed someone was still beside me. I turned to see it was Norman.

"Shall we?" he asked, his slight French accent suddenly appearing.

Was it just me? Or was the deep rumble of his voice irresistible? Ordinarily he spoke with the same Americanized intonations as the rest of us. Tonight the French lilt was a little more prominent than usual. In formal situations, Norman Depardieu reverted to his Francophone origins. Some sort of social defense mechanism? Certainly his powerful physique was more than enough to dissuade anyone from overtly slighting him. But the Frenchness gave him a sophistication, which made me believe that at one time he was something other than a bodyguard. Like Luke, Norman possessed dark secrets, but who was I to dig them up?

He was dressed more conservatively than was his habit tonight in a white shirt and dark jacket, and looked impeccably sexy. Curious how almost any man could look attractive in a suit. This was especially true of Norman.

He curved his arm for me to take. I looped mine into his and allowed him to escort me into the gathering.

The size of the Atrium and the volume of guests overwhelmed me. I had a sense of feeling impossibly small. It was the kind of sensation that could only be overcome with a good stiff drink. And I glanced swiftly around for a waiter or a bar.

Norman released my arm and encouraged me to mingle with the guests while he stood by the door with the other security.

It's strange. I have been to many events similar to this, though perhaps without a guest list quite so besieged by VIPs. Usually I was dateless. I might as well be dateless now. Luke had completely forgotten about me. I knew no one among the guests because I rarely travelled in his social or business circles. I was one of the lowly employees, a museum illustrator (albeit the head of my department at the ROM i.e. Royal Ontario Museum), and yet I felt like a

'Nobody' amongst these directors, curators, members of the boards of governors and multi-millionaire and billionaire donors. This particular event was meant for the movers and shakers in the museum world and I was neither. Besides, everyone was speaking Italian, French or German. I even heard a little Mandarin and some Arabic. And though I recognized the cadences of all of these languages, my vocabulary amounted to little more than *Bonjour*, *Grazie*, and *Dankeschön*. My Mandarin was nonexistent. And my Arabic nada. Although to be perfectly honest my French was mucho better than my attempts at any other language, thanks to having been educated in Canada where high school French was required.

I tried mingling. Most of the guests were acquainted with one another or else they were familiar through reputation, *or* they were simply famous from being a staple of the news media. I stepped up to a likely person who, similar to me, appeared to be at a bit of a loss. She smiled when I approached her and introduced herself as Amelia Krakow, an assistant curator from the Moscow Museum of Archaeology. I complimented her gown. She did the same for me and then the conversation turned to rare antiquities. We soon ran out of steam on the subject as I could sense her disinterest. If she was that bored why did she work in a museum at all?

She politely inquired about my job at the ROM. How *did* I manage to stave off the ennui if what I did was sketch objects all day? I frowned. What was this? Polite curiosity? More like mindless chitchat. I tried to explain how my daily routine involved other interesting tasks, including exhibit layouts. Her eyes darted sideways. Talk about a waste of effort. The whole ten minutes of our interaction, her gaze kept flitting beyond my head to see if someone better didn't come along.

Someone did. The pale eyes, which were focused beyond my shoulder suddenly brightened, and her mouth broke into a radiant smile. She excused herself—with me in mid sentence—and dashed off. I stood staring at an empty space with my mouth half open.

What a surprise.

A uniformed waiter approached me with a silver tray and offered up a glass of champagne. I glanced at the multiple flutes and accepted one. "*Grazie*," I mumbled.

As I took a sip, and then another, I realized it was quite a promising vintage, and sideswiped another glass before the waiter could slip away.

"Hullo," someone said to me. His English was heavily accented, but good.

This time I was prepared for the snub. I put on my nonchalant expression. To my surprise the newcomer was polite and civil. He was a man and it amazed me that I had caught his notice at all. Amidst the Armani, Versace, Dior and Vera Wang I hardly stood out. My gown was lovely, yes, but so were the gowns of all of these wealthy patrons of the arts. At least my dress was prettier than Amelia Krakow's. This thought arrived with belated venom. But what was the use in feeling slighted? That's what people did at these events. All I could do was refuse to play that game and turn on the charm.

"My name is Sulla Kharim. I work for the National Museum in Aleppo. Or at least I used to," he said by way of introduction.

He was a small man, not much taller than myself (granted I was wearing stilettoes). He had a slightly balding head and a short dark moustache and beard. He was olive-complexioned and wore a neat but definitely dated suit. His tie was too wide and his collar too large. It was obvious that he seldom dressed in formal attire.

"The National Museum in Aleppo?" I said. My heart skipped a beat. He was from the Middle East, from war-torn Syria. How had he managed to get out of the country in one piece to attend this event? It must seem strange to him to be surrounded by all the opulence of the western world. Then I remembered that at one time, not too long ago, Syria was a crossroads to Asia, Africa and Europe. It was one of the most thriving, heritage-rich countries in the world.

"Lucy Racine," I said, extending a hand and remembering to smile.

He gripped it firmly. Then dropped it. "I know."

He knew?

"You are good friends with Dr. Trevanian, the archaeologist, are you not?"

"Yes."

"I have been wanting to introduce myself, but there are always so many people monopolizing his attention."

Monopolizing? That was an interesting term to use, and very true.

I had tried more than once, myself, to intrude on his socializing without success. He would notice me when he noticed me and not before. That went for anyone else who desired his attention.

"He is a busy man. And very popular," I said as though that would excuse him.

"I understand he is interested in antiquities?"

"He is," I said. "But you will have to speak to him about that yourself. Is there something you wish to sell to him?"

"Actually, it is more...." He hesitated before he continued. "I have a proposition he might be interested in."

My internal alarm bells started ringing. Proposition? I knew quite well that antiquities in the Middle East were ripe for the picking. The Syrian government had its hands full trying to fight the rebel Islamic State. They had no time to worry about ancient monuments and art, and so smuggling of antiquities to purchase firearms was rampant. But here was a lone museum curator who needed our help. I looked around for Luke. He was the focus of several important people, and not one of them was Arianna Chase. Where *was* she anyways?

D'Agostino, the director of the Naples museum, seemed to be anxious. He was snapping at his assistants and asking questions. They were on the phone, and then *he* was on the phone, and I knew something was wrong. I told Sulla Kharim that I would mention his proposition to Luke at my earliest convenience and made to go to Luke's side. Kharim stopped me with a hand on my arm. Abruptly he removed it realizing how inappropriate it was to touch a woman who was not your wife, sister, or daughter. Or your mother. (In his culture it was considered rude, insulting) And even then.... "Please," he said. "I must meet with Dr. Trevanian. It is a matter of life or death."

I stared at him. He *had* to be joking. Nothing in the museum world was a matter of life or death. "Do you have a card?" I asked.

He withdrew a very plain business card from his breast pocket. It was white with a small burgundy-colored logo of the museum in one corner. "Please," he said. "I must see him in private. He *must* meet me tomorrow. Or it will be too late."

"Can you tell me what it's about?" I asked.

"I can tell only *him*."

"Where should he meet you?"

He indicated to me that I should return the business card. He flipped open a pen and scribbled an address on the back of it. It seemed to be a restaurant or coffee shop.

"I'll see that he gets this," I said as he extended it to me.

I shoved the card inside my pearl-beaded evening bag and hurried across the floor. The sense of tension in the room was gaining strength. Despite the fact I paused. What was really bothering the Syrian curator? And why was he so melodramatic? Evasive? I looked back to search for the strange little man. He had vanished.

"What's happened?" I asked Luke.

His companions stopped talking the moment I arrived. It was the perfect moment to interrupt. As he turned to me, the others speculated over the director's peculiar behavior and the lengthy delay. "I'm not sure," Luke said. "Bruno seems extremely agitated. Excuse me, Lucy. I'll go and find out."

Everyone here was a stranger to me. Although they

smiled appreciatively and politely, and gave me the requisite how dos and pleased to meet yous after I'd introduced myself, it was obvious they were only humoring me. There were things on their minds other than entertaining Luke Trevanian's current lover. All gossip as to what could possibly be distressing the director had ceased. I was an outsider. I was not privy to their conjectures.

I spun to face the exit and caught Norman's eye. He had remained in his original watchdog position. His face had become alert. He too detected an anomaly in the situation. According to the program the speeches should already have begun. The director should have introduced Arianna Chase from the Royal Ontario Museum. Her big news was to announce a multi-million dollar endowment made by Luke Trevanian to link the National Archaeology Museum in Naples with the Royal Ontario Museum in Toronto as sister institutions. The cash would enable the two to build a travelling exhibit and tell the comprehensive story of Pompeii. For the first time, the contents of the 'Secret Chamber' would be studied in full, and a selection of artifacts made available for foreign audiences.

Hanging around these people was useless. I still had no information. I sought out Luke in the sea of faces. He had disappeared along with the Italian director. I left the Atrium, went past Norman, into the corridor. The next thing I knew, he was beside me.

"Do you know what's going on, Norman?" I asked.

He shook his head.

I started down the corridor, my long gown swishing against my legs. I scowled. Why had Luke deserted me again? "Where's Arianna? She should be here by now."

"I think maybe that's the problem. She hasn't turned up. It's not like her to be late for an important event. Especially when she's the keynote speaker."

"You mean she hasn't arrived yet?"

"No one has seen her as far as I know."

I guess he *would* know. He was on familiar terms with

Luke's ex. Myself, she was a figurehead who wouldn't remember my name if you asked her. I turned a corner, and said to Norman, "You don't have to stay with me. I'll be okay. Just come and look for me when it's time to go home." It was meant to be a joke.

He laughed. "Seriously. Why should you have to babysit me? I'm an adult woman. I'm okay on my own."

"Luke pays me to be with you," he said.

I darted him a sideways glance and kept walking. I had no idea where I was going. I felt agitated and helpless. I ended up at a gallery that made me stop in my tracks. It was the gallery of erotic art, the secret chamber that had been locked up out of the public view in the 19th century and then reopened in the mid 20th.

A large sign identified it:

THE CHAMBER OF SECRETS

There were dozens of stone penises, phallic wind chimes and oil lamps, and what I could only describe as naughty mosaics. The pièce de résistance was a stone statue of a satyr having sex with a female goat. These were only a tiny sampling of what was hidden in storage. Most of the erotic collection was considered too risqué for the public. But the promise of Luke's generous endowment had convinced the museum that this collection was what people wished to see, and furthermore it would help both museums out of their burning deficits.

I forced myself not to blush. I was a professional after all. I only wished that Norman had not accompanied me when I stumbled across this find.

"I should leave," I said, awkwardly. "Luke might be looking for me."

"Yeah, he might."

I felt stupid but it was a struggle to tear my eyes away from the goat. What a look of naked fondness in her carved eyes, while his—the satyr's—was that of lusty pleasure.

Norman chuckled. "What else could you expect from a satyr?"

I smiled. He had a way of putting me at ease.

"Better get back to the party." I sighed. "I hate these events. I always feel out of place. This is Luke's world and whenever I come to something like this it just shoves home to me that I'm a lame replacement for Arianna Chase."

He was silent for a moment. "He never compares you to her."

"But *I* do."

"You should stop it. She's the past. You're the present."

"I still don't know why he wants me around." I looked into Norman's face. He was a tall, muscular man, and the warmth in his expression contradicted the overt masculinity of his body. "I've asked him, you know. I've asked him why he wants me around. But he never really says."

"What does it matter? He wants you."

And *what do you want?* Why was it so much easier talking to Norman?

I was still nursing my second glass of champagne and found it was empty. Norman took the flute from me and shoved it into his pocket.

"Let's get out of this gallery," he said. Then he stopped. There was a set of silver in a display case that had caught his eye.

"What is it?" I asked.

He looked at me; then directed his stare back at the case.

I saw what had snagged his attention. The silver was arranged like a dinner place setting, as though any minute someone would sit down and pick up a spoon. On either side of the plates and silverware were oil lamps shaped like oversized phalluses. The wine goblet however was merely that—a goblet. This wasn't what had caught his eye. Because now my sight was also fixed on the display.

"Do you recognize anything about that dinner set?" he asked.

My head bobbed up and down. It was identical to the pattern on the smugglers loot that we had recently rescued from a cave in Positano.

And something else.

Should I elaborate on his observation? No. If my brother-in-law was involved in something shady I wanted to learn what it was first.

"That grape motif on the cutlery. I've seen it before."

Roman silver was a common find in archaeological sites. But I knew what he meant and I mustn't draw attention to it right now. I must feign ignorance.

So I giggled. I pointed to the phallus-shaped lamps. Did they make him uncomfortable too? Or did they trigger the giggle button?

I was never to know. He placed his hand on my lower back, just beneath the dripping folds of silk and nudged me back into the corridor. "Come on. Let's go. Luke will be missing you at the gala."

I thought not.

When we returned to the Atrium, Bruno D'Agostina had bad news. The chartered aircraft carrying Arianna Chase from Florence to Naples had crashed in the countryside with all four passengers aboard presumably killed.

CHAPTER
2

The shock on Luke's face disturbed me even more than the announcement had. D'Agostino was flustered as to what he should do. Would it be disrespectful to continue with their evening's entertainment after such a horrible revelation? Should they cut short the event or should they proceed? I went to Luke and looped my hand through his arm.

"You must speak in place of Arianna," I said.

"I can't. What can I say? Oh my God, Lucy. Arianna is dead!"

"Are they sure of that?"

"It's dark now but the plane has been located. It burst into flame on impact and has incinerated most of the bodies. They won't be able to tell if there are any survivors until tomorrow morning when it's light. After that it will just be a matter of identifying the remains—" His voice broke. "—*If* there are any remains left to identify."

I was just grateful that at the last minute my brother-in-law Shaun had bailed on coming to Naples for the ICOM meetings. He was curator of Classical Collections at the Royal Ontario Museum where Luke's ex-wife was the director. He was a member of the International Council of Museums, and he was constantly involving the ROM in foreign concerns. It was he who convinced Arianna to approach Luke about the twin endowments. Had he accompanied Arianna, my pregnant sister would be a widow now....

D'Agostina was looking around desperately. He still stood at the podium after relating the devastating news. "Perhaps we should reschedule?" he said aside to his assistant.

I urged Luke to take the podium. "For Arianna," I said. I know it was asking a lot of him. But he was a strong man. That was one of the things that had attracted me to him in the first place. As he rose to speak to the audience I saw his public persona supersede the private one; and his emotion was firmly reined in. But something bubbled beneath the outward appearance of calm causing my attention to wander off-course. Had Luke really ever gotten over his ex-wife?

We spent the night in Naples and the following morning Luke sent Norman to buy us some street clothes to wear for the next few days. He had no intention of returning to Positano and the dig, until he knew for certain that all that *could* be done concerning the plane crash *was* done.

He contacted the Agenzia Nazionale per las Sicurezza del Volo (National Agency for the Safety of Flight) for details, but they had no more news for him than he could find on social media.

Air Traffic Control had lost contact with the aircraft on the outskirts of the ancient town of Bagnoregio. The old town, known as the Civita di Bagnoregio or just the Civita for short, sits on a steep outcrop of rocky cliff in the middle of a vast green valley and is reached by a long footbridge, hanging high above the ravine and leads to the modern town. It was luck that the pilot had retained the presence of mind to divert his flight path from the populated area of the modern settlement and had crashed the plane into the side of the outcrop in the gorge.

The Civita di Bagnoregio had not been touched, but the few residents reported seeing lights in the sky, then a fireball at the bottom of the gorge. The witnesses were unreliable because the old village was practically deserted except for a few street cafés and restaurants and souvenir shops. And those that resided there were elderly with various vision and hearing issues. During the summer months the small community was usually inundated with tourists, which also brought in workers from the new town, raising the population from ten to almost one hundred. But this summer for some reason the tourists stayed away, serendipitously for the old town, otherwise the bad press might have sealed their fate permanently. Nonetheless, the Civita was pretty much a ghost town.

Luke was warned to stay away from the crash site that night. It was too dark to see. The following morning he was told that, because of the personal nature of his relationship with one of the passengers and the cargo she was carrying, the director of the aircraft investigation could get him special permission to be on site, at earliest, the next day. Meanwhile if he came to their branch office in downtown Naples his identity could be authenticated and papers drawn up for the permit. At that time he would be apprised of whatever updates were available.

"What special cargo was she carrying?" I asked.

He ignored my question. "Do you mind spending the day on your own, Lucy? I need Norman with me for this meeting. I'll be in conference all day. There are so many people I need to get in touch with. I hope you don't mind. But none of it would be any fun for you. We'll meet you back at the hotel, for dinner?"

It wasn't a question. He wasn't asking my permission. He was informing me that I had to find some way to occupy myself in Naples until he was free. Fine. After breakfast we kissed goodbye. "Just don't fly off somewhere without telling me," I teased.

He gave me a weak smile. He was exhausted. None of us had gotten much sleep last night. Norman avoided my gaze.

I had a whole day to explore the city, but what I had

really wanted to do was join Luke in his inquiries. I understand why he thought I'd be bored if I went to this meeting with the aviation authorities. They had very little information, and mostly it would be paperwork, explanations of how the investigation was going to proceed and other bureaucratic red tape that excluded me. If that was the case, why did he want Norman present? Norman was his bodyguard. Surely Luke was perfectly safe on his own in some government minion's office?

I glanced down at the tourist brochures I had in my hand. I had taken these from the hotel. Should I go back to see D'Agostino at the archaeology museum? Maybe he had heard from Arianna just before the flight. Maybe something she had said would provide some insight into the accident. But was it my place to ask questions? He would wonder why I was doing that. My curiosity was personal. I knew Arianna meant a lot more to Luke than he had ever let on.

Luke had cautioned me to keep to the Vomero, that section of the city above the seedier Spanish Quarter, where gentrification came with the territory. In its earlier history, the hilltop that now housed the bourgeois neighborhood of the Vomero (which simply means 'handheld plow') was home to terraced orchards of lemon trees and broccoli fields, overlooking a stunning view. Today all of that is gone, replaced by museums, cathedrals, gardens, parks, and up-market shops, bistros and cafés to service the growing volume of tourists, as well as apartment complexes and a number of hotels. I was dumbstruck by the streetside vistas and the panoramic views of city, bay and volcano as it sprawled beneath the piazza at the end of the Via Tito Angelini. Mount Vesuvius made a spectacular landmark in the background.

I'd had my fill of churches and cathedrals and it seemed most of the brochures were describing either one or the other religious institution. In my left hand I held a flyer advertising something called the *Sotterranea*. It was a historic site situated underground below the Naples old town. I was used to subterranean sites so decided on this. It was a complex labyrinth of chambers, tunnels, cisterns and cavities. The underground aqueducts were used to transport water to the city, as well as transporting sewage away. There was a theater, shrines, burial chambers and road tunnels. I went with a tour and saw the whole thing within an hour and a half. I remembered nothing of what I saw or heard. My mind was pitifully preoccupied. I was worried about Luke and curious as to what had caused the crash. And yes, belatedly, I felt awful about Arianna. She was the director of my museum. What a terrible loss.

The tour ended up at the ubiquitous souvenir shop. I perused the usual items and then settled for a postcard of the underground city to send to my sister Colleen.

As I was digging out the coinage to pay for the postcard something sharp pricked my finger. I withdrew my hand and sucked on my fingertip. No blood, so no real injury. Then I dug further into the bag to see what I had almost skewered myself with. This morning in our hurry to get out of the hotel so that Luke could get on with his inquiries over the plane crash, I had simply reversed my evening bag (from the night before) inside out and into my usual oversized handbag, where I carried everything in one unorganized mess.

My hand searched deeper and I came up with the culprit. It was the business card from the Syrian curator. I cupped a hand to my mouth. Oh dear. I had forgotten all about this. I had neglected to mention it to Luke. Mostly because he was so distraught after hearing about the accident. Why was he so hell bent on being personally involved? What could he do? I supposed if they needed resources to speed up the investigation he could supply those.

I studied the business card. It read:

Sulla Kharim, PhD
Curator of Antiquities
National Museum, Aleppo

I flipped it over and there was the address of a coffeehouse. I fished for my phone and saw that it was almost noon. I could still make it and send Luke's apologies. I'm sure Luke would have contacted the man—if not actually shown up at this meeting—if not for the horrible news of last night.

The place was called the Arx Café. It had a spectacular view of the Castel Sant'Elmo, Mount Vesuvius and the bay area of Naples. The height momentarily set me back when I arrived in the vicinity. I took a deep breath and followed the escalating road uphill. It wasn't a bridge, I reminded myself. I could do this.

I wondered why he had chosen this place. It seemed like a tourist haunt to me. Well, maybe that was the reason.

No one matching the curator's description was there when I entered the café, and walked out to the patio and took a seat where the waiter indicated. I told him I was waiting for someone and ordered a caffe latte from the menu.

A fortified castle-like structure with twin turrets occupied my gaze as I turned to take in the view. Beyond it was the infamous Mount Vesuvius. It was known for its catastrophic eruption in AD 79 and for burying alive the inhabitants of Pompeii. In fact it was considered the most dangerous mountain in the world because of the density of population surrounding it, and because it had a twenty-year cycle of activity. No one knew exactly when it would erupt again. The last time I'd heard was in 1944. That was a long time ago. It was due for another major eruption.

People had become complacent, however, as they always did, when predictions failed to bear fruit. Mount Vesuvius was now a popular tourist haunt. The area around the mountain was made into a national park in the 1990s. There was access by road to within 200 feet of the summit. After that, access was by foot only and there was a spiral walkway around the volcano from the road to the crater. Luke had always talked about visiting the summit. To be honest I had no desire to make the exhausting hike uphill to see the bottom of a crater. Why would anyone want to do that? Oh well... to each his own. I had my own reasons for disdaining mountain climbing. Even if it was only a steep uphill walk. I glanced at the time on my phone. The waiter brought my coffee. I took a sip. The man was late. I was beginning to get restless. Was coming here a mistake? I finished my first latte and ordered another. I would give Dr. Kharim another half-hour and that was it, then I would leave. I was only here as a courtesy anyhow. He had wanted to speak to Luke. He would hardly be expecting me instead. I frowned as the mystery burrowed deeper into my consciousness.

What, I wondered, could possibly be so cryptic that the Syrian curator had to meet Luke in private? I tried to think of what I knew about the country. It was physically small as were most Middle Eastern countries, with around 23 million in population. It bordered Turkey, Iraq, Jordon, Israel and Lebanon and was served by both desert and fertile valleys. And its history reached into biblical times. The war broke out because of a demand for change. It was not a religious war—at first. The long-reigning aristocracy consisted of Islamic moderates, but they had outworn their welcome and the people wanted change. The long promised economic and political reforms had failed to materialize. So began the public protests followed by imprisonments by a brutal regime. The Syrian government cracked down on the rebellion with military force, and the FSA, the Free Syrian Army was born. Local tribal groups, disaffected military and locals formed militias. But to have any chance of winning they needed manpower and weapons. So when the Islamic extremists appeared, they formed a loose coalition until the original rebels lost control to the terrorists.

Pretty soon it all got out of hand and both sides were killing. In the chaos that ensued the very land they loved became a war field and the ancient ruins battlements. Gunfire and bombs rampantly destroyed antiquities until some members of the rebellion realized they could fund the war by selling artifacts. That was when the looting became serious, and priceless objects, frescoes, and broken bits of temples, tombs and shrines were smuggled to unscrupulous dealers in the west. Some local civilians pitched in because it was the only way to earn enough cash to feed and house their families. The militants went full tilt on the looting to pay for guns and munitions.

Was this what Dr. Kharim was involved in?

I almost stood up and fled at the thought of negotiating with a disreputable antiquities dealer. My imagination was sending my heart into a tizzy as I stared over the stone balustrade at a panoramic scene I was no longer seeing.

A shadow dropped over me. I turned my head, looked up and the smallish, olive complexioned man gazed back. He did not look like a dangerous extremist. His eyes were kind. I stuffed the images of my over stimulated imagination to the back of my mind where they belonged.

The waiter gestured to a chair and the man sat down across from me and ordered an espresso. I recognized him instantly because of the dark facial hair and the solemn expression, which today looked more haggard than ever. He was dressed in a casual pants-and-jacket combo, and had omitted the tie.

"Dr. Kharim," I said, semi-rising, and controlling my nerves, and shaking his hand.

"So nice to see you again, Miss Racine."

I noticed as he stretched out his hand that they were neatly manicured, and small for a man's. The other one lay flat on the table where he braced himself and I caught a glimpse of a yellow gold band on his finger. "Please, call me Lucy."

He smiled cautiously. Was he evaluating me as I was evaluating him? It was hard to tell. "I guess you are here to tell me that Dr. Trevanian will not be joining us?"

"No, he can't. There was a terrible accident last night. I'm here to apologize for him. You heard about the plane crash? His ex-wife was aboard that flight. You can understand he has inquiries to make and arrangements—"

Before I could finish explaining, he cut in, "It was *not* an accident."

I stared at him. All of my prior notions concerning his intentions vanished.

He nodded without elaborating.

There could be only one thing he meant. I jumped to the conclusion before he could confirm it. "It *had* to be an accident. Why would anyone deliberately sabotage that plane? There were only four people aboard. One of the other guests for last night's gala, Arianna Chase and her assistant Sherry, and the pilot." I frowned. "Are you telling me, Dr. Kharim, that someone wanted one of those people dead?"

At this point, the waiter returned with our beverages. "*Grazie*," I said. I took a sip before shifting my attention to Kharim. Dr. Kharim left his coffee untouched.

"I warned you." His voice had dropped to a mere whisper. "A matter of life or death."

A chill involuntarily slipped up my spine. How could he know that the plane crash was deliberate unless he was part of the plot? Possible terrorist connections returned to taunt me, to fill my head with fabrications. I had a moment of absolute horror, before I managed to rein in my impending hysterics. "But how could you know?" I asked.

My mind had run foul of all possibilities. Who was this man, really? Why had he approached me last night to warn me of some imminent disaster? If he had known the crash was going to happen why not go to the authorities or tell somebody sooner? He had only warned me of the 'matter of life or death' an hour or so before it actually occurred. I tried to remember what he had said. Something about a proposition for Luke. Something to do with antiquities.

"Where did you disappear to last night?" I demanded. "If you knew something was going to happen, why didn't you warn someone who could do something about it?"

"I had no idea they would crash the plane."

"*They?* Who? Who is 'they'?"

"I wish I could tell you, Miss Racine. But I would be

putting your life in danger with that information."

"Then at least tell me why you just vanished. I looked everywhere for you. You left the gala."

"I had to try to stop them."

"Stop who?" When he refused to answer, I asked, "Where did you go?"

Dr. Kharim shook his head vigorously. "I've told you enough. You must tell Dr. Trevanian to contact me. Eye Sore needs him."

Eye Sore? What was that? Was I even imagining the words correctly? But that's what it sounded like.

"Not until you tell me why."

"I'm sorry, Miss Racine. I cannot. Please give him my card." He wrote five upper case letters onto the back of a duplicate of the card he had given me last night.

I squinted at it. "What is ISORE?" It was either a name or an acronym.

He left some money on the table to pay for our coffees, before rising. "I wish Dr. Trevanian had come instead of you."

So did I. I got up to run after him, but he had woven through the busy café. By the time I reached the door, swung it open and ducked outside, he had vanished.

***

I returned to my table to finish my latte and ponder what had just happened. My eyes moved from the espresso cup, untouched at the other side of the table, to the balustrade and the view beyond. The mountain appeared through the orange haze as nebulous as the comments of Dr. Kharim. He had left all of my questions unanswered.

I had no reason to stay much longer. Staring at Mount Vesuvius was not helping. The scene made me think of the buried city of Pompeii, and that only generated more questions and no answers. What did Pompeii have to do with any of this? Kharim had made no reference to Pompeii, and yet I kept thinking there had to be some connection.

I found my way back to the hotel and met Luke and Norman for dinner. Neither of them felt much like talking, but I did. I was bursting with my news. How to broach the subject? Dr. Sulla Kharim was a strange fellow. Could I trust him? Was he telling me the truth? But the burning question was: Who would want Arianna Chase dead?

I had decided that if any of what he had said were true then the only person whose death might be of value would be hers. The other curator on the flight was a woman from Sweden. She wasn't known for much of anything. The pilot was a pilot; why would anyone want him dead? And Sherry Louie was only an assistant. There would be no motivation for her death either.

We ate in the hotel's bar because we were too tired to go out for a bite. I ordered pasta primavera and bruschetta. Luke ordered a steak with fries and Norman had the braised lamb shank with mashed potatoes. We preceded that with a glass of hearty red house wine. Norman abstained. I wondered if it was because he considered himself on duty.

"Luke, I have something to tell you."

"Can it keep, honey," he said. "I'm really wasted. I desperately just want to hit the sack and get an early start tomorrow. The aviation authority has given me permission to join the search team."

"Did they find any evidence of Arianna?" I asked cautiously.

He shook his head. "Not yet."

Norman noticed that I felt a little out of sorts with Luke's casual dismissal of my enthusiasm. Why was it that Norman could always tell when I had something on my mind, while Luke seemed oblivious? Norman took a long pull on his water glass—he knew it was not his place to mitigate our disputes and usually remained impartial—then asked, "What did you do with yourself today?"

He was giving me the perfect opening. *Thank you.* I seized the opportunity before it could be intercepted. "I met someone at a café."

They both looked up, showing some unexpected interest. "He was the curator from the National Museum in Aleppo."

Was it my imagination? Or did both of them seem to prick up their ears.

"He gave me his card at the gala last night." I turned deliberately to face Luke. "He wanted to meet you."

Luke raised his shoulders tiredly. In direct contradiction to that motion was the distinct spark in his eye, which only served to pique my growing suspicions. "Last night?" he inquired. "I never saw anyone from Syria last night." He paused to muse over last night's museum guests. "But then there were so many people at that thing and of course all hell broke loose. So, I wouldn't have been paying strict attention to every face and name I saw or heard.... What did he want?"

They both looked expectant. There was something they knew about this man that I could hardly guess at. "Are you acquainted with him?" I asked, returning my full attention to Luke. "His name is Sulla Kharim."

Something happened between them. I swear. It was as though they recognized the name but refused to let on. Why not? The brief shared flicker of a glance lasted maybe a quarter of a second, so short, in fact, that I almost thought I had imagined it.

They were familiar with this man, but for some reason wanted to keep it hidden from me. I knew I should tell Luke what Kharim had said. That the plane crash was deliberate, and that Arianna was the target. Okay, Dr. Kharim had used different words. But he had implied it. He had allowed me to assume that that was the case. He had encouraged me to guess that someone wanted Arianna dead. His exact words were: *It was not an accident.*

It seemed they intended to hide whatever secrets they were harboring. Fine, I could do that too. Until I knew more about the situation I was going to keep this bit of info to myself. And if I were to learn anything further I must ensure myself a seat on the trip to the crash site tomorrow. I knew

Luke. I knew how he felt about putting me in danger. He suffered from a 'hero complex.' And that was okay because my fantasy was always, since I was a teenager, to date a real hero. By that I meant a man who was driven to do the right thing, even if it meant going full speed into danger. That was Luke, so I thought. But I had grown since then. Did I really want a man to control my life? For the time being, if I was to help solve this mystery I had to be as mysterious as they. And if they wanted my cooperation, they would have to take me with them.

"Do you know him?" I repeated.

Luke seemed to muse things over. I know it wasn't because of a lack of trust. His reasons for keeping me in the dark were always more pragmatic than that. "No, I don't know him personally; we've never met," he finally answered. There was an edge to his voice, anticipation in the arch of his brows and the tenseness of his muscles. "Why? What did he want?"

"He wanted to meet you. He said he had a proposition that you might be interested in, but never got around to saying what it was. He also warned me last night before the accident, that it was 'a matter of life or death'." I paused. I still believed it to be a strange remark. "He repeated the same thing today. What could he possibly have meant by that?"

"Give me his card," Luke said.

"Only if you let me join you tomorrow at the crash site."

"Why do you want to go there? It will be unpleasant. You'll hate it."

"I want to help," I said.

"You'll help best if you stay here."

I stared at him. My feathers were ruffled and I refused to cave in to his will. "No."

I had two of Dr. Kharim's business cards and I separated them inside my purse (which happened to be unzipped on my lap), but I refused to surrender one.

I waited for him to speak. He went quiet.

"I'll give it to you tomorrow at the crash site," I said.

CHAPTER

3

The following morning, Luke landed his helicopter a small distance away from the smashed plane and had the pilot wait after we debarked. The authorities were understandably impatient with our presence, however they knew Luke by reputation, and understood his concern since the accident involved the loss of his former wife. And now that the director of aviation safety had given him a signed permit to enter the crash site, they were forced to comply. He was warned, however, not to touch things.

The plane was located in the valley at the side of the cliff about five miles from the nearest road in a gorge. The aircraft was so badly fragmented that the only evidence of the cockpit was the flight control mechanisms. The course the flight took was distinguishable in the pattern of the debris. The engine was located at one end. The remainder of the body was scattered behind in intervals.

The man in charge informed Luke that everything that could be done was being done. The best thing he could do was return to his yacht in Positano, and to his life. The relevant authorities would contact him if there was anything significant to report.

But Luke was obstinate. He wanted to search on his

own. It wasn't that he mistrusted the experts he assured them; it was just that he was acquainted with some of the passengers and might recognize oddities they could miss. "Like that for example," he said under his breath to me as we hurried off to search on our own. On the ground was a white and gold Gucci handbag, soiled now, and partly charred. Luke recognized it instantly. "I gave that to her for our fifth anniversary. I remember because she specifically pointed it out to me in a boutique."

Luke picked it up. As per strict regulations regarding discoveries on the crash site, he was forbidden to rifle through its contents. It was unnecessary. He was certain who it belonged to. Still he was tempted to take just a peek.

The authorities shuffled us away as soon as one of the searchers spotted us poking in the bag. Despite written consent from the Agenzia Nazionale per las Sicurezza del Volo (National Agency for the Safety of Flight) or—as us North Americans like to refer to any title with too many words—the ANSV, his billionaire status had no real weight in the current situation. He had been asked to leave things untampered with. He had ignored the warning. We were in the way and the investigators were losing patience with our snooping. Luke stared at the torn designer purse that was taken away from him and placed inside a plastic bag. There was only one wealthy woman on the plane's passenger manifest. It must be Arianna's.

"You will have to leave the vicinity, Dr. Trevanian," the lead investigator said. "Please let us do our work."

Luke was about to object. I seized his hand. "Look." I reached into my purse to distract him and fetched out one of Dr. Kharim's business cards. It happened to be the one with ISORE written on the back of it. "I meant to give this to you first thing this morning."

He didn't even glance at the card. Whatever it had meant to him last night was nothing compared to the trauma of seeing the scorched fragments of airplane debris and the smell of burnt human flesh. The sight of Arianna's torn purse brought home the horrific reality.

"There's nothing more we can do, Luke," I said as softly as I dared, trying to soothe him. I should have done this last night. I should have quelled all of my suspicions and negative feelings and been one hundred percent available to him. It was amazing what jealousy could do. The woman was dead. It was heartless and immature of me to feel threatened by a dead woman.

I shoved the card into his breast pocket. I placed his hand up against my cheek; then let it slide to my lips. "I know this is hard for you. Those officers are right." I pointed towards the search party, most of them in uniforms and many of them men. "They need to do their jobs and we're not helping by interfering. They'll call us when they've identified her remains."

Luke nodded. He slid his fingers between mine and clasped them tight. "I can't believe she's gone."

The two of them had not gotten along in the last quarter of their marriage, but old habits died hard. She was still an important person in his life and I reminded myself of that.

"Do you think they might have seen anything from the old village?" he asked. "If there were survivors, that's the closest place they could go to for help."

Norman and I exchanged troubled glances. The accident had hit Luke harder than we'd thought. And until the authorities determined the cause of the crash and accounted for all of the passengers, Luke would refuse to get the accident out of his mind. He even reminded us of the broken airplane tail. It had survived intact. If she was sitting there, despite what had happened to the rest of the passengers, couldn't it be possible...? I looked up at the steep rocky bluff. Even had she survived, it would be quite a climb.

But the one question that clung to my mind was: What was she doing in Florence before boarding the ill-fated flight?

"Maybe if we went to the village and asked around," he continued.

"I'm sure the authorities will do that," I cut in.

"Not if they think she's dead."

She is *dead, Luke.* But neither Norman nor I said so out loud.

"What if she survived? What if she managed to crawl up to that old village? We have to go and see."

"Luke." Norman was an old friend after all, not just a bodyguard. His eyes shot across the greenery to the burned out crash site where the tail of the plane had broken off scorching the soil, but everything else was shattered into charred fragments, including the seats and luggage. From the looks of things there was no hope. Norman was trying to be rational and realistic but his words came out a little cold. "When the remains have been identified, you'll know for sure."

"That could take weeks, months, even with monetary incentive to make her case a priority. I told the folks in charge I'd give them payment in advance if they'd rush the job but you saw how they shrugged. It's not up to them. It's not up to anyone. You know how slow they are in these sleepy little countries."

"She's gone, Luke," Norman said. "I'm sorry. We had our differences and she didn't much care for me, but I always respected her. She was not only beautiful, but also incredibly smart. She was a good woman."

"She's *not* dead, goddammit."

Norman and I were both chastised to silence.

Finally I asked, "How do you know?"

He said nothing, because he *didn't* know. He was merely hoping.

"The tail of the plane," he whispered. "That seat is not charred."

It dawned on me painfully that maybe he still loved her. The thought had occurred to Norman too because when I lifted my eyes I caught him looking pitying at me. I lowered my lashes and stroked Luke's hand. There was nothing left to say.

I tugged him toward me and started walking. "All right. We'll go to Bagnoregio and ask around. Maybe someone saw something."

Bagnoregio is actually two towns—the modern settlement where the majority of people in the community live and work, and the medieval settlement of Civita di Bagnoregio. The old village, which is referred to simply as the Civita by the locals, lies seventy-four miles north of Rome. It has a permanent population of just ten people who live amid twisting stone paths and centuries old houses that are perched atop sheer cliffs overlooking deep gorges to the sea.

Luke's helicopter took us up the slope to the road where we debarked. He would have dropped us off right inside the Civita but there was nowhere on that clustered landscape to land.

I was impressed at the view. Here the road met the footbridge, which rises high over the deep cuts and ridges in the landscape and links the old town with the new. It would have been breathtaking if not for my concern over Luke's behavior—*and* my raging fear of high, narrow bridges. Why was he so certain that Arianna had survived the crash? I had seen the remains of the aircraft. No one could survive that. Not even had she sat in the tail seat... Unless... unless she wasn't on it?

Why was it so important to him that she be alive? (Not to be morbid or anything or show disrespect to the dead.) After all she was my boss, or rather my boss's boss. But Luke had told me that they hated each other, and that they could barely stand to be in each other's company. The only reason they showed civil manners in public was to keep the paparazzi from inventing outrageous stories about them. Not that it worked.

I realized now as we approached the imposing bridge on foot that part of my reluctance to search the old village was due to my aforementioned terror of high places. It was an irrational fear, an inexplicable fear. Scads of people were terrified of flying. Not me. My sudden loss of control over my panic impulses had nothing to with flying. I looked up at the departing helicopter as confirmation. Planes and helicopters did not frighten me. Something about being enclosed, despite being suspended in the sky, made me feel safe. (Didn't I just say it was irrational?)

I think it was the vertigo that I often experienced when out in the open near a cliff top or a high bridge that was the culprit. It was the fear of the *fear* that was irrational, and the unpredictability of it all that terrorized me. I was not expecting it and it was suddenly upon me. It was happening to me right *now*. I had made it one quarter of the way following behind Luke and Norman when the overwhelming terror suddenly struck. I was paralyzed, my legs refusing to budge one step further. I had made the mistake of looking over the edge and seeing just how far it was to the gully below.

When the fear began it was all I could think of. The more I thought about it the worse it became.

The bridge was supported by multiple thin steel footings. The handrail was about midriff level on me, but it might as well have been ankle level. This thin spindle-railed barrier was all that stood between myself—and imminent death.

I couldn't breathe. Oh God. Nothing like this had happened to me in years. It was as though the air had suddenly thickened and I couldn't get enough of it into my lungs. I was going to pass out from oxygen deprivation and fall.

"Lucy!" Norman called to me. He had turned around and was worried. "What's the hold up? Why are you just standing there?"

It was obvious that I hadn't paused to admire the view. I was frozen in the middle of the footpath between the two rails. My face had gone pale, I could feel all the blood drain out of my head, leaving my brain numb, and my fingertips icy.

Luke turned around. He was almost halfway across the

bridge. There was no one else using it except us, so I didn't have to worry about making a fool of myself in front of strangers. No—I only had to worry about making an idiot of myself in front of the two men I cared about most.

CHAPTER
4

"What's wrong? Hurry up, Lucy. What's the matter with you?"

At this distance Luke could not see that there was something desperately wrong. I still hadn't moved. The fear was overwhelming me, and it might as well have been a flood of water. That was how helpless I felt. I felt like I was drowning. I could. Not. Breathe.

"I think she's having a panic attack," Norman said.

"What?"

I had carefully hidden my fear of heights from Luke over the span of our almost two-month-long relationship. He was an adventurer and would never understand this type of fear. It hadn't been hard to conceal it from him. How could I possibly expose myself? It wasn't like we'd ever gone mountain climbing. And like I said, aircraft were not the same. He was totally oblivious of my phobia.

"Lucy! What's the matter with you?"

I tried to speak, to explain, but my throat was dry and my voice shackled.

Luke's hands were in the air in a gesture of impatience.

"Come on. Let's go." He started to come towards me and I could see that the impatience was changing to annoyance. That wasn't helping. Not at all.

Norman sensed my turmoil. "It's okay, Luke. You go ahead. I'll get her."

Luke exhaled, slightly exasperated, and spun to resume his trek across the footbridge. For some reason I was relieved. That was one less person to shake their head at me, and shrug in disbelief.

Norman faced me. His voice was throaty and soft. "*Ça va, petite chou. Viens à moi.*" Other than swear words, Norman seldom spoke French to me. It seemed he thought the mellower sounds would soothe me. He was wrong. He switched over to English and said, "It's okay, sweetheart. You're okay. You are not going to fall. I won't let you."

I tried to move towards him but my feet refused to obey. My eyes were wide with terror. I could feel my eyelids stretching and my eyeballs lambasted by the hot wind. "Come to me. Can you come as far as to me?"

No.

"Lucy, there are railings on either side of you. You *can't* fall."

It wasn't the railings I was worried about. It was the damned height. We were so high, the bridge was held up by such measly posts. And it wasn't even that. It was the fact that I could *not* breathe.

Norman's hand was outstretched to me. All I had to do was take it. I couldn't even get my arm to lift.

Norman glanced around as though summing up the situation. The wind had died a little, but I could still feel the tremor of the bridge as he approached. My heart hammered. My pulse raced. Finally he reached me and took my hand. I lunged at him and hugged his arm.

"It's okay, Lucy." He paused. "Why didn't you tell us you had a fear of heights?"

I thought I was over it.

"If I'd known I would have left you behind."

I didn't want to be left behind.

I was shaking and he wrapped a strong arm around me.

"I'm sorry, Norman," I whispered. I was afraid that if I spoke too loud the bridge would wobble.

"Nothing to be sorry about," he said. "Everyone is afraid of something."

Not you.

He smiled, reading my thought. "Even me."

I looked up at him. *Really?*

"Really," he said. "I'll tell you about it sometime. Not now. We have to go. The longer you stay here, the harder it will be for you to get moving."

That was so true. I didn't feel like I could walk back the way we had come, or go forward to the old village atop the outcrop.

Ahead Luke was almost at the end of the bridge. *Please, please, don't tell Luke about this.*

"Is Luke mad at me?" I asked.

"No. Just confused. He's a little impatient because of the stress. He's really upset about Arianna." He sighed. "I really had no idea she still mattered that much to him."

"They *were* married for ten years."

"Yeah, they were."

"Do you believe she's still alive?"

"I don't know. How can anyone know until they've analyzed all of the forensics?"

"What about that tail piece? It wasn't cracked or charred."

"The impact alone would have killed her. You saw how the rest of it smashed into bits."

I paused and glanced up at him. "I wonder what she was doing in Florence before she boarded that charter flight."

Norman shrugged. "She's a museum director. They travel all over the world for various reasons."

"Yes, I suppose." I sighed. "It's just that fate is strange. If she hadn't been in Florence, she wouldn't have boarded that particular plane and then she…" I exhaled heavily. "I don't understand how he could possibly believe that she's still alive."

"That's Luke for you. Stubborn as hell."

By the time he stopped talking we had reached the end of the bridge. "There," he said, disentangling himself from my stranglehold on his arm. "We made it."

I stared in disbelief at the firm rock beneath my feet and the rubble path that led into the village. Behind us the footbridge curved over the gorge to a sea of green citrus and silver olive trees. In front of us the ancient stone buildings of the village, glowing pink and peach from the sun, rose as though cut directly out of the rocky hill. Cascades of color and lush green fell from window boxes and steep-sided walls to the dusty cobblestones below.

A young lad in trousers torn off at the knee and a bright tie-dyed T-shirt with GRATEFUL DEAD printed across the chest suddenly appeared out of nowhere with a handful of crudely made miniature Roman pots. He must have been around twelve or thirteen years old. His English was good, though accented. I wondered if he was a fan of the Grateful Dead or if this was just something he had found in a thrift shop in the big city. He held out his armload to make sure I noticed his wares.

"You like?" he asked, juggling the goods precariously, which made me believe that they probably weren't terribly valuable. "The pretty *signorina* like my pots? Is genuine *Roman* pot. You take home and impress your friends, yes?"

I laughed, my rattling heart slowing down. "Did you make those yourself?"

"No," he said as though he couldn't have been more insulted. His face brightened when it dawned on him what would please a tourist most. "I dig them up from an archaeology site."

"Don't encourage him," Norman said.

"It's okay, I don't mind."

"He'll swindle you if he can," Norman warned, lips twitching.

"I *did* so dig them up from an archaeology site," the boy argued with the distinct appearance of someone who was insulted.

"Oh, did you? And where is this archaeology site?" I asked.

"In the valley—" He tilted his head to the left. "Where my uncle grazes his sheep."

"All right. What's your name?"

"Franco," he said.

"How much for that pot?" I pointed to a crudely made clay bowl.

"Ten euros."

"Ten euros!" Norman exclaimed and guffawed.

"Stop it." I admonished him. "Don't pay any attention to that man," I instructed the boy. "Here—here is your money."

"Oh, thank you so much." He handed me the bowl with one grubby hand while juggling the remainder of his wares in the opposite arm. "*Grazie.*"

I pretended to admire my new purchase before slipping it into my oversized handbag. The boy pocketed the bills and said, "The pretty *signorina* and her husband stay at the hotel in Bagnoregio, yes?"

I cut him off quickly, waving a dismissive hand in Norman's direction. "Oh, he's not my husband. He's just a friend."

"Your friend then. You stay at the Hotel Bagnoregio? Is very good hotel, the Hotel Bagnoregio. My cousin Giorgio work in that fine establishment. I will tell him to slip you extra grappa tonight. The gods will smile on you."

"I'll bet," Norman said, chuckling. "Do you like grappa, Lucy?"

Not particularly. Grappa was a local Italian liquor, of the brandy family, that as far as I was concerned was an acquired taste. I had tried it once or twice since our arrival in Italy and not once had I enjoyed it. Out of politeness, however, I drank it when it was offered. The flavor was strong and hit hard. It was made from the pulp (and by that I mean the grape seeds, skins and stems) leftover from winemaking and, honestly, tasted like it.

Norman made a sweeping gesture to usher me past him. "Let's go find Luke."

I was breathing fine after that little encounter with the street urchin, my heart no longer banging against my ribcage and my hands warm. I stood in wonder of how Norman had distracted me so that I could cross the bridge. And bartering with the boy had further diverted me. Nothing like *that* had happened to me in so long I was stricken with embarrassment. But I felt just fine now, almost elated, and looked back and saw simply a beautiful vista of blue, cloud-swept sky, hanging over the narrow overpass. Only briefly did I ponder how I had managed to cross that bridge.

"You did it, Lucy," he said noticing the path of my gaze, and gently elbowing me in the side. "Wasn't so bad, huh?"

My eyes rolled up to his and I shook my head. "How did you do that?"

"It's a technique I learned in the army. Tell you about it sometime." His lips twitched at the corners, and it amazed me how I had never noticed before the strong angle of his jaw and the statue-like bone structure.

I turned abruptly away; Luke was coming towards us.

Neither of us spoke, but by his expression I could tell he had received some news.

"No one claims to have seen a woman resembling Arianna," Luke said.

His eyes glittered with excitement and I wondered why. This was *bad* news, not *good* news.

"I guess that's it then," Norman said.

"No." Luke's voice lowered and he jutted a thumb over his right shoulder towards a vendor's stall. "That shopkeeper I was talking to? He's lying or I'm a monkey's uncle."

"How could you tell?" I demanded. I was really beginning to worry about Luke. He was behaving irrationally. That mad gleam in his eyes was the first sign of it.

There were two other elderly folk, or maybe they were simply middle-aged, who now wandered down the path with a couple of goats in tow. It was hard to determine the couple's true age because the locals mainly worked outdoors in the wind and sun. Their skin was weathered and brown, although they smiled. But that was the strange thing. The moment Luke asked them about any survivors from the plane crash the smiles vanished. Luke tried again even going so far as to pursue them as they goaded their goats with wooden walking sticks, but they simply said gruffly, "*Non capisco. No parla Inglese,*" and shook their heads and hurried off.

Their behavior was off kilter for a country known for its friendliness toward strangers. For a town that depended so completely on tourists the blatant rudeness was incomprehensible. If I'd questioned the local boy would he have reacted the same?

"*Buona giornata!*"

Luke had wished them a nice day. They never looked back. They scurried down a hilly alley and disappeared behind a crumbling stone wall. Luke shook his head as he returned to us. "Did you see that? I was polite as all get go. Why are they behaving as though I have mange or something worse? No, Lucy, Norman, I am not crazy. They know something. And I think I have an idea what it is."

His eyes returned to the stall of the old street vendor. He glanced back our way and said, "I saw something back there. I have to be sure."

The sounds of clinking pottery caught our ears. It sent all three of us staring at the souvenir stand. The old man was rearranging his wares and briefly glanced up. Luke took my arm and waved Norman to follow. "Here, let's move out of earshot, and out of the sun. It's getting hot. And I don't want that creamy complexion of yours to get burnt." He touched his lips to my cheek.

We ducked under the shade of a bay tree, and he mopped the sweat out of his eyes with the back of his sleeve. It was clear he was agitated and excited at the same time.

"I don't think that shopkeeper understands English, but you never know…" Luke paused after a few more steps.

"This is good." The tree was about twenty feet from the shop and the vendor stopped darting suspicious glances at us. "Now, as I was saying. I saw something, and you two have to see it as well. We are going to go back to that stall. Norman, I want you to stay here and keep an eye on things. Signal me if the old guy shows any sign of turning around. And you, Lucy, turn on some of that Canadian charm. Pretend you want to buy a souvenir from the gift shop. Keep him occupied. I have to get him out of the stall so that I can search his inventory."

I raised my voice, just a bit. "Luke, what did you see?"

"Wait until I've double checked, then I'll tell you everything."

CHAPTER
5

Reluctantly, Norman and I humored him. There was only one way to find out, wasn't there? We did a careful reconnaissance; the cobblestone alleyways were pretty much empty, the goat herders had long since disappeared, and the street urchin was nowhere in sight.

We retraced our steps to the tattered souvenir place, which wasn't really a shop, but a sort of semi-covered stand. The roof consisted of sheets of corrugated tin attached to a small open-air room connected to a larger stone building. At night a wire gate was drawn across to seal off the back room where all the valuables were stored.

On the dusty countertop were small sculptures of Michelangelo's David, a few Madonnas with Child, replicas of Roman frescoes and mosaics, plus small clay pots like those of the street boy's, and some not very well made miniature Roman soldiers. A large number of dated postcards were filed in a wire rack. On the walls were tacky clocks and more cheap, fake frescoes.

Behind the owner, who just happened to be a rather weathered-looking old man, dressed in traditional peasant garb of dusty black trousers and blousy white shirt that looked like it had suffered too many washings, were stacks of cardboard boxes with presumably more of the tacky souvenirs, and behind that, what looked to be a studio or workshop.

Don't ask me why I had Gorgons on the brain, but I did. The Medusa was a famous figure in Greek myths adopted by the ancient Romans. Would it be so odd for me to ask if he had any replicas of it? I tried in my stilted Italian. "Medusa?" I gesticulated with my fingers to create imaginary snakes around my head. "*Per piacere.*" I hoped I was using the correct phrase. "Please, do you have a sculpture of the Medusa?"

He shook his head and brought me a cheap imitation of the goddess of love, Venus. I picked it up and strategically banged my elbow against the wire rack containing the postcards and spilling the lot onto the floor.

I apologized profusely, set the statue of Venus back on the countertop, and crouched down to pick them up. The vendor came around to my side to help. Meanwhile, Norman who was standing some distance away from us pretending to be sightseeing, turned to keep an eye on the movements of the vendor and myself. Luke popped out from around the side of he souvenir stand and ducked into the shop and over to the cardboard boxes.

While I was busily apologizing and dropping postcards all over the place and watching the wind snatch a few, and then chasing them, the vendor finally ran to me and said," *Signorina, per cortesia,* stop. It is all right. Do not bother."

"But your postcards," I mourned. "Someone must pay for them."

"Fine. It is five Euros for the lost postcards."

I made a fuss of looking for the money in my purse. When it looked like the old man was going to kick me off his property, Luke slipped out of the shop and came to my rescue. "A problem, *Bella?*" he asked.

"No," I said, and smiled sweetly at the grizzled face of the vendor. He shook his head, gave me something that might have been a smile but looked more like a scowl and returned to rearranging his postcards and finding something with which to permanently anchor the wire display rack onto the counter. The street urchin in his bright T-shirt reappeared from between some stone buildings and dropped his armload of pots onto the counter of the stall. As we left I smiled at the boy and he rewarded me with a beaming one of his own. Then he tossed a curious glance at Luke, and when he questioned his grandfather, I noticed the old vendor turn his scowl onto the boy. They began arguing about something although I was out of hearing range.

The three of us reunited at an outdoor café, and claimed a table with a fabulous view of the valley. There was a stone wall to keep anyone from falling off the cliff side and on top of the coping sat heavy ceramic flower boxes containing lovely red geraniums in full bloom. On the ground large pottery urns stood proud, bursting with summer annuals like petunias, verbena, million bells, impatiens and in the shadier parts begonias.

We ordered, and then Norman and I turned to Luke. "Well...?" Norman said.

Luke faced in my direction. "You know that Gorgon's head I gave you to draw? Well, it was one of three in a triptych. That one you have is Medusa. It's a head broken off the main piece. She has two other sisters. I saw the other sisters. Back there—" His thumb angled briefly.

"How do you know it's from the same piece? It's probably just a replica of a generic Gorgon's trio. These souvenir places are full of cheap copies." From my handbag I dug out the pitiful pot I had purchased from the local boy as proof.

"I'm pretty sure," Luke said.

"How? How can you be so certain?"

He shot a glance at Norman.

"Because Arianna had the other two pieces in a locked Pelican case among her luggage," Norman replied for him. "I know, because I'm in charge of security. I was supposed to take the case from her assistant after their arrival, and protect it until our return to Positano."

"You mean the Gorgon belongs to her?"

"As much as any historic relic belongs to anyone." Luke pulled at his chin, thinking on his feet. "It was a purchase for the ROM. She wanted my lab to run tests on some peculiar residues, and naturally, she wished to have you, Lucy, visually document it. She also thought it'd be safer stored aboard my yacht."

"And you think this vendor has the remaining two figures?"

He hesitated. "When I was there earlier asking about any sightings of a beautiful blonde woman who might have survived the plane crash, I caught a glimpse of the edge of one piece in a cardboard box behind the vendor. I recognized it instantly. Don't ask me how I could tell, on so little evidence. It was a gut feeling, like I'd seen something similar before."

And that something was the Gorgon's head?

He nodded like he'd read my mind. "Now, I'm positive."

Luke removed his phone from his pants pocket and tapped it on. He swiped through several photos. He had captured these while I was chasing postcards to distract the vendor from the workshop behind his stall. The images were representations of the Gorgon heads all right. And Luke had managed to photograph the edges so that we could hopefully match up the fresco (as one would do with the pieces of a puzzle) to the one in the yacht's lab. He was texting Emily, as we spoke, to attempt the match on the basis of the pictures.

"And you touched them? They're authentic?"

He pressed SEND. "As far as I could tell without doing some standard tests. But if those fracture lines match up, we'll know these three pieces belong to the same triptych… and look here—" he pointed to some rusty discoloration on the face of one of the photos. "—It looks like the same residue that's on the fragment Emily is testing."

I stared at Luke. I knew what he was thinking.

"They could still be fakes," I said. "You saw all those cheap replicas they have for sale. And in the back of the store I saw the workshop. There's a kiln and heaps of unfired clay sculptures."

"I know," Luke replied. "I was *back* there, remember. But this is the clincher—" He swiped the screen of his phone and stopped at a photograph of something yellow and black. A sawed-open Pelican case in two pieces. Inside was packed with solid foam.

"Why would a peasant like him have an expensive Pelican case? Why would he even know what a Pelican case was?"

"A Pelican case would survive the impact of a plane crash?" I asked.

"Yes," Norman said. "Depending on where it was stored during impact."

"This one is Arianna's," Luke insisted. "I know because I gave it to her."

Yes, for your fifth or sixth or seventh anniversary. I avoided his eyes and was grateful that none of that had been spoken aloud. I had to stop this jealousy and the sarcasm. It was ugly. "Pelican cases all look the same," I said calmly.

"But they don't come inscribed."

I cleared my throat. "Are you sure it's the same one that you gave her?"

"I wasn't when I was photographing it. Didn't have time to decipher the lettering. But I noted an inscription so I shot a picture of it. Read what it says."

I squinted at the photograph. It was a bit fuzzy, although parts were quite legible. Before I could repeat the words aloud, he calmly recited: *"Whatever you keep in here will always be safe. Along with my heart."*

That was exactly what it read.

"You had that inscription engraved on the case?" I asked.

He nodded, not noticing how awkward I felt.

"It was one of the first gifts I ever gave her."

Why should I be surprised? Luke was generous with his money. I had only been dating him for a month and a half, and he had already bought me more clothes and jewelry than I could have bought for myself in ten years. And that was without calculating the expense. Because of course I couldn't afford the quality of the gifts he showered on me.

My thoughts were going off on an irrelevant tangent. I forced myself back to the current issue. If all of what Luke was saying was true, then it meant that the crashed plane had been looted before the arrival of the first responders.

It did not, however, mean that Arianna Chase was alive.

"I know," Luke said, perceiving my thoughts. "It's not proof that she survived. But it *is* something."

"When you questioned the vendor, did he say anything about seeing a survivor?"

"No, I got the same kind of blow-off as I got from the goat herders, but then—" He waited. "Why would he? If that vendor were stealing things from the plane why would he admit to seeing anyone alive?" He clicked shut his phone as the waitress arrived with our food. I had ordered an iced coffee and a slice of tiramisu. The men drank their coffee hot and black, and snacked on meatball sandwiches.

The waitress left quickly. Was she worried we'd question her too?

"This is going to be harder than I thought," Luke said. "No one is talking. Why are they so cautious? Even nervous?"

I had to agree. The behavior of the villagers was uncharacteristic. Normally places like this were full of cheerful locals eager to please. Not just because it was in their natures but for the generous tips North American tourists were prone to give. He glanced around. I followed his gaze with my own.

This rustic, ancient, picturesque town was in dire need of a facelift—and not *just* a facelift. Beneath its fading splendor the infrastructure was crumbling. I didn't need to be an engineer to see that. The buildings seemed unconsolidated.

They were ready to collapse at the slightest vibration. A windstorm could dislodge a stone from one of the walls and send the entire building to the ground. However, on a clear, warm day like today, when everything was dry and the air at the moment quite still, the destruction that could be just around the corner, if there were even a minor earthquake or a rumbling from a nearby volcano, seemed not only improbable but also impossible.

I was unfamiliar with the people who lived here. Obviously, they loved their village enough to stay—despite few and sporadic services. The place was dirt poor. They could not hold on for much longer, especially with the tourist industry dwindling. To what lengths would these people go in order to remain living here? History exuded from every cobblestone alleyway and limestone edifice. Lives were lived and lost here. Babies were born and families raised. But that was now all in the past. The few holdouts were mostly older folks. They rejected the modern world of computers, fast cars and cellphones. There were no young people anymore. Except for that boy in the Grateful Dead shirt. And the waitress. Well she was probably from Bagnoregio and only came up to the old town to work in the summer. Anyone with dreams had moved to the cities for work and opportunities, and for the chance to enjoy the luxuries of modern life. I was pretty sure there was no Starbucks or Wi fi here, although they did make a mean iced coffee. I sipped this now as we discussed our options, and I dipped into my tiramisu with extra whipped cream.

"They will do anything for a buck," Luke was saying. "Short of murder."

"Don't be ridiculous," I objected. "These people are not criminals, they're just poor."

"You'd be amazed how poverty can motivate people."

"What are we talking about anyway?" I demanded. "So they looted the plane. I'm sure that poor old guy has no idea how much those frescoes are worth on the black market. Do you think that's why the villagers are all acting so weird?

There's some kind of racket going on here?"
Luke and Norman exchanged glances.
"Seriously?" I said. "Even if that persnickety old man knew he could get some money for them. What does he know about selling? He'd have to have contacts in the underground." I widened my eyes. "You *think* he has contacts?"

I shouldn't have been surprised that this was the tangent their minds were taking. After all, they were in the business of acquiring antiquities. And the provenance of precious artifacts was dubious at the best of times. There were disreputable dealers and legitimate dealers but sometimes it was hard to tell the two apart.

"You mean you think this might be a front for a smuggling ring?"

"I didn't say that," Luke answered. "But I'm not dismissing it. No. All I know is, this village has the motivation. And everyone is acting like they've got something to hide."

"So what are you going to do? Go up to him and ask where he got the frescoes? How are you going to explain how you know he has them? If he's involved in anything suspicious he's going to deny having them, and you know it."

"That's why I'm not going to ask to look at them."

"No, Luke." I recognized that set of his jaw and the sharpness in his eyes. "You can't steal them. That would make you as bad as him—if in fact he *is* a dealer." I sent a swift sideways glance in the direction of the shop. Instead of catching a glimpse of the vendor I saw his grandson watching me. He waved briefly; then darted out of sight like he had been caught doing something he wasn't supposed to.

"You got a better idea?"

Luke's question brought me back from my thoughts. "First of all, I think we should wait until we get the results of the forensics tests," I said. "And worry about authenticating the frescoes later."

Luke decided that it was best we stay in close proximity,

and he postponed our return trip to Positano. It didn't matter anyway. He was independent of a time schedule, other than the one he imposed on himself. As we rose to pay our bill I caught a glimpse of the street boy once more.

***

That afternoon, after we returned to Bagnoregio, Luke got on his phone again. He was outside on the balcony of our hotel room trying all of his connections to speed up the identifications of the dead passengers. I'd had a shower and was watching him from the bed where I perched in my bathrobe, combing out my wet hair. The small TV was on and the news was blaring. He must have gotten the call while he was catching up on world events. I turned from the TV to study his lean masculine body as he paced the small balcony. There was a time when Luke could not resist seeing me like this. Now he was oblivious of my presence. How had things changed so fast?

That was an easy question to answer. Arianna.

Luke's thoughts were on her twenty-four/seven. It took her death to bring out what she really meant to him. How had I not seen it before?

I was debating whether I should just drop my robe and step out onto the balcony and rub up against him and see if he noticed, when my cellphone suddenly chimed and I picked it up off the dresser. The caller ID told me that it was my brother-in-law Shaun in Toronto. I fumbled for the remote to lower the volume to the TV as I answered it.

"Hi," I said quietly, "you heard?"

"Yes," he said. "Lucy, are you okay? I've been calling and calling you. Where've you been?"

"I'm fine," I said. "A little shaken up. But it's Luke whose taking it the hardest. When did you hear? It just happened."

"Twitter," he said. "Yesterday."

Of course. "You probably shouldn't let the word out until everything is official."

"I don't think I can stop it. I'm at work. Everyone in the museum is talking about it. Lucy, is it true? Is Arianna dead?"

The director of the ROM was not a popular person. She was one of those people that made you feel small. She didn't have to say anything; she only had to look at you to make you aware that her world excluded you. However, that didn't make her a bad person. Just a very intimidating boss.

"Do you need me to come, for identification purposes or anything like that?" He didn't sound like he wanted to come. He sounded like he was repeating what was expected of him. "Or just for moral support? Colleen has been hammering me to let her come see you, but she's getting big. I don't want her flying. Especially after what happened with Arianna's flight."

"That was a small chartered plane, not a passenger liner. She'd be safe enough." But I didn't bother to convince him. I wasn't sure my sister was the person I needed right now. She could be incredibly self-centered; not deliberately, mind you, but that was her personality. And with the baby on the way, why wouldn't she think she was the most important person in the universe?

"I could catch the next flight out."

"It's not necessary, Shaun," I said. On the TV screen I saw a news report about the plane crash. The camera was panning over the crash site where men were still busy searching for evidence. So they had allowed reporters onto the scene.

"You don't need to come," I repeated, dragging my attention back to Shaun.

To be honest I wanted to keep some distance from him—both physically and emotionally. I have long suspected that Shaun was involved in something cryptic concerning the museum's acquisitions but I didn't want to get into it at the moment. He sounded relieved, which made me wonder even more. I was pretty confident Shaun was not a crook. If he was involved in anything clandestine, I was certain it was indirect and probably quite innocent, but I had no time to investigate. And that was also why I was avoiding talking to Colleen. She was unaware of my suspicions, and it would cause her unnecessary worry to think that her husband possessed knowledge of some illicit activity at the museum.

I glanced at my phone while Shaun was still speaking and saw that Colleen was on the other line. I would have to decline and call her back another time. Gossip mistress that she was, she would want all the sordid details and I was not in the mood for spreading rumors just to entertain her.

"I'll keep you in the loop," I promised Shaun. I would have to remember to return Colleen's call within a few hours or else she'd be leaving me messages like crazy. My phone pinged. There was one from her already.

I ignored it and raised my head. On the TV screen was an image of carnage. I reached for the remote and raised the volume. "Shaun," I said. "I have to go. Talk to you soon."

I cranked up the volume some more. Luke came in when he saw what I was watching and joined me without a word.

Militants were on the move the newscaster said. There were scenes of shooting in an ancient temple. Broken columns and frescoes lay scattered about. A stone tomb, exquisitely engraved with everyday scenes smashed into pieces. "Antiquities are under siege," the newscaster reported. "Some of the most valuable treasures have been destroyed as collateral damage in the shelling and crossfire between government forces and rebel factions. Others have been sold off in exchange for guns or food, or for passage out of the turmoil into Europe and the hope of a better life—overseas."

Now satellite images showed historical sites with the soil so completely pocked by holes, the result of thousands of illegal excavations, they resembled the moon.

"Destruction and looting on an industrial scale," she continued. "And then there is the Islamic State, the terrorist group whose conquering of vast areas of land in Iraq and Syria has turned the destruction of heritage into wholesale butchery."

Up came an online video of militants gleefully attacking priceless artifacts with jackhammers, and rampaging through museums destroying collections with gunfire.

Now, they were in Palmyra.

Luke's attention was completely focused on the TV. These events had particular significance for him. Why?

For some reason I was thinking about the Gorgon heads.

CHAPTER
6

"Luke?" When I awoke in the middle of the night, my heart was pounding. I had a creepy sensation that someone was in the room. Although I could barely see, could barely even make out the shapes of the furniture in the darkness, some inner sense told me Luke was gone. And I had company.

I cried out one more time in desperation. Was I mistaken? He should have been in bed beside me. If that wasn't him, where was he? "Luke!"

Had he gotten up to use the bathroom? I half rose but my eyes were still blurred by sleep, as well as the dim light coming through the thin drapes over the French doors.

The night was peaceful, and the sounds of insects and the rumble of the odd car came from outside. A shadow moved. "Who's there?"

Did they have 911 here? Or was the emergency number a different set of digits. My mind fumbled. I bunched myself up against the pillows, drawing my knees to my chest. I was suddenly alert and grabbed my phone. I squeezed it tight. If nothing else I could throw it at the intruder.

"Who's there?" I shouted again.

No answer. Were my eyes playing tricks on me? But it

wasn't just what I thought I had seen. It was what I had felt. I woke up, not because of a bad dream or a sound outside. I had awakened because I had the distinct sense that someone had touched me.

"Lucy?"

A loud rapping came at the door.

"Lucy, are you all right?"

The door clicked open. Did I forget to lock it before going to bed? I had retired before Luke. Now, come to think of it, had he even come upstairs to join me under the covers? I wished my brain were less fuzzy.

A dark figure entered the room and rushed to the bed where I was still huddled, confounded by my own muddled thoughts.

"What happened? Are you okay? I heard you cry out."

It was Norman's hand that found mine and cupped my fingers in his strong grip.

"I'm fine," I said. "I'm sorry I woke you."

"What scared you? You were shouting."

I blinked my eyes several times to get the dryness out, and wet my lips. "I'm not sure."

"Where's Luke?"

Why was he asking me that? Wasn't it *his* job to know the whereabouts of his boss? He was Luke's bodyguard; I was just the girlfriend. Or was I? Unfairly my thoughts turned in a suspicious direction. Just what was I suspicious of?

"I thought he was with you."

Norman's split-second hesitation was barely perceptible, and it did not fool me. I knew that generally Norman would only go to bed after Luke. Was this guilt? And if so, what were the two of them guilty of? What was *Norman* guilty of? He was protecting Luke. I could see that.

"Luke told me he was turning in," he answered, innocently enough. "So I did, too."

He turned to switch on the bedside lamp. I heard the click. Strangely, no light came on. He swore thickly under his breath in French. The bed creaked as he rose; it sounded like a scream. Now I realized what I had found so odd when I woke up. The hotel was quiet. Too quiet. The electricity was out.

"I'll have to go see if the entire building is experiencing a blackout or if it's just our floor. I noticed when I came round to your room that the hall lights were out..." He hesitated again as though measuring his words. "What time did Luke leave?"

I shook my head, and spoke with equal caution. "I don't know. I don't know if he ever came upstairs. I was asleep."

Norman still held my hand even as he got to his feet. I deliberately disengaged myself from him. He looked toward the French doors. A breeze gently stirred the drapes, which were drawn against the night.

"Did you leave that open?"

"No." My mind replayed my last actions before bed. I was quite certain I had bolted the doors and windows before undressing and doing my evening routine. I answered firmly, "That door was locked. I'm sure of it."

He moved a few feet to check the balcony. I followed him. Outside it was warm and breezy, the small enclosure empty. We were two stories up from the street. This was a small hotel and not exactly a Five-Star establishment, but it was the best we could do on short notice. What it had going for it was authenticity. It was charming and rustic. And the people who ran the place were exceedingly helpful and polite.

Lampposts illuminated the road every few blocks. Norman was leaning over the rail to peer down into the balcony below. He scoured the street. He then turned to check the balconies on either side. "No one here," he confirmed. He removed his phone from his pocket and pressed it on for light. "I'd better check inside, just to be sure."

He searched under the bed frame and inside the wardrobe, and in the small bathroom, waving the light from his phone in all the black corners. "Nothing. You can go back to sleep, but first I'd better make sure that French door is secure." He approached it and stopped.

"Is something wrong?"

He shook the doorknob. It rattled. "This is loose. Was it like this before?"

"I don't know."

It was disturbing that I should feel so cold when it was warm outside. He looked at me and could see that I had my arms wrapped around my shoulders, my thin silk nightgown slipping slightly as I rubbed my arms.

"You'd better get under the covers," Norman said, his voice growing hoarse.

I gripped myself tighter. "I don't think I can sleep. I don't want to be alone."

"It's all right. There's no one here. I checked everywhere."

He was right; there was no other place anyone could hide.

"Do you want me to stay with you until Luke gets back?"

I still had the sense of lingering tension. I couldn't have imagined it, could I? I felt the creepy crawlies all up and down my skin, but that could just be from the fact that I was scantily dressed.

"Norman," I said my voice hanging on a quiver. "Someone was here."

He paused. He was skeptical of whether these were hysterics or if I had seen something. His voice was unconvinced. "Who," he asked. "Who did you see?"

"I didn't exactly *see* them."

"Then what..." He went quiet and waited for me to elaborate. I was still standing in the middle of the floor, my bare feet beginning to get cold.

"I felt somebody touch me."

I shivered. That was what was giving me the creepy feeling, the idea of someone touching me while I was asleep and vulnerable. A stranger. An intruder.

He came to me and sat me down. Then he seated himself on the bed next to me. "Tell me why you think that."

How to begin to describe the disturbing sensation? My heart started to palpitate and my breathing to grow shallow. The palms of my hands were cold and damp. How to describe what it felt like? Except that one moment I was warm and calm and totally relaxed in sleep and the next I was hyper alert, though my eyes were closed and my brain barely registering consciousness, feeling the gooseflesh ripple along my arms.

"It woke me up. The feeling of cold fingers on my skin." I shuddered.

He put his arm around me to still my trembling. "Are you sure it wasn't Luke?"

I hesitated before I answered. "Yes. His fingers have never felt that cold. Besides, when I opened my eyes he was gone. It couldn't have been him. He wouldn't have just left like that without saying something. And not that fast." I stopped. There was also a scent, something familiar. It was on the tip of my tongue. Oh why, why, why couldn't I identify it? And then I knew what it was. "I smelled lemon blossoms." He stared at me but I remained steadfast. "Yes, I know it's a strange thing to notice. But that was what I smelled. And I know for a fact that Luke has no shampoo, aftershave or lotions that smell like that."

It occurred to me now that Norman was dressed in lightweight pants and a T-shirt, with his socks and shoes on. Why was he fully dressed if he had just gotten out of bed? Where was he intent on going when he heard me cry out?

I removed myself from his hold and went to my suitcase to pull out my clothes. I found a loose blouse, the color of which I could not distinguish in the semi-darkness, and a pair of skinny jeans. I went to the bathroom and dressed in the dark while he silently waited in the bedroom.

I returned, tugging my blouse around my waist, and strapped on sandals as he rose from the bed. "Where do you think you're going?" he demanded.

"Same place you are."

He stared.

"He told you to stay with me to make sure I was safe, didn't he? But you got it into your head to follow him. Where did he go, Norman? And why does he think I'm in any danger?"

"Lucy, you should stay here."

"You lied to me. You knew Luke was going out. Give me one reason why I should do what you say."

"You'll be safer, here."

"Someone broke into my room." I went to the lamp and switched it on and off. "They killed the lights on my floor, in my room. Why? What were they going to do? Who are they, Norman? Tell me!"

"Quiet, or you'll wake up the whole place."

I shoved past him toward the door. He went after me and stopped short just before grabbing my arm. "All right. Stop moving. I'll tell you what I know."

I swung around, and he released me. "Begin with the Gorgon heads."

His eyes widened in surprise. I know he was thinking of sidetracking me by making up some story to keep me from pursuing what was really going on.

"What did you two find out after I went to bed?"

Norman glanced quickly at his cellphone. Was he expecting a call from Luke? The bright digits shone 2:08 am.

"All right, all right." He exhaled in exasperation, caved in. This time I hoped he meant it. Because if he didn't...we were going to spend a very long night together. "I'll tell you what I know."

"Is Arianna alive?"

"We think so."

"You mean *you* think so, too?"

"Emily texted us the images of the three Gorgon heads that she digitally matched. The broken edges fit exactly. They are all part of the same triptych. Furthermore, that residue on the original is human blood."

"That's not proof that Arianna is alive. It merely means that the old shopkeeper looted the crash site... And the blood, well that could mean the exact opposite—was it Arianna's?"

"No. DNA testing showed it came from someone with an Arab ethnicity, but that's not surprising." He quickly changed the subject. "Do you remember that street urchin at the old village? He just happens to be the shopkeeper's grandson. Yeah, well, the boy managed to get a message to Luke. Apparently he overheard Luke asking about survivors from the plane crash. After you were so nice to him—you realize ten euros is a fortune to these people?—it dawned on him that we three were together, and he wanted to help. I believe he also thought there would be some monetary incentive. So he contacted his cousin Giorgio at the hotel and left a message for Luke. There's a strange woman he said living with a tavern owner named Giovanni Zia. She matches the description of Arianna."

"And Luke's gone back to the Civita? At this hour?"

"The boy's grandfather has forbidden him to speak to us. That also tells you something, doesn't it? They're hiding something. So the boy sent a message through his cousin Giorgio for us to meet him in secret."

"That's where Luke is now?"

Norman nodded. "It was just luck that Luke and I happened to be having something to drink in the bar. Giorgio was our waiter."

"I'm coming with you," I said.

"Are you sure you want to do that?" He hesitated. "There is a reason Luke kept this meeting hidden from you."

I glared. "You can't leave me out of this. Arianna Chase is the director of my museum. If she's alive and needs help, I want to help her."

"I have no doubt that you do. We are meeting Franco back at the Civita. We will have to cross the bridge on foot. Are you sure you want to do that?"

I shivered. "Yes."

CHAPTER 7

It helped that it was dark and that the bottom of the gorge was out of my visual range. Believe me I made no effort to look. The moon was out and gave us enough light to see our way. Norman parked the rented Audi A8 behind Luke's vehicle, an S-class Mercedes, by the roadside and we got out into the balmy air. I could see Luke's lean, shadowy figure on the footbridge. He was alone. He was well over midway across.

I took a deep breath and begged to all the gods in heaven to prevent me from having a panic attack. I started to walk behind Norman and then I realized I was paralyzed. I was physically unable to move. I refused to call out to him to wait for me. It would not only make me look pathetic, but prove to him how right he was, how right they both were, to try to leave me at the hotel where I was safe.

I tried to stare at the dark cluster of buildings atop the outcrop. If I could focus, if I could crowd out the terrifying thoughts... But I knew I wasn't going to make it across. Already my breathing was labored and I had hardly taken more than a few steps.

Norman sensed that I was no longer directly behind him. He made a gesture to Luke, who had jerked around at the sounds of our approach, and turned to look for me. I gazed at him helplessly, angry at myself for being so weak. Why was it so hard for me to cross high, narrow bridges? It didn't make sense. I could fly in an airplane or a helicopter. I was okay on rooftop patios or anything with a solid stone or brick wall between me and the mountainside. But these thin narrow bridges were my enemy.

It seemed to me an eternity that he watched me without speaking. I couldn't have spoken had I tried. All of my thoughts were taken up with the feeling that I could not breathe. My heart was palpitating, my mouth dry and my hands damp. My lungs strained despite the fact that I stood perfectly still.

Luke turned back to face the Civita and I saw through my terror a black figure running silently down the gradient towards the bridge. The boy gestured to Luke to turn back and they both started towards me. Norman swung about, too, and waved me back in the direction of the cars.

When he reached me, he said nothing about the panic incident. Luke arrived shortly after with the boy Franco. He did not seem surprised to see me.

"My grandfather will come looking for me soon if I don't return," Franco said. "He heard me get up to leave the house and asked where I was going. I told him I heard something outside and was going to check to make sure no one had broken into the shop. I cannot stay long."

"Thank you for coming at all," Luke said.

The boy gestured that we find somewhere out of sight in case his grandfather came as far as the bridge to look for his grandson. He started down the slope just where the bridge began and reached a hand out to me. "The beautiful *signorina* is here, too?" I caught a flash of white teeth in the dark, and then, "Let me help you." He extended his arm further and I graciously latched onto it.

Luke and Norman exchanged amused glances, and then followed down the gentle slope to a wide ledge of rock and shrubbery just below the road.

"It is safe here," Franco said, his face quite clear in the moonlight. "No one will see us."

"Franco," Luke said, squatting and directing his question to the boy who was sitting cross-legged on the ground beside me. I had my back up against the hillside, although the ground was lumpy, and felt quite safe. "Where is this woman that you saw?"

"She is at Giovanni's but the tavern is closed now."

"You saw her?"

"Yes."

"What did she look like?"

"Light hair, like the sun. And she is tall and beautiful like the goddess Athena. Like you, beautiful *Signorina*," he said, showing me his white teeth.

I smiled back. "Thank you, Franco. I'm flattered that you think that." Of course, he was exaggerating. I looked nothing like the elegant and sophisticated Arianna Chase. And my hair was not exactly blonde. But the description was accurate as it pertained to Arianna. It could be no one else.

"Did you talk to her?"

"Oh, no. Giovanni will not let anyone talk to her. He says she is shy, that she is his sister from the north; that is why she is not dark-skinned like our women in the south. They are not blessed with so much sun as we are."

"His *sister?*" I echoed.

I saw Luke swallow and control his voice. "He claims to have a sister?"

"It is what he says. So she must be. She lives with him."

"How long has she lived with him?"

Franco shrugged. "I only saw her yesterday."

"Then when did she arrive?"

"He says it is weeks ago. I don't know. Maybe she did not come to help in the tavern at first."

"Then it can't be her," I said to Luke.

I saw again that cryptic exchange of looks between the two men. "Giovanni. The snake. He's lying," Luke said.

Norman agreed.

"But if he says she's his sister?" I was horrified as I thought about what this potentially meant. Poor Arianna.

"What time does the tavern open?" Luke asked.

"At six o'clock," the boy answered.

"Thank you, Franco. You'd better go back now before your grandfather comes looking for you."

Franco half-rose and peered over the gorge toward the old village. "Yes. I see him. He has a light. He will whip me if I do not return."

My hand shot out in objection. "No. Franco. Really?"

The boy flashed me his white smile again. "Not really. How do you say? I am joker?"

"Joking," I said. "You were just joking. I'm so glad. I'd hate for us to get you into that kind of trouble."

Luke jerked to his feet and removed several euros from his wallet. "You've been a great help. Now you'd better hightail it out of here."

We watched Franco hoist himself energetically over the shallow buttress and onto the road, then he saluted us American-style and took off across the footbridge like a rabbit. Luke followed next and stretched a hand down to help me up. Norman came up behind us.

"Get in the car with me, Lucy," Luke said. "Norman, go back to the hotel. We'll be right behind you."

I have to admit I was a little concerned that Luke might be upset that I had tagged along with Norman to their rendezvous. But when he turned to me after starting the car back in the direction of Bagnoregio his face was calm.

"Lucy," he said. "I'm sending you back to Positano tomorrow morning."

"No."

"It's not safe for you here."

I scowled. "Both you and Norman keep saying that. What exactly is going on? I refuse to leave until you tell me."

"I can't tell you. It would put you in danger."

"I'm already in danger, Luke. Someone broke into our room tonight."

I felt the car jerk as his foot jolted on the gas pedal.
"Who? What happened? Did he hurt you?"
"No. And I don't know who it was; I didn't see him. But I felt him and he left the French door open so he must have come in through the balcony. And left that way."
"I told Norman to keep an eye on you."
"Did you tell him to sleep with me?"
He stared. "What?"
"How else could he keep an eye on me except to sleep in the same room as me?"
Luke was well aware of the sarcasm but he ignored it. "That's why you can't stay. If you stay, then I have you to worry about as well."
"How do you know they won't just come after me if I go back to Positano?"
He was silent. He was used to getting his way and I was thwarting him. The dark scenery slipped by. There was still traffic, but nothing like what it was during the day.
"Tell me what you think has happened to Arianna. Because if you don't, I'm going straight to the police with this story."
"Your Italian's not good enough. They'll never understand you. And even if they did, why would they believe you?"
"I'll tell them about Giovanni and the tavern. I'll tell them about the Gorgon heads." That didn't get a rise out of him, so I added, "I'll tell them about the broken Pelican case at the street stall, how it was looted from the plane. Listen to me, Luke, they *will* be interested. There's an investigation going on, remember? There was a plane crash. If they don't find any evidence of her body along with the others, they'll be very interested in my story." I turned to face him and stared hard at his profile. It was difficult to read his thoughts; he was concentrating on driving. The road was quite empty along this stretch and required little attention. "She's alive, isn't she? You were right. Giovanni has her. Now, what I want to know is why were you so certain she survived?

You're not the only one who cares about her, you know." My last sentence came out angrier than I had intended. I had not meant to reveal my emotions. But if it was the end of my relationship with Luke, then I had a right to know.

He was silent. He continued to resist revealing his secret. Why?

"Does Norman know?" I demanded. "Does he know why it's so important that she's not dead?"

Luke turned to me. "You sound like you want her to be dead."

"Of course I don't want her to be dead! But there's something else going on here. I am not just imagining it." I was almost in tears. I felt like I didn't know Luke anymore. Hell, maybe I had never known him. Wait a minute. What was I thinking? I *didn't* know him. He had bulldozed me into coming to Italy with him. And he was hiding things right from the beginning. Before that he was just some billionaire in the news, as unreachable as the stars. That was all. And now? Oh, what was he to me now…?

"Are you still in love with her?" I asked.

My voice had softened. I had gotten control of my feelings. Whatever reply he gave I would accept. It was all for the best. At least that was what I told myself. Whether I believed it or not was a different matter…

We had arrived back at the hotel and he had parked. We were sitting inside the car in silence. Eventually, he darted a glance my way.

A knock came at the window. It was the concierge from the hotel. "*Prego*," he said. "You cannot leave the vehicle here. I will park it for you."

The silence that followed lasted only a few seconds. "I'm sorry, Lucy," Luke said. "We have to get out."

He turned off the electronic ignition with a push of his thumb, removed the key fob from his pocket, exited the car and handed the key fob to the concierge. I got out on the other side and went into the hotel ahead of him.

CHAPTER
8

We sat at the bar. It was half-past three in the morning and the bar was closed. Most of the chairs were overturned onto the tabletops, and Luke and Norman had tipped three back to the floor for us to use. There was no one to serve us, so Norman removed three S.Pellegrino waters from a vending machine and we drank straight from the glass bottles. The electricity had returned. The lights were half-cast and moody, which perfectly suited the atmosphere of Luke's creating. Apparently the outage was nothing more than a blown fuse in our section of the hotel, on our floor. But Luke and Norman were still suspicious, although they mentioned nothing to the night attendant when he returned after parking our cars.

I was willing to accept the explanation of a blown fuse for lack of a more convincing one. But I refused to accept Luke's silence on the matter of Arianna.

Luke was trying to outwait me. He wanted me to go to bed so that he could avoid answering my question. Norman had joined us; we had no privacy. I refused to pose the question again with him there. I asked instead, "Why do you both think I'm in danger? I mean it, Luke. I will not go back to Positano unless I'm satisfied with the answer."

Then something horrible occurred to me. Luke had a past history of working with smugglers. Just a few weeks ago the Interpol Agent Alessandra Piero had joined his team undercover as a fresco expert in an attempt to expose his involvement in a cold case that took place when he was a university student. Fortunately for him his involvement was proved to be pure fabrication. The Black Madonna was never in his possession. But *un*fortunately for Piero the real smuggler had killed her.

My suspicions were bringing back unpleasant memories. I had known Piero under her alias Marissa Leone; she was a good person. And she had died because of these dirty dealings.

My intuition had me shivering. Had Luke and Norman reentered the trade? How could Luke do something like that after all we had been through to clear his name of any further association with the black market antiquities game? He promised me he had quit but now I questioned his ethics. He was not a traditional archaeologist. He had not entered the business in the usual way. He had bought his way into the business through his wealth.

"It's not what you're thinking, Lucy," he said.

"Tell me what I'm thinking."

When he was silent I exploded. "It's *exactly* what I'm thinking, *isn't* it? It's the only thing that would account for you putting me in danger. Who are these crooks you're working with? And if you've gotten Shaun involved too…"

I could hardly breathe at this point in my tirade. How dare he get my brother-in-law involved? Especially now that he and my sister were starting a family. He could end up in jail! And poor Colleen; that did not even bear thinking about—

"Lucy, calm down. It's nothing like that."

"Like what? How do you know what I'm thinking? Unless it's *exactly* what you're doing?" I could barely look at him I was so angry. I shunned Norman's eyes as well. I was certain whatever shady activity Luke Trevanian was involved in Norman Depardieu was in it just as deep.

"If you'll calm down, I will tell you."

My head felt like it was going to explode but I forced myself to breathe. "Okay, fine. I'm calm. Tell me what you're hiding."

"Arianna was involved in something."

A scowl was on the verge of appearing on my face. Was that how little he thought of my intellect? "That's obvious. What was it? Did she get Shaun involved, too?"

"I don't know," he said.

You don't know? This time I failed to repeal the emotion. What did he mean? That he was unaware of what she was *involved* in, or whether *Shaun* was involved? Either way, I could scarcely believe him.

"It is not illegal." He paused. "Well, okay to some people it might be considered illegal. That Gorgon head did not come from anywhere in Italy. No—" He correctly read the question in my eyes. "It came from the Middle East. Palmyra."

"What?"

"Arianna had picked up the remaining pieces of the triptych in Florence before arriving here. They were secretly brought over the border from Syria into Turkey and transported west. The piece I gave you to draw arrived first with some Roman silver. She thought her contacts had lost the remaining pieces of the triptych so she went in person to claim them when they were located. I warned her not to—"

"She's a...smug...smuggler?" I had trouble getting the words out.

He looked at me and shook his head. "She—well—*smuggles*—for lack of a better word—precious antiquities in order to protect them from the rebels looting archaeological sites in Syria."

I finally understood. Some of the most valuable heritage sites were being dug up. Rebel groups were selling artifacts to fund terrorist activity in the Middle East. The current government was helpless to stop the rampage, and maybe it wasn't even a priority since human lives were at stake. But Syria had some of the oldest artifacts in the world; they represented the most ancient civilizations—and all of that was being destroyed. And Palmyra was home to some of the oldest Roman sites and hence some of the most precious antiquities.

"She was trying to save them and got caught in the crossfire," he said.

"And you knew about this?"

"Only superficially. I told her it was dangerous and refused to be a part of it. It's a long road between Palmyra and Toronto. There are various stages to go through which is why they call it a smuggling ring, but it's really more like a chain. First there are the looters in the east, then the buyers, and then the runners, then the dealers in the west and finally the collectors. That's where the big money comes from. Unethical collectors. Arianna tried to intercept this process and get the goods directly from the crooked buyers in the east, using her own people to then run the stuff across Europe. I told her I couldn't be a part of it and that she shouldn't either. She was putting her career in jeopardy. If the board of governors ever found out she could lose her job as director of the ROM... Stop looking at me like that, Lucy. After all, you wanted me to quit smuggling. And it *is* still smuggling, even if it *is* for the greater good. Remember," he said, when he caught the persistent judgment in my expression. "I swore off the business for good."

"But this is different. Those rebels, the Islamic extremists, are killing anyone who tries to stop them from destroying what they believe to be pagan symbols. And it wasn't until they realized they could sell off some of the stuff to questionable collectors in the west that they started to dig them up or break them into pieces and sell off the parts so that they could buy artillery."

I knew all about the situation in Syria concerning antiquities trafficking. After all, I worked in a museum and had some training as an archaeologist. But never in my wildest dreams did I suspect Arianna Chase of being a philanthropic artifact runner. She always seemed so self-centered to me, and officious. She did everything by the book and made sure that all of her employees did also. I was beginning to have a growing respect for her, despite the fact that she was breaking international law.

"And you've known about this how long?"

"She only told me about it a year ago. I don't know how long she's been involved. She knew how I felt about antiquities trafficking and that I would disapprove. She told me to think of it as a salvage operation. That we were rescuing precious objects from destruction or worse—from being sold on the black market to fund terrorism."

I gasped. What a brave woman... and all this time, to think that I believed she was some high society gal who had never even picked up a gardening spade no less dirtied her hands with dusty artifacts... "And none of us suspected. And you *knew*—" I had no words to express what I was feeling.

"That was to protect *you*. To protect all of her employees... So, you see why this is dangerous, Lucy, and why I want you out of it."

I wondered for a split second if that accounted for the animosity between him and his ex-wife. Arianna Chase wanted to save the heritage of Palmyra for posterity and Luke Trevanian wanted to protect his reputation. There was a huge gap in the two ways of thinking and I was leaning towards camp Chase. "Why would anyone be after me?"

"Because of *me*." He thumped a fist against his chest. "I'm getting too close to learning the truth."

"That Arianna is alive?"

He nodded.

I frowned. "Who do you think has her? I mean I know the name is Giovanni Zia, but who is he? What's his role in all of this? Is he mafia? A terrorist?"

"Oh, I doubt if he's a terrorist," Luke said.

At this point Norman cut in. "He's nobody important. He is just doing the grunt work. He's slipping the goods out of the country and into the hands of disreputable dealers. And it's possible that Franco's grandfather has been innocently recruited as well. Don't forget, these people are incredibly poor and their village is about to be condemned. There will come a time when the government of Italy will evict them against their will. It will be too dangerous for them to live there, what with the crumbling buildings and broken roads. This is one way to get the money to repair the unstable infrastructure of their ancient town."

"I hate to think they've involved those boys in it too. Franco and his cousin Giorgio."

Norman shrugged. "Things are different here."

"That's why the first order of business is to definitively identify Arianna," Luke insisted. "If they have her then we have to get her out. There's no doubt she's being held against her will. The problem is how to get her out of there without creating a scene. We don't want whoever's trying to sabotage Arianna's rescue efforts in Syria to know that we're on to them." He stopped to take a breath.

I piped in, "I think I know who can help or who might know something."

"Who?" Luke demanded.

"The director of the National Archaeological Museum in Naples. What was his name? D'Agostino."

"Why?" Luke asked. "Why do you say that?"

Norman perked up at this point in our conversation. "Because of the Roman dinner setting?" he queried looking sideways at me. "You think those pieces of silver came from Palmyra as well?"

"Yes." I nodded. So Norman had also remembered seeing the dinner set at the museum in Naples, and had drawn the same conclusion. "Because the ROM has similar pieces that must come from that collection. They had a distinct pattern on the borders, a grape motif. I saw the Roman silver downstairs in Shaun's lab." Did that mean my sister's husband was part of the illicit plan to save Palmyra's heritage too? "If Arianna was sneaking the artifacts from one museum to the other, then someone would have to receive them. Someone she trusts."

"Well that's a connection. But a loose one. I can't exactly come out and accuse D'Agostino of being partner to Arianna in stealing Roman artifacts from Syria. But now it makes sense why she wanted the twin endowment. So that the two museums would be legitimately linked and no one would question the trading of artifacts...." He paused to think, sighed. "Well, we'll cross that bridge when we come to it."

Then another name occurred to me. "What about Dr. Kharim?"

"What about him?" Luke asked. I felt the tension return.

"You might as well tell me now. I know you're acquainted with him, or if you're not, you recognize the name."

"I've never met him," Luke said, finally relenting. "But you're right. I recognize his name. He *is* one of Arianna's associates."

The pieces were coming together. "And he came to the gala to find you. He knew something was going to happen this week. He knew something was going to happen to Arianna and when he couldn't get hold of her to tell her that her life was in danger, he came looking for you." I slumped back in my chair, triumphant.

"Only it happened earlier than he expected."

I leaned forward. "He still wants to see you, Luke. I think he has some information."

"I agree, but my first priority is to get Arianna away from Giovanni."

"I wonder why she hasn't tried to get away on her own? She could easily cross that bridge and into Bagnoregio to the police."

"Maybe she doesn't want to leave?" Norman suggested. "Maybe it's her way of finding out who's behind sabotaging her plane."

"You mean you think one of her team might have

betrayed her?" I asked.

"Anything is possible," Norman said. "Remember, these are rebels we are dealing with. They can easily slip among us and walk beside us and we'd never know. Their religious beliefs may be the only thing that motivates them, but they know how to behave in western society. They know we value individual lives, and if anyone has a family connection with the Middle East, it may be possible to coerce them into helping the rebels."

"No," I said. "No one that we know or that Arianna knows would switch sides even to save the life of someone they loved."

Norman shrugged. Luke smiled at me tenderly. "My sweet Lucy. Always wanting to see the best in people. That's why I want you to go back to Positano. You're too trusting. We are not dealing with nice folks. They will kill with the right motivation."

"But who *are* they?"

"I don't know. And at this point I'm not sure who we can trust. This man Sulla Kharim, did he say anything else?"

"Only that the plane crash was intentional. Someone wanted Arianna dead. Someone wanted to put a halt to her artifact rescue efforts."

"Well, we can't get a visual on Arianna until the tavern opens tomorrow night. So I say, first thing in the morning I go look for Sulla Kharim. While I'm doing that, Norman, I want you to go back to the Civita and find Franco. Get him to keep a watch on any sightings of Arianna, and make sure you don't let on that you know anything about the smuggling. He's willing to help us because he thinks it's only Arianna that concerns us. If he knew we were onto his grandfather, we'd get no cooperation from him or Giorgio. And we might need help from both of them before this operation is over. Then do some reconnaissance yourself. Find out what you can about Giovanni Zia. I want to know what's going on before we attempt a rescue."

"And I'm coming with you," I said to Luke.

***

It was clear to Luke that I would go to bed only if he went also. He suggested we turn in. He had given me much to think about. I was certain I wouldn't sleep a wink.

I was right and not for the reasons you might think.

Because of the possible danger to him and myself, and because someone had broken into our room earlier tonight, Luke decided Norman should share our room. I could see how Norman might object. There was only one bed and despite it being a Queen it was inadequate for three.

Where was Norman supposed to sleep? The furnishings excluded a sofa. As a luxury accommodation, the Hotel Bagnoregio missed the boat.

Or did the job of bodyguard require Norman to go sleep deprived?

Luke was in a thorny mood. No surprise. He had no intention of making love tonight, and even if he had he wouldn't have cared all that much if Norman was in the room. But I did.

I was in the bathroom brushing my teeth while they worked out the sleeping arrangements. At this point I was too tired to care. When I returned to the room Luke was stripped to his shorts and lying on one side of the bed while Norman lay on the other with shirt off but pants still on. They both looked amazing and it took immense willpower to shift my gaze from their half-naked, spectacular physiques to their faces.

Where did they expect me to sleep? I stood in the middle of the floor in my white silk negligee and turned to Luke.

I dodged even peripheral eye contact with Norman as I raised my hands palms up. I fully suspected Luke had done this on purpose to avoid being alone with me. He was still ducking my earlier question, and worried that I would ask it again. And I *would* have—had it not been for Norman's presence.

Was Luke still in love with Arianna?

Luke got up to use the bathroom, and indicated that I get into the center of the bed. Oh great. This was all I needed. To know that Norman was sleeping next to me. When Luke closed the bathroom door I crawled gingerly into the bed beside Norman, leaving a space on the other side for Luke. "Didn't think you were a threesome kind of girl," he joked.

I peered through my eyelashes at him, giving him what I hoped was a withering look.

He grew quiet. "Look, Lucy. If you feel uncomfortable with me here, I'll go sit on that chair."

The chair he indicated was made of wood.

That would be cruel.

"No. It's okay. Stay where you are."

I remained on my haunches and studied the two pillows against the headboard, one of which Norman was resting on. If I took the other one, Luke would be pillowless. And I for one could not sleep without a pillow. Norman recognized my dilemma and slid the pillow out from under his back. "Here, you have it. I don't need a pillow."

It was one of those long pillows meant for King or Queen sized beds. I shook my head. "No. You have it. I'll share with Luke."

"Luke doesn't share pillows," he said.

"Really?"

His lips jerked slightly at the corners. "He's a billionaire; he doesn't have to share pillows."

I laughed. Why was it that Norman could always ease the tension out of a tense situation?

All I had to do was not look at his throat, his shoulders, his arms or his chest. Yes. I could do this. I settled myself against the left side of the pillow and patted the right. I *could* do this.

He shifted his weight so that I could pull the covers over myself and sat a little more upright against the headboard. I don't know why I felt suddenly shy. It wasn't like Norman had never seen me half-naked before. In fact he had seen it

all. Maybe *that* was the problem.
I patted the right side of the pillow again. "That means you can use this side. I don't really have that big of a head."
His eyes looked bemused, then shot through with humor. "Probably best if I don't, but thanks for the offer."
He searched the nightstand for his cigarettes and popped one out. "Mind if I smoke?"
"Yes," I said.
He glanced over and down at me, his broad back still leaning against the bare headboard. He put the cigarette back in the box and stared straight ahead.
"Can you turn out your light," I asked. "It's shining in my eyes."
He switched out the lamp.
I closed my eyes, my face slightly turned his way. I could feel him observing me. Or at least I thought I could feel his gaze on me. I opened my eyes and found that it was true. My sudden stare into his face left him unfazed.
"What are you looking at?" I asked.
"Was I looking? I didn't mean to." He turned his vision back toward the far wall at the door.
Why did I want to reach out and stroke his arm? He had incredible muscles. *Eyes front and center.* I must not look. Luke would be back any moment and he would catch me ogling his bodyguard.
"Go to sleep, Lucy," Norman said.
At that moment, Luke returned and rolled into bed beside me. I was now sandwiched between two of the most gorgeous men this side of Mount Vesuvius.
"'Night, Lucy," Luke said.
"Good night."
No term of endearment was expressed. He had simply addressed me by my name. Why did that bother me?
Luke fell asleep almost immediately. I could hear his even breathing. I lay awake staring at the ceiling, feeling the need to curl up in someone's arms. Clearly it was not going to be Luke. And Norman was out of the question.

How many women had the opportunity to bed down with two hunky men and be forbidden to have sex with either of them? I rolled over to watch Luke's back. He had perfect back muscles and strong arms and nice shoulders. I felt Norman move on my other side and I stiffened. I was never going to get any sleep. Not with him there.

I turned and rolled smack into Norman's chest. He had rolled over at the exact same moment, and now we were in an awkward lover's embrace. His arm accidentally flung over my shoulders to land somewhere near my butt. And my right hand slammed his collarbone.

We should have separated immediately. But for a long, very long couple of seconds we remained in that position. It felt wonderfully arousing and at the same time safe.

"Sorry," he said, and disentangled himself from me, as his erection grew against my thigh.

"Sorry," I mumbled, embarrassed.

This was not going to work. What was Luke thinking?

Norman flung himself onto his back; I did likewise. I was hot and breathless. And sleep was a million miles away.

The mattress bounced ever so slightly as he swung his legs to the edge and sat up slowly. He still had his pants on. And although he had stayed on top of the covers, that had not prevented us from an awkward horizontal tangle.

I raised myself on one elbow. "Where are you going?"

"For a smoke," he whispered in a gravelly French toned voice.

"It's the middle of the night."

"It's actually closer to morning... I'll be on the balcony," he said.

And I'll be here, I thought, *wishing you were here.*

What was the matter with me? I turned my face into the pillow to hide my guilty thoughts.

I raised my head to watch Norman's sexy torso go behind the heavy curtain, out the glass door and onto the balcony. He spent the rest of the night out there, and only returned indoors at dawn when Luke woke up. He went to his own room to shower and shave.

CHAPTER

9

Morning came with sunshine and scattered clouds. Norman had drawn the drapes wide open before he left. Luke and I got out of bed and took a shower together. There was a time when we couldn't have showered together without physically reacting to each other. It didn't matter how sexy I looked or felt, Luke resisted me. How could I blame him? And yet I did. But my insecurities would have to wait. This was neither the time nor place. A life might be at stake.

He got out of the shower first and called the number on the Syrian curator's business card. It was long distance to Aleppo. The secretary at the other end informed Luke that Dr. Kharim was currently at the ICOM meetings in Italy.

We had forgotten all about the meetings. Naturally the International Council of Museums would not cease all activity because of one deceased member. Attendees had flown in from all over the world to meet in Naples. There was a good chance we would find Kharim still there.

Luke decided since we would be flying back to Naples that he wanted his bodyguard with him. After Norman instructed a more than eager Franco to keep an eye on Giovanni's house and tavern for signs of the alleged sister, he returned to us and we traveled by helicopter back to Naples.

From the heliport we took a taxi downtown to the Museo Archeologico Nazionale, aka the National Archaeological Museum. Since we weren't expected, Luke decided not to startle everyone with our sudden presence. He wanted to keep a low profile to avoid having to answer questions concerning the plane crash, and the never-ending river of condolences.

There were conference rooms on the upper floors of the building. We slipped into the back of a symposium that was in session. It was hard to isolate the members of the audience from a rear view, but I thought I might be able to recognize our target by his height and build and the color of his hair. It did occur to me as we were sweeping the room with our eyes that he might have given the lectures a miss. After that conversation I had had with him, it appeared to me that he had no interest whatsoever in ICOM's boring talks.

I nudged Luke out of the room without attracting too much attention our way, while Norman followed and told Luke when we were safely ensconced in the corridor that I doubted Kharim would be attending any conference sessions. "His whole reason for coming here was to meet *you*. I don't think he even belongs to ICOM."

One way to ascertain that. Luke led us to the administrative offices and asked for a list of members. The secretary was hesitant to comply until Luke showed his credentials. Then she greeted him with a fabulous smile. Who hadn't heard of Luke Trevanian, world adventurer and billionaire archaeologist? After he turned on the charm we were considered quite the celebrities. She bent over backwards to accommodate us. And if Luke were inclined to reciprocate her obvious flirting, I would have meant that literally!

We ran down the names and saw that indeed Sulla Kharim's was absent from the list. So where was he? And how could we find him? We returned the list to the office and Luke asked if the secretary had ever heard of Dr. Sulla Kharim. She shook her head.

Perhaps Dr. D'Agostino was acquainted with him? She shrugged. Perhaps, but she wouldn't know. She punctuated the response with a coy smile.

"Can we wait for him?" Luke asked. "Bruno and I are good friends. He won't mind. Can we wait in his office?"

"I don't know how long he will be."

"Well, we can wait for a half hour. If he doesn't show up we will leave."

Luke was cranking up the charm. He had mesmerizing eyes. They were a cross between green and blue, but more green. Was it the effect of contact lenses? Not a chance. He had no need for corrective lenses. His vision was perfect. But there was something about the way he looked at you, the crinkle at the corners of his eyes and the twinkle itself that could almost hypnotize, and well Luke knew it. And not only that but it seemed to work on men as well as women. Somehow the intensity of his gaze elicited trust. It had worked on me, and now I noticed that it worked on almost everyone. Having that sort of power was a gift. It annoyed me to watch women swoon all over him like this.

The secretary had a kind of dreamy expression on her face as she clung on every word that left Luke's lips. I glanced at Norman. Was he noticing this? Or was it just me—and what most people would consider a lover's jealousy?

Norman's lips twitched in amusement; I returned the sentiment. It wasn't like Luke ever did anything on purpose. He just seemed to evoke that kind of response in people.

I inwardly shrugged as Luke waited pleasantly for an answer. Of course, she should stop us entering the director's office in his absence. But did she? No. What was *wrong* with her? She drew the keys from her desk drawer as though she were some kind of robot, and opened the adjoining office and let us in. Luke gave her a brilliant smile, ushered Norman and myself inside, and closed the door.

"You realize that woman is going to be in deep trouble?" I said to Luke.

"Not my problem. Look around and see if there's anything to tell us if he knows Sulla Kharim."

"Look, here's an address book. I think. Holy cow. Do people really still keep paper address books?"

"Bruno does," Luke said.

I flipped to the K's and ran my finger down the rows of names and addresses. "There he is. There are two numbers. One is his museum in Aleppo. This other one looks like it might be local." I looked up at Luke. "What made you think Dr. Kharim knew Bruno D'Agostino?"

"Nothing," Luke said. "I was just taking a shot. I was going to ask Bruno if he knew him since he had shown up at the museum's gala the other night." He glanced swiftly at the closed door. The window there was frosted. No one could see our actions. "Take a photograph of that page," he instructed Norman. "I guess we don't need to wait for Bruno now."

We all turned to leave when the door opened and D'Agostino walked in. His face was controlled and pleasant, but I sensed an underlying tension. I wasn't surprised. No responsible secretary allowed visitors into the boss's office while he was away. That was unheard of. But D'Agostino was gracious, and if he was exasperated with his staff by our impromptu visit, he hid it well.

"How can I help you, Luke?" he asked.

Luke decided to come clean. He told the museum director what he suspected and asked him to keep it mum. He omitted how he thought Arianna was alive. The fact was unconfirmed, and he had not actually seen her with his own eyes. However, he did relate how Sulla Kharim had hinted at sabotage.

D'Agostino's eyebrows shot up. "That is quite the assertion, Luke," he said. "What kind of proof do you have?"

"Personally? None. It's only his word, which is why I need to find him and talk to him. The authorities will want to interrogate him as well, to learn why he thought this."

"And he told you the plane was tampered with?" D'Agostino said to me.

Something about the director's controlled patience made me cautious. I nodded. I was more nervous than I cared to be. "More or less. Luke was too busy to see him and then the crash happened and he was busy with that, so I went to the coffeehouse to meet him."

D'Agostino's face showed very little emotion. I wondered if the last few days had drained him as it had done us. This tragedy was having wider implications than any of us could have imagined, and it wasn't over by a long shot.

The director sighed. "Such a tragedy. And now this. Foul play? Oh, what next." He went behind his desk and invited us to sit. There were only two visitor's chairs so we declined, although Norman would have stood by the door to stand watch as usual.

"We have to go," Luke said. He pushed the chair in for emphasis. "I just stopped in to ask if you might have a local address or phone number for Dr. Kharim?"

It was difficult to pretend nonchalance. I fought the mortification that threatened to expose me as the three of us stood tensely awaiting his answer. We couldn't exactly admit to having snooped in his address book and found it ourselves.

D'Agostino absently nudged the black address book towards the edge of his desk and slipped it into a drawer.

"I'm afraid not," he said, silently shutting the drawer. "Kharim. Sulla Kharim? No. The name rings no bells. I'm certain we are unacquainted." He smiled. "I may have met him at one of these meetings but—" He shrugged. "I meet so many people all the time... so, no. I don't have his number."

We escaped giving ourselves away by avoiding any exchange of glances, but now I wanted to leave as quickly as possible. Bruno D'Agostino was aware of more than he was willing to admit. There was a tension in the air so thick you could taste it. And Luke knew better than to call him on it before Arianna was securely out of harm's way.

***

We left the museum as though it were a condemned

building ready to collapse onto our heads. None of us spoke until we were safely out on the street.

"He lied," I said.

Luke nodded. "But why?"

"It seems to me that D'Agostino is in on this, too," Norman said.

"It doesn't mean he's the bad guy. He may be protecting Sulla Kharim."

"But if he *is*?" I asked. "The bad guy I mean?"

"That's why I didn't ask him. I almost told him that we knew he was acquainted with the curator from Aleppo. It would have been quite revealing to see how he reacted."

Luke scratched his head. His beach boy curls caught the breeze.

"But if he's smuggling for the rebels."

"Unlikely," Luke said, frowning at me.

"Then why deny knowing Kharim?"

"That's what I need to find out. But right now let's look at that phone number. I want to call him."

Norman turned on his phone and showed Luke the number from the page that he'd photographed from the address book. Luke punched it into his keypad. The line rang. There was no answer. "Is there an address?" Luke asked.

There was. It was the address of a cheap hotel on the darker side of town. The Spanish Quarter.

"Maybe we should grab a bite to eat, then if there's still no answer we'll go to his accommodation."

That was a good idea. It was hard to think on an empty stomach and we had skipped breakfast. I was starving now and so were the men. We found a nice restaurant and went inside to fill our grumbling bellies and rest our tired legs.

An hour and a half later, we were sated with pizza and salad, and were back on the street. Luke tried the phone number one more time. When still no one answered, he hailed a cab. He told the driver to take us to the street address of the seedy hotel.

When we got there twenty minutes on, a number of

police vehicles were at the scene.

CHAPTER
10

The Spanish Quarter looks nothing like the postcard Naples that tourists are more likely to recognize. This part of town lacks the medieval palazzo style of architecture characteristic of Italian cities with their paved courtyards and roads. It is impoverished, a refuge for criminals. There is no colorful laundry dripping from picturesque buildings drenched in sunshine. Street-side shrines appear intermittently, and children chase after feral cats, mongrels and chickens. Vespas are the vehicle of choice as the streets are so narrow.

Our taxi crawled between the lively alleyways almost scraping the walls of thin buildings. There were women sitting outside on kitchen chairs with babies and vendors on the street corner hawking stolen cigarettes, lighters, and bottled water and lottery tickets. Most of the alleyway turned into stairs up and down the hillside from shabby-looking buildings. From here we would have to walk.

Luke paid the cab fare and we got out. The neighborhood was foot-bound and close-knit. The one or two-room apartments were all ground floor, and we saw that the hotel where Kharim was registered was not really a hotel but a boarding house. With the police there, traffic had no room to move. They had arrived on motorcycles. A single ambulance blocked the entrance.

Oh my God, what had happened? Luke debated whether or not he should reveal his presence and barge into the crime scene to make enquiries. We were assuming it was a crime scene, otherwise why so many police? Two or three reporters had arrived as well.

Luke traded quick glances with Norman. "What do you think? Should we go in? I have to learn what happened."

"Might not be such a good idea," the bodyguard answered. "Maybe I should go. If you're recognized the media will pounce on you. And worse, they'll think you're involved somehow. Because, what other reason would you have for being on this side of town and concerned over a little known Syrian smuggler?"

Smuggler? Was this true? Did Kharim actually run the goods or was he only a stopgap, using his museum to temporarily store the objects before they were snuck across the boarder into Turkey?

My imagination was going into overdrive.

"That would jeopardize our mission to rescue Arianna," he continued. "The authorities and the media will delay you. And we don't want either one of them following us."

"You're right. It will have to be you, Norman. Glad I didn't leave you behind in Bagnoregio."

"*Mon Dieu*," Norman said. "What is she doing?"

I was no longer listening. I had just caught the oath as I slipped past the men and out into the open where a crowd was gathering.

"She's going to do it herself," Norman said.

"Lucy, get back here!" Luke shouted in a loud whisper. "You don't understand enough Italian."

He was wrong. I understood enough of the local lingo to learn why the police had been called. Like it or not I was their best bet. Either of them could be recognized. While I, on the other hand, blended in quite well with the street folks. He continued to reprimand me in a low voice. I ignored him.

"What's happened?" I asked the first person I came across.

The woman glowered at my English. She stared at me uncomprehendingly, muttered something in Italian and went away in a swirl of ragged skirts and the piquancy of sausage. I approached the next person. He was smoking, dressed in grubby black slacks and shirt with a sloppy thin jacket. I was about to speak to him when I caught, out of my corner vision, an unlikely sight. Most of the people in this neighborhood were poorly dressed, which was what made this person stand out. My glimpse of her was brief; long enough to identify her as female and to note that she was taller and thinner than most of the people in this crowd. She was an outsider. Her face was obscured by the horde—visible for a split second, and then gone. But I did remember a flash of red. Her blouse? A jacket? I frowned. Why did that ring bells in my memory?

And then the police officers at the front door of the building started ushering people away. They had a gurney with a body on it. The face was uncovered. I recognized the beard and the olive complexion and the small neat hands with the plain gold band. The left arm had fallen loose and was dangling off the side of the gurney. One of the paramedics noticed the arm and hauled it back onto the victim's chest. Dr. Kharim? The white sheet over him was soaked with blood. That's when I froze. Was he dead or merely injured?

Yes. I was pretty convinced now that this was foul play and not an accident. The man had not suffered a heart attack or some kind of seizure. There was too much blood. This was not some sort of a medical emergency.

"*Va'via!*" The police officer shouted, waving his hand to scatter the crowd. In my mind I was translating, *'Go away. Nothing to see here.'*

"Excuse me. *Chi è quello?*" I hoped I had asked the right question. I needed confirmation. My accent was terrible but I repeated the question, "*Chi è quello. Signor* Kharim?"

"Kharim?" the policeman said to me. He rambled off in

Italian so fast I failed to translate a single word. Finally, he stopped when he noticed the blank look on my face. "You know this man?" he asked in English. "You know the *signore*?"

"I met him a few days ago at a gala at the *Museo Archaeologico*." In my nervousness I was pretty certain I had pronounced every syllable incorrectly.

"You are a friend?"

"No, I only met him once."

"Then why are you here?" The officer's English was infinitely superior to my Italian.

"We both work in museums and he gave me his card." I swiftly fetched the business card out of my deep handbag and showed it to him. This one was the first card he had given me, the one he had handed to me at the museum gala. It had the address of the coffeehouse scribbled on the back of it.

"I will keep this," he said.

"Of course."

He took out a pen and uncapped it. "You will give me your name and a number where I can reach you."

I stared like a dimwit. "Of course." I gave him the name of the hotel where we were staying.

"Why do you stay in Bagnoregio?"

"Sightseeing," I answered lightly. The trip from Naples was a three to four hour drive depending upon which route you took. I couldn't very well tell him we had our own personal helicopter. "We are only here for a conference and are headed to Bagnoregio to see the sights this evening. Our hotel is already booked." I was a little worried at this point that he'd tell me to remain in town, so I laid it on thick, "I can assure you, I know nothing about this man. He told me where he was staying and when a group of us from the museum meetings, ICOM—Have you heard of the International Council of Museums? (I knew he hadn't but I had to make my explanation as boring and confusing as possible so that he would lose interest in me.) It's an organization where museum workers come together from all over the world to meet and discuss our museums' goals. Anyways, we decided to go for lunch, and we included Dr. Kharim on our guest list."

"*Si, si,*" he said, disinterestedly. "All right, so why do you come in person? Why not just telephone him?"

"Oh, I did," I said. "I phoned him and got no answer, so I came down in person to invite him to join us. I was in the neighborhood. Sightseeing, you know."

He arched his brow. *Yeah, I know.* What was to sightsee in this neighborhood? The Spanish Quarter, an ancient seaport was five minutes downhill from the lovely bourgeois Vomero district by the funicular railway, and if that wasn't explanation enough, let me reiterate. It was an old seaport full of seedy characters, the smell of boat oil and garbage.

Architecture, I thought. Yes. The Romans, the Greeks, the Spanish and the Moors had all left their mark on this city. "I am interested in the old architecture."

"I see. But it is dangerous here for tourists. You should go to the Vomero. There it is nice."

The Vomero is home to Naples' middle class, and a popular neighborhood for tourists. "I will," I promised, to show I appreciated his concern. "Please, before you chase me away, I must know. Is Dr. Kharim alive? And do you know what happened to him?"

"It is not for me to say." The policeman scribbled something down on a pad. The curtness had returned. "We will be in touch."

Officially, he was forbidden to speak. I realized that. Gossip or hearsay could jeopardize the case. But I was certain he knew, was aware, at least, of whether or not the man was dead. I shot a quick glance at the ambulance, but Kharim's body was already inside and they were closing the doors. Things were done differently here, especially in these poor neighborhoods. It would be presumptuous of me to guess at the victim's condition based on my knowledge of medical and police procedure in my own country. The officer let me go and I returned to Luke and Norman.

I waited until the policeman had turned his head away to consult with one of his colleagues before I spoke. "It's Sulla Kharim. I recognized him."

"Did you find out what happened?" Luke asked.

I shook my head. "The officer was very pleasant, but naturally, he wasn't allowed to say."

"The face wasn't covered," Norman said. "Does that mean he's alive?"

"I don't know. He didn't *look* alive." I added, "Nothing we can do about that. If he's still alive he won't be able to talk. His injuries looked serious. There was blood everywhere."

Luke glanced at his phone for the time. "Let's go find a café, and figure out our next move. We can't go for Arianna until tonight so we have plenty of time to think things through."

As we left the rooming house and followed the narrow road I could see why the police had arrived on motorcycles. The streets were viciously tight for cars. It would be a nightmare for the ambulance to navigate this maze if not for the fact that most people were too poor to own cars anyways.

I understood now why Kharim had sought a room in this neighborhood. It was out of the way and no one would ever think to look for him here. It also had a strong Arab flavor. Centuries ago the Spanish drove the Moors (who were of Muslim descent) out of Naples and left Moorish architectural details, memories of the golden age of Andalusia. The two shopping streets, Pigna Secca and Emmanuele de Deo were so crowded as to rival any Middle Eastern marketplace. It was bustling and noisy so we continued to weave our way through the clots of humanity. There were numerous trattoria where rich smells of fried seafood, tomato sauce, garlic, basil and lemon thickened in the air.

We passed a few locals seated outside indulging in octopus and pasta, and red wine served in carafes. I almost wished we had passed on eating earlier; the delicious smells made me hungry. But this was a precarious place for a rest stop. Luke urged us to move faster. He wanted to leave the neighborhood because we looked too obvious. We strolled by several painted murals and a theater house. I was grateful once more for Norman's presence as we ducked the sullen stares of street gangs and the impish grins of urchins just itching for a chance to lift our wallets.

Above the local theater, the Teatro Nuovo, we sighted a gem of a hotel. The Toledo stuck out in the neighborhood like a swan in a lake of ducks. It had a rooftop garden restaurant and it was towards this oasis that we headed. We were seated by a very suave host at a small table amidst small palms, lemon trees, cockatoos and tortoises. We ordered iced teas and bent our heads to pool our knowledge, and take a well-deserved reprieve from the hot afternoon sun.

CHAPTER
11

Dusk came at last. It was all I could do to get Luke to stop pacing. We had returned to our hotel in Bagnoregio an hour ago. He wanted to arrive at the Civita's main tavern as soon as it opened. Both Norman and I dissuaded him by insisting that being the first customers at the bar would make us conspicuous. We waited another hour.

Once again we parked the rental at the roadside just before the bridge. Norman glanced at me as I snatched at a breath and a glimpse of the footbridge ahead. Luke had completely forgotten about my fear of high bridges—if he had ever acknowledged it. He was already forging ahead of us, while Norman looked back at me.

"You don't have to come with us," he said.

"I'm coming," I insisted, clenching my teeth. I would not, *could* not miss this rescue mission because of some stupid reaction my body had towards walking across a steep, narrow overpass.

"Put on your sunglasses, and look straight into the setting sun," he said.

"Won't I go blind?"

"No. The sun is already down. That's just the afterglow. Pretty soon it will disappear and you won't be able to see anything anyways. Here...take my hand." He wiggled his thick fingers and I grabbed on.

Luke never looked back. So much for worrying about him wondering why his girlfriend and his bodyguard were holding hands.

"You know it was foolish for you to go off questioning the police like that on your own." Norman was referring to our adventure of this afternoon.

"I know. I'm sorry. But neither of you two could have done it. They would have asked you why you wanted to know, what your connection to the Syrian curator was, and then they would have taken you both downtown for questioning. I, at least, had an excuse for being there. I had met Dr. Kharim at the ICOM gala; he had given me his business card. And I could pretend quite convincingly that I was in the neighborhood doing some sightseeing."

"And the cop bought that?"

"He did. He took Kharim's business card, and my cell number, but didn't drag me downtown for questioning, now did he?"

"Clever girl," he said with a smile.

"Norman," I ventured tentatively. "Is the ROM really involved in Arianna's artifact running?" I refused to call it smuggling even though technically she was sponsoring the removal of artifacts illegally out of Aleppo. But neither the Syrian government nor the rebels were making the monuments or objects a priority. If they had to, the government forces were blowing up valuable heritage sites to kill the rebels, and the rebels were digging up archaeological sites and toppling ruins to sell on the black market to finance the purchase of guns. Either way valuable antiquities were being destroyed or lost to the world.

"I find it hard to envision her as a crusader," I said.

"She always had a lot of moxy."

Which reminded me that I didn't.

Norman noticed my silence and quickly said, "She has the means and the network."

I found myself wondering once again whether Shaun was directly involved. Where did the artifacts go once they landed at the museum in Toronto? Surely, Arianna had to account for the extra collections. Who did she report to? Did directors of museums report to anybody? Or could they make independent executive decisions? Whatever the logistics, the objects would still have to be stored. And hidden. Were they actually stored at the Royal Ontario Museum? *My* museum?

I realized now that I didn't care if they were. She was doing a good thing and I wanted to help. Thousands of years of art, culture and history should not be wantonly destroyed like that. These were unrenewable resources; valuable information about civilization and the migration of the Romans could be gleaned from Syria's rich heritage. But if the Syrian government should find out about her activities?

"I know I've asked you this before, but please tell me the truth." I flicked a tentative glance at Norman. "Dr. Kharim was such a nice man, so sincere and kind. What was his part in Arianna's rescue campaign?"

"I believe he was the first stop in the entire thing. He would buy the goods from local looters and store them until they could be removed and transported safely out of the country."

"I see," I said. "Did you know him?"

He shook his head.

I peered at him in the dark. Yes, the last of the sunlight was gone and the sky glowed eerily beyond the cluster of stone buildings. "You're telling me you know nothing of Arianna's activities?"

"I only know what Luke knows."

"But you knew that the Gorgon triptych was from Syria. You admitted to being retained by Arianna to escort it to safety."

He nodded.

"That means you and Luke are both part of it."

"No. We were doing her a favor."

"I'm not judging you, Norman. I've come around to her

way of thinking. I admire what she's doing, dangerous though it is."

"That triptych came from what we believe to be an important Roman temple in Palmyra. It is only part of billions of dollars worth of precious remains. Rumor is that the temple hides something even more valuable. Whatever that is, we won't know unless we join forces with Arianna's team and slip into Syria ourselves. Luke said No, but we did agree to escort the Gorgon heads because if we left them in her possession they might not be safe. She knew it and so did we. Unfortunately, the cargo was intercepted at some point along its long and arduous journey—and broken in the process—before Arianna went in person to sniff it out, and recovered the pieces."

"She found those pieces in Florence?"

"It seems that way. Whoever had stolen them, transported them to Italy and tried to pass them off as legitimate items. Arianna bought them back for an exorbitant price from a local dealer who had no idea they were stolen, (of course she never revealed that they were contraband) and meant to transfer them to my safekeeping when we met in Naples."

"But she never made it." I mused pensively. "If she recovered those pieces, she must know who stole them from her people in the first place."

"That seems to be the issue. There's a mole in the network. She wanted to recruit us to discover who it was."

"And Luke said No?"

"That's right. He wanted nothing to do with her crusade for the illicit rescue of antiquities out of Syria."

"He's still worried that his old criminal files could be reopened? But Norman, he was a kid back then. Surely none of it's relevant now? Especially since he discovered who had stolen the Black Madonna. And don't forget, it was he who returned it to the church."

"He can be stubborn that way, and now with what's happened to Arianna there's no possible way he would ever change his mind."

"And *you?*" I asked.

His shoulders lifted and I felt the movement through my arm and into the hand that he held. It was an odd sensation of pleasure, security.

"What *about* me?" he inquired.

"Don't you think Arianna was doing the right thing... *is* doing the right thing?"

He glanced up. Luke was way up the road, flanked by the town's towering stone buildings. His dark figure stood impatiently, fidgety, waiting for us. Norman dropped my hand. We had crossed the bridge and were on the opposite side at the entrance to the old village.

I exhaled in relief. He had done it again, and I almost reached up and kissed him for distracting me long enough to get me across the bridge.

"Who is the mole?" I whispered. I didn't want Luke to overhear what we were discussing as we approached him. He would disapprove of my meddling and would fly me back to Positano—maybe even back to Toronto—if I continued to probe.

"Well, I don't think it's Kharim."

I also had my doubts. But one thing I did know. I wanted to find out where the leak was.

CHAPTER
12

The old tavern was rustic inside. A few tourists and locals from Bagnoregio had come to drink and share in the day's gossip. I could identify the locals by the strange way they stared at us as we walked through the door single file. The whole room went silent on our entry. Then resumed their quiet buzzing as the regulars drew their eyes away when we looked. They behaved like a village with something to hide. If Luke's theory about the threat to their homes was accurate, were they all complicit to the secret inside that kitchen? I had not yet got a glimpse of Arianna but someone other than Giovanni was working behind that swinging door.

No one came to show us a table so we found one by ourselves. The place was half empty. The voices were muted. Was it because of us? It seemed to me there were a few boisterous voices before we entered the room. Perhaps it was my imagination. The night was young. No one was drunk yet. It was Friday evening. Did the Civita's local drinking establishment ever draw a crowd? There were so many more interesting (not to mention *cleaner* places) in the new town.

It wasn't just a drinking establishment. From the warm smells it was clear that they also served food. Good. Because I was famished. The service was casual and after leaving our things at the table, Luke led us up to the counter to order drinks and some dinner.

It appeared that there were also no menus. The evening's offerings were written on a chalkboard on the wall behind the countertop. The dishes were traditional, some of which I could not translate, and so I settled for something familiar: spaghetti with meatballs.

We returned to the sticky wooden table and sat down. Norman brought a decanter of the local red and two short stemless wine glasses. He himself had ordered a bottle of S.Pellegrino.

Luke poured and we sipped the wine. Despite its homely look, it was good. Norman twisted the cap off his bottle of fizzy water and drank from the bottle.

The door to the kitchen flashed open while the tavern owner came out. Inside I caught a glimpse of someone in peasant dress, with her hair tied back, straining pasta over a hot steaming sink, the flames from a gas stove fluttering blue and orange.

Arianna? I turned to catch Luke's eye. He was staring at the now closed door. There was a glass porthole currently fuzzy with condensation.

"Do you think Giovanni ever lets her come out to serve people? Or does she just do the cooking?" he queried.

How incongruous. If that was truly Arianna Chase, then she was even more impressive than I had thought. To think that the great Dr. Chase, director of the Royal Ontario Museum was at this moment slaving over a hot stove, cooking pasta for a local eatery was mindboggling.

"I need to get her out of there," Luke said.

"How?" I demanded. "You can't just walk in there and take her, especially if she doesn't want to go. It's not like she was tied up and locked away somewhere out of sight. From that short glimpse of her, she looks like she has all her faculties."

"Lucy's right," Norman argued. "She's here because she wants to be."

Luke's brow glowered. "I don't care if she's here of her own free will. I still have to find out why."

"Lower your voice, you're drawing attention our way."

The owner, a stocky, dark complexioned man with an ample beard and scruffy clothes looked in our direction. We bent our heads towards each other around the square table as though engaged in some fascinating tourist anecdote.

The door to the tavern opened and Franco walked in. *"Va al diavolo!"* the owner shouted at the boy. The owner had to be Giovanni Zia. He was chastising the boy. Had he owned a wooden rolling pin he would be threatening him with it right now. It was true that Franco was underage to drink in a tavern but I was pretty sure that in the Civita no one paid any attention to age.

"Signor Luke," the boy waved frantically, before indicating the door.

"*Si*, I'm coming." Luke rose and signaled to Norman to follow. "Stay here, Lucy."

Giovanni was bringing me my spaghetti and meatballs so I stayed put. The men ducked outside with Franco and I nodded and smiled at Giovanni. "*Grazie*," I said.

He scowled at the front door as it swung shut behind the men and set down an enormous platter meant for three, alongside a stack of rustic pasta bowls layered with cutlery rolled in white paper napkins. I would have given anything to know what he was thinking. But he said nothing to enlighten me.

He marched back to the kitchen. A few minutes later he returned with a basket of fresh crusty bread and some wooden tongs for serving the spaghetti. Clearly food was consumed family style here.

He said something that I think meant *'do you want cheese on that?'* And I nodded, "*Si. Prego.*"

He went away, and a few minutes later, a peasant woman came out with a small bowl of newly grated Parmesan. I was about to thank her when I realized she was no peasant. Sure she was dressed in the traditional garb, a drawstring neckline and short puffed sleeves with the blouse tucked into a long black skirt of some coarse material. Her dark blonde hair was twisted into a sloppy bun. It looked more brown than gold, with loose tendrils streaming everywhere along her long, white neck. She would have remained incognito if it wasn't for the fine cheekbones, the well-formed mouth and the intelligent eyes. She wore no makeup, but that only emphasized the quality of her skin. She was now a subtle, almost ethereal beauty, masked by the lack of immaculate grooming and the shabby clothes. Did she recognize me? If she knew me she made no sign of it.

It wouldn't surprise me if she thought I was a stranger. Although she was the head honcho of my museum I had only met her in person twice in the entire time that I worked in the ROM's art department.

"Arianna?" I said very softly.

Either she failed to hear, could not understand, or she was ignoring me.

"It's all right Dr. Chase. It's me; Lucy Racine your head artist from the ROM. Luke is here. We're going to get you out of this place." All the time I spoke I kept my head down and my voice low.

"*Non capisco,*" she said. She rattled something off in fluent Italian and left the bowl of grated cheese with me.

Maybe she was afraid to talk to me in a public place. Although the room was nowhere near full, there were enough people to cause a scene. She wiped her hands on the apron that was tied over her long black skirt and sought the Ladies Room. I tried to follow her but apparently tavern washrooms were meant for single person use. I'd have to wait for her to exit.

Back at my table I slipped a plate out from under the rolls of cutlery and filled it with steaming al dente noodles, rich red sauce and spicy meatballs. I picked up a spoon to sprinkle some of the freshly grated Parmesan onto my spaghetti. It smelled wonderfully delicious. I struggled with the idea of feeding myself over going outside to search for

Luke and relate my encounter with his ex-wife.

My stomach won out. The information would keep. She had not recognized me and seemed to perceive English as a foreign language. How could that be? A forked meatball was halfway to my mouth when another question occurred to me. Was it possible that she had amnesia? If she had escaped from the plane crash it would make sense that she had amnesia. But she appeared uninjured otherwise. I took the succulent meatball between my teeth and chewed. Local folk were correct when they said that, sometimes, simple taverns and trattorias were superior to the city ristorantes.

I sipped my wine and watched the door. Arianna exited the washroom and wove her way to the kitchen. Giovanni, the owner, had returned to the tavern the same moment she left for the kitchen. The alleged siblings merely nodded at each other but no words were exchanged. Giovanni went to attend to some customers at the opposite side of the room.

Now was my chance to corner Arianna. I went to the counter to peer at the steamy porthole. As I was wondering if I should just wander into the kitchen on the pretext of searching for the bathroom, the front door opened and a gust of air washed over me. I ignored it because I could see movement beyond the kitchen door. But before I could do anything, a man came up to me, bearing the fresh green smells of the outdoors. He leaned on the counter blocking my view. He was greasy and dark.

"*Salve*," he said.

"*Buona sera*," I uttered, hoping he'd leave after giving his order. Unfortunately for me, Giovanni had not returned to the counter. Arianna came into the tavern when she sighted us waiting, and asked for our selections. I had no choices to make since my order had already been filled. The sleazy Italian ordered a glass of rustic red wine for himself and a Prosecco for myself. I thanked him and refused it.

"You are tourist?" he asked.

"Yes," I said. "But I'm with friends." He was really annoying me because I was trying to get to Arianna. After serving the drinks she made to return to the kitchen. "Wait!" I said, calling out sharply to her back.

"*Si?*" she asked, turning slightly.

My mouth opened but no words came out. I was stumped as what to say. She turned her back to me and left.

"I don't want your drink," I said to the man as he pressed it on me. He appeared to be a local. He was getting positive feedback from the single men at one of the tables. "It's very kind of you but I have drinks already." I hoisted myself away from the countertop where I had been straining to follow Arianna with my eyes. The man grabbed my wrist.

"*Perchè no.* Why not, *Bella?* It is free. It is good. What is wrong with my drink? It is the Italian way. Do you wish to insult the hospitality of my country?"

It was *not* the Italian way. No Italian male had ever behaved this way with me. When was the last time anyone in this country had pushed an unwanted beverage on me? And I did not wish to insult his country. Then I paused. Something made me wonder if this *was,* in fact, his country.

He dusted his knuckles down the top of my hand and I noted the black hairs growing there. A chill went scooting along my arm. I jerked back and when I tried to move away he stepped in front of me.

By now my heart was racing, and the man had locked eyes with me. Who was he? What did he want? I got the feeling that this was not just a standard pickup in a bar. I swallowed uneasily. He pushed the glass of Prosecco towards me.

"No. No, thank you," I whispered, trying to sound more polite than terrified.

Suddenly, I felt another gust from the doorway. A few seconds later, someone else stood behind me.

"Ladies like this drink," the greasy local insisted. "Taste it. You will like it."

He was insistent. Why? Had he drugged it?

"No, thank you," I repeated.

The man's hairy hand came towards me again.

"You heard the lady," Norman's voice said softly from behind me. "She doesn't want the drink."

The man's eyes jerked up. "Who are you?" he demanded.

"I'm her boyfriend."

My head jerked back to catch Norman's hard eyes warning him to back off. Relief flooded my system as the man glared, then scowled, then lifted his wine and went to a table by the east wall to sit with one of his buddies. I raised my eyes to Norman, and he pushed the Prosecco away.

"Why aren't you at our table?" he demanded.

"I saw Arianna," I said. "I thought I might talk to her."

He shook his head, exasperated. "Come on." He took my hand and led me back to the spaghetti and meatballs, which continued to steam.

"Do you think you can stay out of trouble for just ten minutes?" he asked.

I was about to respond with a taut, defensive remark when I caught the glint in his eyes. He was kidding of course, and I smiled sweetly, and lowered my head to my heaped plate. "*Boyfriend?*" I said with razor-sharp sarcasm.

"It got him to leave, didn't it?"

I shot a swift, nervous glance in the greasy man's direction. Now I know why I had thought this joker's actions weren't that of a routine pickup. He reminded me of Dr. Kharim, only much less nice. His coloring was the same and the way he wore his beard. Not to mention his voice. It had a distinctive Middle Eastern inflection to it. He was not a local.

But before I could relay my suspicions to Norman, Luke returned and sat down beside me. He looked distracted, which made me forget all about the Prosecco-pushing terrorizer.

For some reason Luke's appearance always commanded attention. What news did he have from Franco? Norman and I were both silent as we waited for Luke to speak first.

"Giovanni will be out of town tomorrow. His 'sister' Justina goes to the market on Saturday morning. We can get her alone then."

"He calls her Justina?" I asked.

He nodded. He reached over to help himself to the spaghetti while Norman took a chunk of the crusty white bread.

I leaned over and placed my hand on his. "Luke, I think she might have amnesia."

He paused. Then said, "Why?"

"She came to the table to bring me the cheese." I tapped the bowl that he was about to scoop from. "She didn't recognize me. And when I spoke to her she registered no recognition whatsoever."

"That's not surprising. You said you'd only met her once or twice to speak to in person. The museum is a big place. It's unlikely she'd remember anyone except for those she sees regularly."

That was true. "When I spoke to her in English, she showed complete bewilderment. I would swear that she doesn't understand a drop of English."

"I need to talk to her," he said, semi-rising.

Norman grabbed his wrist. "And say what? And how are you going to get past *that*?" He darted a glance at the tavern owner who was now watching us. "Sit down and eat. We are drawing way too much attention to ourselves."

Luke grunted his discontent and slumped down. Norman took the tongs from him and filled a plate. The three of us ate in silence, mostly because the day's work had built up an appetite, but also because there was nothing we could do until Arianna reappeared at our table. I hoped she would.

We polished off the platter of spaghetti and the bread, and washed it down with the rest of the wine. Giovanni came to the table to collect our dishes. We had all been hoping that it would be 'Justina' the sister, but we must have raised suspicions and now Giovanni was keeping a tight rein on her.

"I have to get into the kitchen to talk to her," Luke said.

"I don't think Giovanni is going to allow that. Don't worry, Luke, she's not going anywhere. We can talk to her tomorrow, catch her on the way to the market," I said.

He clenched a fist around his fork. His teeth were clenched as well. "I wish we could stay here all night. It's too bad they don't have a hotel in the Civita."

"They do, Luke," Norman said. "Franco mentioned it to me earlier. It was shut down due to the lack of tourists but it is owned by Franco's grandfather, Landolfo."

"Then we'll get them to reopen it. I'll pay for every room in the place if I have to. I'm staying here until I can get some face-time with Arianna."

"We will need some overnight things," I said.

"Right. After we eat, you and Norman go back and fetch all of our belongings. I'll go make things right with Franco's grandpa."

We finished our meal in silence. Luke paid the bill and we left the tavern. Outside, the night was warm and the moon bright. Shadows moved.

Norman glanced at me. His question? Could I stand to make another crossing over that footbridge? The way he was looking at me made me feel invincible. I turned to seek out Luke, but he was already heading along the road to find Franco and the hotel.

***

Luke had called the Hotel Bagnoregio to inform them of our change of plans. The owner was quite understanding and Norman and I made our way up to our rooms to pack. Luke and I each had a small suitcase. We had never intended to spend so much time away from Positano. I put everything I could find of ours into the two suitcases, and then I went to the bathroom to pack all of our toiletries. It did not take long. As I said we had few belongings. I had finished packing my suitcase and was tucking in the last of Luke's things when I noticed some tidbits remaining on the desktop that should either be discarded or slipped into my purse. The first was a receipt for our refreshments at the Toledo hotel's rooftop patio, above the theater house, where we'd had iced tea amidst the exotic birds and plants. The second and third pieces were a pamphlet from my visit to the underground city, along with the postcard I had purchased and forgotten to mail, and the fourth was Sulla Kharim's business card, which I had given to Luke yesterday.

I flipped the business card over and read the word penned in black ink.

ISORE

While I was absorbed in pondering the meaning of the letters, my iPhone pinged to notify me that I had a text. I thought it was from my sister, Colleen. She had been texting me regularly when I failed to return her phone calls. I glanced at the message. It was from Sulla Kharim. He was alive!

Come to see me at the hospital.

Norman came to my room and walked in through the opened door. He also had a single bag. I looked up. Should I tell him? I was about to, but I had a few questions I wanted answered first.

"Ready to go?" he asked, glancing around.

I shut off my phone, and raised Kharim's business card and pointed a finger at the letters. "What does this mean?"

"What a beautiful night," he said irrelevantly, and looked past me at the view through my gaping French doors to the sparkling skyline. He was pretending he hadn't heard me and had moved strategically toward the balcony.

I stepped in front of him, and if he were going to continue moving he would have to knock me over.

"Who is ISORE?" I demanded. I pronounce it like 'eye sore'. "Or should I assume, since it is written in capitals, that it is not the name of a person, but an acronym?"

Norman placed a hand on either side of my shoulders and stepped back so that we weren't breathing each other's exhaled air.

"Don't try to blow me off," I warned. "I want to know."

Norman's face was blank but I could read him like a book. He refused to tell me anything, but I knew eventually he would. When he still said nothing, I stepped up nearer once more, ignoring the slight thrill I received from being in such close proximity with him. I said, "Is this the organization Arianna works for?"

Norman sighed. He pinched his lips together, still trying to decide how much to divulge. Finally, he nodded, said, "Luke didn't tell you? I thought he had, since he had already let you in on Arianna's cryptic activities.... Well, I suppose it doesn't matter that you know. You're aware of everything else. It's just that the less you know the better off you will be."

My head bobbed up and down, everything dawning on me at once. "I want to join."

The expression on his face was all I needed. "It's too dangerous, Lucy. You are not equipped to deal with the consequences."

"And Arianna is?"

"She has a network. One she created."

I stuffed the business card with the acronym into my pocket. "Sulla Kharim is—*was* part of ISORE, wasn't he?"

Norman exhaled.

"What does ISORE stand for?"

"International Save Our Ruins Effort."

The irony struck. I smiled grimly. "Yes, what the civil war has done in Syria and other unstable countries in the world *is* rather that." It had left great big, gaping eyesores on the landscape where looting was done with grenades and shovels, and whatever tools the rebels could get their hands on.

"I want in."

Norman stared at me in disbelief. "Do you understand what you're saying?"

"Yes."

He paused and rubbed his forehead, then looked up. "It's not up to me. I don't work for them."

"I know. But you know the people who do."

He went silent as he pondered my comment. I wasn't sure exactly what was going on in his mind but I knew that it wasn't on my side. "Do you know how to handle a gun?" he asked.

"No."

"Can you drive a truck?"

"No."

"Can you decrypt code?"

"No."

"Can you detect patterns in data?"

"What do you mean?"

"Can you disappear among the locals and speak their language?"

"No."

"And here's the biggest one of them all. Can you lie? Can you keep a secret?"

I stared at him. I was keeping one now.

"And here's another nasty. If you were caught by one of the extremists would you mind being raped?"

My heart was racing and my voice was trapped between fury, insult and resentment. How dare he try to undermine me? I knew they employed women. The founder of the organization was female. But I also knew he wouldn't stop bombarding me until I saw reason.

"Arianna doesn't do any of that," I said petulantly.

"Are you sure? Even now she's either pretending to be that Italian barkeep's sister or she actually thinks she *is* his sister. If Giovanni Zia wants to marry her off, she will have to do what he says."

"But..."

"Can you fight and kick and scream? Do you know any of the martial arts?"

All right. Enough, I thought.

"Then what good are you to ISORE?"

Mortified to rage, I was about to ask Norman if he could do any of those things himself, when I realized that, of course, he could.

"I could work behind the scenes," I suggested.

Norman resisted a snide comment.

A light rap came at the open door and a young waiter entered with a tray and two glasses holding a very clear liquor. I shot a glance at Norman to inform him that the subject was not yet closed. He shook his head at me to refute it. As far as he was concerned it was shut *and* closed. But I knew something that he didn't and so it wasn't. Not by a long shot.

"Compliments of the house," the waiter said.

I welcomed him with a friendly smile to spite Norman. The waiter possessed the same affable charm as Franco, and I concluded that this must be the cousin, Giorgio.

"I promised to give the lovely *signorina* the grappa. I had promised. I forgot before now, my apologies."

"Thank you, Giorgio. You *are* Giorgio, Franco's cousin?" I asked.

"I am. Thank you for recognizing me. How did you know?"

"You and Franco are very like. Both so handsome and charming."

Giorgio was delighted. "I give you extra grappa. You just call me when you finish this."

"Oh, no. Thank you. But no, Giorgio. This is quite enough. We're on our way out. And," I added superfluously, since our luggage was packed and waiting at the door, "in a little bit of a hurry. We'll be staying at the Civita tonight."

"But you *will* come back?"

"I hope so."

He left the tray on the desk and Norman tipped him generously. The young man flashed me his debonair smile and closed the door.

Norman turned to me and we stared at each other and laughed. Norman knew I hated grappa.

"You don't have to drink it. I can dump it down the sink."

"It's okay, Norman. New things take time to acquire a taste for."

I handed him a glass. All of my antagonistic feelings had abated for the time being. I debated on whether it would be to my advantage to reveal Kharim's text now. The man had not mentioned my bringing anyone with me. And maybe if I handled this task on my own it would prove that I might be of value to ISORE.

Norman was totally oblivious of the debate that was going on in my head. He took the liquor and stared at it. It was clear and looked like water but when you sniffed it, it smelled anything but.

A grin broke through on my face despite my efforts to suppress it. "Don't you like grappa either?" I asked.

He set the glass back on the tray, next to my glass, which I had left untasted. "Actually, I don't drink at all."

I stared at him. "You mean you *never* drink?" Come to think of it I had never seen him consume alcohol. There were only three reasons why people did not indulge. One, they hated the taste. Two, for religious or moral reasons. And three, for health reasons.

I stalled, unable to stop the question, because my eyes did it for me.

He nodded. "I *can't* drink."

"Oh."

I was embarrassed that I had put him in this position. "I'm sorry, Norman. That was thoughtless of me."

He shrugged. "How could it be thoughtless? You didn't know."

"I feel so… stupid. Awkward." I twisted my fingers together because I was flustered. Besides what else could I do with them?

He separated my hands and sat me down on the bed, away from the grappa, where the full glasses taunted. He edged in beside me. "Please don't."

"But I should have known…"

"Why, sweet Lucy. Why should you know?"

"Because I have observed that you never drink anything but coffee and water, and occasionally tea. But I didn't want to ask…"

He gave me a lingering look. I swear there was amusement in the twinkle of his eyes. But when he spoke his voice sounded less than amused. "How astute of you to notice…. Are… you asking now?"

I was silent. It was none of my business. We were barely even friends. Why should he divulge this most private detail of his life? Who was I to him? Only nobody. Luke's girlfriend. And for how long? The way things were going…. Well, I didn't want to think about it. Norman's job was to keep me safe, the same as it was for Luke. I was wrong to ask. I should let it go. But I wanted to know. I was making an awkward situation worse by not leaving well enough alone.

I felt his warm thigh pressed against mine and tried not to think about that. I wondered if he was even aware….

He swallowed and stared across my head towards the windows. His hand came down on my knee. It was a very intimate gesture and yet the expression on his face showed no connection between the act and what he was thinking. "Remember when we were on the bridge and I told you that *every*one is afraid of something?" He lifted his hand off my knee and dropped a sideways glance at me.

I nodded.

"Well, one of my greatest fears is to fall off the wagon. Believe me, I am tempted everyday."

"When did you know?" I paused. "If you don't mind my asking."

"Before college. A whole bunch of unpleasantness related to my drinking happened then. I can be pretty thick sometimes and it took me a long time to realize that you can't fight genetics." He sighed and took a long breath to assemble his thoughts.

"Luke and I were good friends. We used to go drinking

every night. He to drown out the misery of having disappointed his rich father, and me to drown out the misery of not having one at all. My shithead of a dad abandoned my mother, my sister and me. He was a drunk. Squandered away all of his savings and left my mom and us kids destitute. We moved from Montreal to Toronto and my mom and sister went to work for various companies as low-level office staff. I worked in the shipyard and then on numerous ships, but never for long. I couldn't hang on to a job; I drank too much. Then I joined the army. But I was miserable there too. I kept drinking and getting into fights. I was discharged.

"And then I met Luke. Ironically, it was in a bar. Things were great for a while, until I made the stupidest mistake of my life. I almost beat the crap out of a guy for stealing my whore of a girlfriend. Luke intervened. He made things right, kept me from going to jail. Made me see that the girl was not worth it. He paid for all the damages to the bar and to the guy; then told me about this venture. He had been to Italy the previous summer and was offered a lucrative opportunity that would make us both rich. Only thing, he said, was that I had to be sober. Our lives might depend upon it. After our summer on the Amalfi Coast—smuggling artifacts as you have probably guessed—I enrolled in some college courses and eventually got a degree. Luke was hoping to do a PhD by then. But it was only when I started school and thought I could drink socially that I realized I could not. There was a reason for all of those pub brawls; I was out of control when I was drunk. Booze was anathema to me. And I could not seem to stop at just one."

"So you quit, cold turkey?"

"I did. And now it is a struggle everyday not to tie one on. Because—*everyone* drinks."

"Wow. That is so brave."

"No more brave than you are." He turned his head and his lips curved gently. I suddenly noticed that all this time he had been speaking in that sexy, low, French-accented rumble that he reserved for times when he was alone with me. I realized then that this was his real self and I felt privileged that he trusted me. "I'm pretty sure you can walk across that footbridge now without any help from me," he added.

I felt my lips twitch, and I picked up the other glass of grappa. I took one sip, grimaced, and ran to the bathroom and dumped the contents of the two glasses down the sink. "You aren't missing anything," I assured him when I returned, empties in hand. "But at least I tried it. Poor Giorgio. He was being such a sweetie."

No comment came from Norman. I searched his face, feeling lighter and freer than I had in days. The look on his face was sad, pensive, and when he caught me watching him, he sloughed it off, and smiled.

He got to his feet. "What say we get going?"

Why did I feel right this second that I wanted to stay? My only desire at the moment was to forget that there was anything else out there except for me and this huge lug of man, who had a heart of gold that nobody ever saw, except maybe for Luke. That was why they were so loyal to one another. And I knew that even if I were inclined it would be impossible to seduce Norman because he would resist.

And that just made me like him more.

CHAPTER
13

By the time we returned to the Civita Luke had booked us into two rooms. It was true the hotel was empty. There were very few tourists this year. The place was rundown and only the innkeeper, Franco's grandfather, Signor Landolfo, his wife Rosa, and daughter Sofia were on the premises. They happened to live there. Luke informed me that at first he'd had trouble convincing Landolfo to give him the rooms, insisting that the hotel was unfit. But after flashing around a bit of cash, the man gave in and Luke felt triumphant, as once again he had purchased what other people could not.

He had called from the hotel to ask what was keeping us. I told him we were on our way.

We were walking down the dark alleyway behind the tavern, heading towards the hotel when the backdoor to the tavern's kitchen opened. A lovely, feminine figure, black against the light of the open doorway, moved away from the building carrying an overstuffed garbage bag, which she promptly dumped into a large, wooden box after lifting the hinged lid.

"It's Arianna," I whispered to Norman.

"You stay here," he said, lowering the luggage to the cobblestones. "I'm going to speak to her."

I was about to object but then I realized that she actually might respond to him. When I had addressed her inside the tavern she had ignored me. Maybe she would talk if it were just Norman. I was close enough that anything they said could be heard. And now that she had turned slightly into the light her face was visible.

"Arianna?" Norman said. "It's me, Norman Depardieu. Luke's bodyguard."

She edged away, terrified. Granted it was getting late, and meeting a tall, large man in a dark alleyway was scary even if you were expecting it. "*Non capisco,*" she said, which I knew meant *'I don't understand.'*

"It's just you and me. Luke's here. He's at the Civita hotel. He's been looking for you. Do you want to come with me?"

He reached for her hand and she jerked it back. Clearly, the idea of going anywhere with him was appalling.

"*Stai bene?*" he asked. "Are you okay?" He tried a few more Italian phrases, proving to be as fluent in the language as Luke.

Silence. She stared in my direction, and I think she recognized me as the woman who had approached her inside the tavern. She mumbled some more Italian, which Norman later translated as, *'Go away or I will summon my brother and he will call for the police.'*

"Norman," I warned. "I think we should leave."

The backdoor suddenly flew wide and Giovanni stood in the frame of the lighted threshold. "What do you want?" he demanded. "Get away from my sister. Justina go inside. And you," he threatened Norman. "Get away from my alley!"

"Arianna!" Luke's voice suddenly came from somewhere in the dark shadows. He must have come down to look for us. "Arianna, it's me, Luke."

Did she pause? It was hard to tell. She was visibly startled. Her body froze for a second and then she shot a sidelong glance in Luke's direction. Was it his voice she recognized or was it just *any* voice coming out of the dark that caught her attention? Giovanni slapped her on the shoulder and she scurried indoors.

"Let me see my wife," Luke demanded.

"Your wife?" Giovanni scoffed. "She is my sister. If she had a husband I would know it." He started indoors, but Luke lunged out of the shadows and tackled him. He fell against the doorjamb and I screamed. The Italian twisted out of Luke's grip and blindsided him with a punch that knocked him sideways.

"Stop them!" I shouted to Norman.

It was taking tremendous self-control to keep from jumping into the foray himself. Norman grabbed Luke by the arm and when the Italian started for Luke again, Norman said, "*Signore*, I apologize for my friend. He has had too much to drink and is seeing things. Your sister very much resembles his wife. I am sorry. I will take him to the hotel to sleep it off."

"I am not drunk!" Luke shouted.

"Pretend you are," Norman whispered into his ear. By this time I was on the other side of Luke keeping a stranglehold on his other arm. I heard every word of their interaction. But the word that stuck in my head was 'Wife.' Luke had called Arianna his wife. *Again.*

Giovanni snorted. "Keep him away from here or I will have him thrown into jail."

That was unlikely when they learned his identity. Luke Trevanian was world-renowned. His sojourn in jail would be brief. Nevertheless, was it smart to risk Giovanni's wrath? The man meant business and it could be a cold day in hell before we got to Arianna in time.

"What the blazes was that?" Norman asked after Giovanni slammed the door in our faces. He was referring to the brawl.

"That was Arianna," Luke said, a wounded expression on his face. "She stared at me like I was a stranger."

I must admit that when I say Luke's expression was wounded I meant it. His eyes had an injured look like he had been struck to the core of his soul. This disturbed me.

"Maybe she didn't want to give herself away. Listen to me, boss; I think it's worse than that. I think she has no memory of us. Come on, let's get away from here so we can talk."

We went to the small hotel up the hill. Franco's grandmother, Rosa, greeted us at the door and gave us a curious look because Luke was a bit messed up from his fistfight with the tavern owner. "And to think," Norman said, sizing up the damage to Luke's face. "*That* used to be me."

"I'm not proud of it," Luke said as his hand came away with blood on it from wiping his mouth. We dumped him onto the bed. He sat on the edge of the mattress with his head in his hands. Should I go to him and comfort him? He was in no mood for my ministrations. He raised his head and his gaze landed first on me then on Norman. "That *was* Arianna. What have they done to her?"

All I could think of was that he had called her his *wife*. Not ex-wife, not former wife, but '*my* wife.' What did that mean for *us?*

"I'm okay," Luke said as I started to fuss (mostly to mask my feelings), and finally he allowed me to examine the cut on his lip. Norman set the luggage down and I went to the bathroom to fetch some tissues dampened with water to wash off the blood.

"That was none too smart, boss," Norman said.

"Yeah, yeah, I know. It was just the shock of seeing her." He slammed his fist down onto his thigh. "I *knew* she was alive!"

"But *we* might as well be dead," I reminded him, returning with the tissues for his injuries. I had decided to keep myself focused by playing nurse. "As far as we're concerned Arianna drew a blank. I've been thinking and thinking, muddling it over like crazy. How Arianna survived that plane crash is a miracle. Did she even have a scratch on her?"

"She might have amnesia," Norman said. "That's not

surprising."

"Is that why she pushed us away?"

"Must be," Luke said. "We have to get her out of there before Giovanni gets it into his head to move her." He grabbed the tissue away from me as I tried to tend to his scrapes. "I'm okay, Lucy. Leave it. It's stopped bleeding."

Luke rose from the bed and started pacing. "We have to get her out of there. She has no idea where she is or *who* she is. That asshole could take advantage of her."

"I doubt it," Norman said. "Otherwise, why call her his sister?"

"Nobody knows what goes on behind closed doors," Luke spat. He went to the small desk near the door where a bottle of expensive whiskey perched. Norman followed.

True, Luke had every right to be concerned. And he was correct. We had to get her out of there before Giovanni moved her. But how?

"He doesn't know who we are," Norman said, placing a glass into Luke's extended hand. "That's to our advantage. We should keep a low profile until tomorrow. It's too bad you showed yourself like that, Luke. Now they'll be on the lookout for you. And might even discover who you are."

But blackmail was the least of our problems. None of us was saying it, but we all thought it. If they dug around to learn Luke's identity, then he might have just put Arianna's life in danger. Arianna was the head of ISORE. If they knew it, they could use the information to force the organization to back off. They could also use the information to extort money from Luke. If they knew how much he cared. Unfortunately, now they did. He had shouted to the world that she was his wife. But no use in pointing fingers. What would that solve? We needed a game plan for tomorrow.

Luke was strung tight as a wire. His nerves taut like guitar strings, the tension so palpable they could have been my own. He knocked back the hard liquor and then poured himself another. I was pretty sure the whiskey would only worsen things; he was in no mood to be antagonized.

Norman eyed the drink. Did he dare tell Luke to dial it back? Did I?

"There's nothing we can do tonight," Norman said affably.

Luke scowled. "We should have just taken her."

"Against her will? She would have screamed and had the whole tavern out, not to mention the neighbors."

"There are very few neighbors. We could have done it."

"And gone where? The Civita might as well be an island. The only way off is across that bridge."

"Or down the slopes," Luke said. "I could have called my chopper pilot to pick us up in the gorge."

"That's too dangerous. And you can't drag an unwilling woman, kicking and screaming down a cliff side." Norman glanced at me. Was he also thinking of what it would have taken to get me to climb down the face of a cliff in the dark?

"Well, what's *your* plan then?" Luke demanded. His anger was as much from failure to rescue Arianna as it was sheer fatigue.

"Luke," I cut in. "Do the extremists know that Arianna is the leader of ISORE?"

"I doubt it. She was always careful not to participate in covert operations. I warned her to stay visible as a museum professional, that way no one would ever suspect her."

"But someone knows," I said. "Otherwise, why abduct an amnesiac woman? Sure, she's beautiful. But that isn't a good enough reason to kidnap her. Without knowing her identity they can't even extort ransom from anybody. But I don't think it's ransom they want. They must know that she's a valuable member of the organization and that she has the power to thwart them…. They must know there will be people looking for her. It was a smart move to hide her in this ghost town. No one would have noticed her here, hidden away inside Giovanni's kitchen. But now *we've* seen her."

"Lucy has a good point," Norman said. "It makes sense. So if the bad guys know who Arianna is, just *who* exactly are these bad guys? I think Giovanni is a pawn. And if Franco's grandfather has anything to do with it, he too is just a pawn. They're oblivious of the bigger picture. All they're aware of is that someone will pay them to hold artifacts until someone else comes along to claim them. As far as Arianna is concerned, I think they've been told to hold her in the village, and that she *really* is somebody's sister. They have no idea that she is a pawn in a more sinister game."

"Yeah," I said, picking up the thread. "They, Giovanni and Grandpa Landolfo are just taking payment for a small part in the chain. They don't care where the goods come from or where they're going as long as they get paid. But I'm sure if they thought Arianna would be hurt, they'd refuse to play along. I'm certain of it," I said adamantly.

Luke shook his head. "I warned her," he muttered. "I told her that this could happen one day. That someone would try to kill her."

"But they botched it, Luke. And maybe Giovanni and Grandpa are unaware that Arianna is part of this rescue effort. Maybe Giovanni found her, realized she had amnesia, thought she was beautiful and wanted to keep her? It wouldn't be the first time a man had tried to do that."

"Then she's still in danger."

"I agree, and first thing tomorrow, we'll figure out a way to get her out of that tavern."

"Which is why we have to keep low tonight," Norman advised. "If they're confident we know nothing, they will stick to the plan for tomorrow. And I think Lucy should be the one to approach her at the market in the morning."

Luke opened his mouth to object. Norman raised his hand to explain. "Arianna doesn't remember us, Luke. That's why she was terrified when we tried to talk to her. She'll be just as terrified of us tomorrow. We have to win her trust. Lucy has the best chance of doing that."

I agreed.

Perhaps it was the whiskey or merely fatigue, but finally Luke came around to our way of thinking. He set down the glass and listened while I explained. Even though my Italian was miles worse than theirs she'd be less afraid of me if I approached her as a helpless tourist.

"Is there anything you have, Luke," I asked, "that might trigger her memory?"

"If my face or my voice didn't do it, what would?"

"Something, maybe, that would remind her of her purpose here in Italy."

The booze was taking its toll. Luke struggled with his thoughts. I wished to high heaven that I could soothe and untangle them. Discussing things with me had always helped him before. He had even confessed once that my insights were the reason he had brought me to Italy. I kept him grounded. But not this time. When it came to Arianna my influence waned.

Then his face brightened. "I might have something. He went to his suitcase and slipped his hand inside a side pouch. "I found these papers in that Pelican case which was where the Gorgon heads were. Franco's grandfather thought they were nothing, so he ignored them. I pinched the lot, and haven't yet had a chance to study them."

He unfolded the papers. They were falsified requisition forms, orders to have the Gorgon heads removed from the archaeological site of Pompeii and delivered to the Royal Ontario Museum in Toronto.

"Who authorized the delivery? Who signed-off on them?" I asked.

"That's Arianna's signature here at the bottom of this page. And over here, that looks like D'Agostino's scribble."

So, the institution of origin was the National Archaeological Museum in Naples.

I had seen requisition forms for objects from Pompeii before. Shaun, my brother-in-law, was cataloguing a shipment of Pompeii artifacts from the Naples Museum prior to my departure for Italy. What time was it in Toronto? Dare I phone him? My intuition told me that I already knew the answer. I wondered if he would deny his involvement with ISORE. And it made me all the more determined to join the crusade. Unfortunately, now was not the time to ask about membership. But finally I understood the Pompeii connection. Those papers were falsified to give the acquisitions the appearance of legitimacy. I had thought that Shaun's alleged special exhibit was taking an inordinate amount of his time. It was also taking an unusual toll on his nerves. The artifacts coming out of Pompeii were not, in fact, from that site at all. They were Roman, yes, but they were Roman objects from war-torn Syria, illicit contraband, smuggled out of the country without the permission of the current government who was too busy bombing rebels, extremists and civilians to worry about whether they were blowing up priceless heritage at the same time. What the rebels failed to sell on the black market, ISORE managed to whisk away in their underground pipeline, of which Pompeii was a pickup point. The objects were then shipped across the Atlantic to Toronto and held in trust via the ROM for the day when the violence and destruction were over, and the artifacts could be returned to their home country safe and sound. Unluckily, Arianna's attempt to save the Gorgon heads had been intercepted. Now the extremists thought they had the upper hand.

Naples, I thought. Naples was the connection at the other end. That meant somehow D'Agostino was involved. And then I thought of Sulla Kharim. What was *his* connection?

CHAPTER
14

Luke was fast asleep. The whiskey had done its job. I kissed him on the forehead and slipped out of bed. Not even an eyelash flickered.

I returned my attention to the bed. Should I wake him? Mention the text I received from Dr. Kharim? Kharim was alive and in the hospital. He wished to see me. Or was it Luke he wished to see, and had only contacted me because mine was the only number he possessed? I had given him my number at the gala. And then forgot.

Poor Luke had been too riled up for me to mention it earlier. And now with the plans to accost Arianna at the market, when would I get a chance to see Kharim? I didn't want to wait too long. It must be important or he would never have contacted me. Why me? I should have told Luke. I should have told Norman. But Arianna had taken precedence. As usual.

And Luke needed to sleep it off. His thoughts were muddy with all that alcohol in him. I shouldn't have let him go at the whiskey like that but he was in pain—physically from the brawl with Giovanni and emotionally because Arianna hadn't recognized him. Was it my place to control his behavior?

A minute passed. Why was I just standing here in the dark? The longer I stood the more wide-awake I became. Sleep was impossible. I slipped the thin silk robe over my short strappy nightgown, and sat at the desk in front of the whiskey bottle. I stared. What it must take to resist temptation.

I shoved the liquor away and rose. I hooked on my slippers and opened the door. The faint creak did not disturb Luke, and I slipped out the door. I needed to use the bathroom down the hall. Flushing the toilet in our own tiny bathroom might wake up Luke.

The hall was dark. The inn was old and had few light fixtures, most of which were not used at night. I found the facilities by memory and fumbled around for the switch. When I came out to return to my room, I noticed that Norman's light was on and his door slightly ajar. By now I was almost as familiar with Norman's habits as I was with Luke's. He sometimes did that, kept his door open so that he heard every sound that went on. There were no other guests in the hotel, only us. He had probably heard me walking down the hall and assumed it was the hotel owner.

Why was I doing this? I should not be invading his privacy. But he couldn't be doing anything terribly private if he had left his door ajar. I peeked inside.

He was in khaki pants, shirtless, sitting on a chair in the middle of the small room facing the bed. His head was bent in concentration, his close-clipped hair showing every nuance of his facial features. The muscles on his chest and arms rippled as he made small movements with his hands. He had what appeared to be a sketchpad and a pencil between forefinger and thumb. What was he doing? Drawing a picture of the bed? This puzzled me. I was the artist on our team. Norman was head of security. What was he doing sketching?

I was about to knock and go in when I felt something brush my arm. Startled, I gasped and turned to look. I must have gasped out loud because a clatter came from inside the room. Norman must have dropped his pencil and sketchbook before he came racing to the door. By that time I had swung around to see who had touched me, expecting it to be Luke or perhaps the hotel proprietor. All I saw was a flash of red. I sniffed the air as Norman's door swung wide. He glared at me.

"*Merde*, Lucy, what are you doing out here?" Norman always reverted to French expressions when I was around, especially if he was cussing. I guess he thought I didn't understand French swear words.

"I'm sorry, Norman, I had to use the bathroom. I didn't want to wake Luke."

"I thought I heard a scream."

"Not a scream, exactly. That was me. I felt someone touch me."

Norman scowled. "Again? Who was it?"

"I don't know. I was so flustered I didn't see."

I glanced around. The hallways were not well lit at night. And the person had been in shadow. I noticed again the familiar lemony scent. I moved up to Norman and sniffed him. He was so tall I had to stand on tiptoes.

"What's the matter?" he asked. And I observed once more that he was shirtless. "Do I need a shower?"

"No. It's not you. You smell nice... I smelled something. I must be imagining it."

He took hold of my arm and swung me about. "Go wait in my room. I'm going to have a look around."

I knew better than to argue with him when he was in bodyguard mode. I obediently entered his room and he shut the door. I stood staring at the closed door for a moment, unable to get the image of his naked back out of my mind. Then I turned to see the sketchpad and pencils on the floor. Why can I never leave a mess alone without attempting to clean it up? I went over and collected the goods. I set the pencils on the nightstand and sat down on the edge of Norman's tousled bed with the sketchpad still in my hands. Clearly he had tried to sleep—like me—but couldn't. So... he had gotten up and decided... to do what? Some sketching?

I flipped to the first page and almost released a gasp as loud as the one I had made outside his door. Oh my goodness. He was good. But it wasn't so much the quality of his work that had elicited that involuntary response from me, but the subject of his drawings. They were nudes, tastefully done. Nothing pornographic about them at all. They were erotic in a subtle, exquisite way. The models were all women: lovely, nubile young women posing in seductive poses. The effect was ethereal, the contrast of light and dark, the transformative use of negative space so that the one blended into the other. The swift light strokes of the pencil and the smudging of charcoal made for striking imagery.

They could have been nymphs and sprites, goddesses and sirens. Were they conjured up from his imagination? They looked too real, almost like he had opened the door to someone's bedroom and caught them unawares.

Some of the women were completely naked; other's partially dressed in flimsy, see-through dresses and shorts. I wondered when he had time to draw. In the middle of the night? Like right now?

I lifted the page, flipped it over to the next one. I was so engrossed in his art that I was oblivious of his return until the sketchpad was wrenched out of my hands.

"What the hell?" he snapped. He was really angry; he had forgotten to use the French equivalent.

I was shaking as I spoke. "I'm sorry. It was on the floor, I picked it up."

"They're not for anyone to see."

It was hard to decipher the exact emotion in that statement. It could be embarrassment or outrage at the invasion of privacy. He was standing over me crushing the sketchpad to his chest like he wished he could squeeze it to dust, the drawing I was just about to view turned inward. I realized, this time, that I had more than overstepped boundaries. I had stomped on them.

"So, did you see anybody?" I asked lightly, trying to

distract him from his anger.

"No. Nobody. Anywhere. Are you sure you didn't imagine it?"

No. I wasn't sure of that at all.

"What the fuck did you think you were doing, snooping through my things?"

The invective hurt like he had physically struck me. Not that I was a prude. But this was Norman. And Norman rarely cursed in front of women. And *never* in front of me. At least not in English.

"They're really good," I said wistfully, trying to cajole him back into good humor. What was the big deal anyway? I knew, like any other man, he enjoyed nude pictures of women. I was not offended—as long as he didn't do it in front of me. There were no spread-legged scenes showing anatomical parts, only sensual scenes of skin and curves and hints of what was hidden behind the fluid limbs. Was the problem that *he* was the one who had drawn them? Was this big, lug of a man embarrassed because he could be respectful and sensitive while appreciating the wonder of the female body? "These are *really* good," I insisted. I tried for a joke. "Better than anything *I* could do—and *I* make my living as an artist."

He was quiet. The rage or mortification or whatever had triggered his outburst was fading. "You think so?"

"I know so. Why don't you want anyone to know that you draw?"

He seemed deflated, went silent. Maybe he thought the reason was obvious. It wasn't obvious to me. Artistic skill was a gift, one that should never be taken for granted. Not everyone was creative and not everyone could draw. Surely, he must know that?

I giggled nervously, hoping to vanquish the tension in the room. "Maybe it's just as well. If Luke knew you were this good I'd be out of a job."

His lips twitched at the corners. He relented. He must see that I never wanted to hurt him on purpose. "I can't do what *you* do," he said.

"Yeah. And why would you *want* to, when you can do that?" I tapped the edge of the sketchpad (that he was still squeezing the life out of) with my fingertip. I was a technical illustrator. I drew artifacts, objects, frescoes, sculptures and pots. He was an artist. He created art.

"Luke doesn't know?" I asked.

He shook his head. "And I'd rather it remained that way. It's just something I do to while away the hours. I spend a lot of time on surveillance. And usually nothing is happening."

I nodded. "Your secret is safe with me. Can I see them again?"

"No," he said.

"Please."

"No. They're nothing, just doodles."

"They're beautiful. Are they women that you know?"

He shrugged.

"Women you've dated? They are all so gorgeous. Or maybe it's just your style. You make them beautiful because to you they are."

"Is there something wrong with looking at pretty women?" he asked. He sounded defensive.

"No. I think anyone you thought worth your time would be flattered. Do they pose for you?"

"No. I draw from memory."

"You have an amazing memory."

"You should go back to bed," he said. "If Luke wakes up and finds you gone he will worry."

"After all that booze? He's dead to the world." And then I sighed, this time sincerely and vigorously. "I'm worried about him, Norman. He never drinks like that."

"And he won't again once we find out what's up with Arianna."

Maybe it was the night, because it was late and I was tired although not sleepy. Maybe being in that state of exhaustion causes the brain to lose its inhibitions. Maybe it causes one to separate the brain from the body and talk about the mind as if it existed on its own. Yes, I was *that* tired. And I was saying and doing things I wouldn't otherwise have said or done.

I flopped onto my back on his bed. It never occurred to me that what I was doing was in any way inappropriate or seductive. Norman had seen me naked. Not often, maybe just once or twice. Luke never gave a thought about flaunting his lovers in front of his bodyguard. It still embarrassed me.

I tangled my hair in my hands to squeeze out the thought, and looked up at him. I felt defeated. "I think he still loves her, Norman."

That pitying look came over his eyes again confirming to me that I was right.

"Did he say so?" he asked.

"He refuses to say so."

"But you asked him."

"I had to."

I sat up, finding it unbearable to have him looking down at me with that expression on his face. I stared at my lap, fiddling with the sash of my robe, twirling it around my fingers.

"They were together for a decade," he said, sitting down next to me. He placed the sketchpad face-up at the foot of the bed and unwound my fingers from my sash. "It's natural that he should still care about her. After all, this is no ordinary situation she's in. We don't know the whole story, whether she's in danger or not."

"What do *you* think?" I asked. "Is this part of her plan? Or does she really have amnesia and is at the mercy of these crooks?"

"That, I don't know."

"You can tell me the truth, Norman. I'm a big girl. I can take it. Has Luke said anything to you about how he feels? About Arianna I mean."

"I honestly don't believe he knows himself."

But you *know,* I thought.

"Stop beating yourself up, Lucy. Nothing has changed."

But it has, I can feel it.
"I just don't measure up, do I? She's like a goddess. I'm like a what? A pixie?"
He laughed. "Oh so now, you think I'm a pixie, too?"
"I never said that."
I exhaled, mournfully. "He always said I had great legs."
"You do have great legs."
"But I'm too flat-chested."
"God, why do women always dissect themselves into parts."
"Because you men do it. That's why."
And that was the thing I loved about his drawings. Each woman that he sketched was a whole person, a complete and necessary part of the composition. He had not dissected them into thighs and breasts and butts. They were a miracle of all these things that drew the eye not to the parts but to the whole.

He sighed. "And why do you care what we think?"
"I don't. At least I didn't use to."
He scowled and was silent for a moment. He seemed to be struggling with his emotions. "If Luke doesn't see what you're worth, then it's his loss... Go to bed Lucy. We have a big day tomorrow." His voice was hard now and I felt something of the anger returning, but this time it wasn't directed at me.

I sighed in turn. "I can't sleep. I feel like I shouldn't even be here. In Italy, I mean. I feel like I don't have a role in anything that's going on."

"As far as I'm concerned. You do. Now get up. I want you out of my bed so that I can go to sleep."

"Are you sure you're not just going to draw more pictures after I leave?"

"So what if I do?"

Yeah so what? I was babbling now. Fatigue was taking its toll.

I stood up. So did he. As I turned to leave my eye caught

the sketchpad again. He had left it on the page that I was just about to view before he barged in and jerked it out of my hands.

My mouth opened. My eyes widened. Something about the picture on that page was disturbingly familiar.

I swallowed, glanced up at him. Color threatened to flush my face but I fought it down. I had sworn to him that I was not a prude. Why did I feel like one now?

"Is that—*me?*"

CHAPTER
15

There was utter silence at first, and then he looked at me. "Yeah," he said. His voice was reluctant, hoarse. Why bother to deny it? It was obviously me. No wonder he hid his drawings from Luke. Had he drawn Arianna, too?

"No," he said before I could formulate the question.

He had read my mind. How could he know what I was thinking?

I lifted the sketchpad off the bed, and this time he let me. The sketch was delightfully simple. And if I wasn't being immodest it was the best of the ones I had seen. The face was mine in three-quarter profile, my hair in soft waves, caressing my cheek, a single lock blocking one eye. I lay stomach-down on a bed; the covers tossed, not really covering anything at all, except for one foot and part of a lower leg. I was propped up on one elbow, part of my breast showing in the crook, the fine lines sweeping towards my hipbone and the curve of my thigh. My bare bottom rose from the covers, round and firm dipping down one side to my lower back and up to my shoulders; the other side sloping along my thigh to my slightly bent knee.

I was experiencing inappropriate sensations towards him. But it wasn't the first time. And I knew he felt them too.

"Why did you have to do that, Lucy?" he demanded. "Why couldn't you leave well enough alone? What I feel for you is wrong."

I ignored his questions. Voicing them aloud made everything too real. I decided to focus on the picture. "When did you draw this?"

He said nothing. My eye turned to the tossed bedcovers and then back to the sketch. I lifted the page and saw that it was the last one. The next page was blank. He had been working on the drawing of me when I interrupted him.

I looked up and our eyes met. I was well aware of the consequences of going to a man's bedroom in the middle of the night. I thought I would be protected by his chivalry. There were very few men in the world like Norman. He had the willpower of an ox. It was wrong of me to tempt him. It was not like I didn't know. And then there was Luke. How did I feel about Luke? Ever since Arianna's accident his world had revolved around her. That should have told me something. Or was I just being selfish? I have been asking myself this question over and over. I have no answer.

Norman gently pried the sketchbook out of my hands. He flipped the cover over and the sketch of me vanished from my sight.

"Let's just forget you saw that," he said, his tone forcibly curt.

"I don't know if I can."

He suddenly softened. "I'm sorry, Lucy. I should never have drawn you."

He placed the sketchbook on the nightstand and came back to me.

"You'd better leave now," he said, his voice quiet. The tension was thick and I could almost touch it. The silence between us lengthened interminably before he spoke once more. "If you don't leave now I won't be responsible for what happens next."

Every fiber of my being wanted to make him responsible, but I had to be as strong as he was. I was being selfish. Luke was in trouble. Because of Arianna. We had to rescue Arianna and then I could decide.

"Lucy?" he said as I approached the door. I turned to see him, standing frustrated and forgiving. "About all the swearing. I am sorry. I never meant any of it."

What came over me? I plunged forward and fell into his arms. If he was surprised it was well hidden. He engulfed me with his powerful forearms and I felt a sudden sensation of utter surrender.

"Lucy, Lucy," he mumbled against my hair. "Stop torturing me."

I had no words to express how I felt, or how any guilt I might have been harboring was totally washed away by the magical feel, and scent and sight of him. I was drowning in a yearning I had been afraid to admit.

"I want you, Norman," I whispered.

"No, Lucy. No."

I felt the tears of emotion well up in my eyes as his hands stroked my back. I knew he was trying to resist me but I honestly did not want him to.

I wore nothing but a thin silk nightgown and a matching robe that was already worked loose, the slippery sash hanging almost to the floor. His hands fumbled against the silk down the curve of my lower back and I felt the jolt of self-consciousness, the sudden realization that I wore no panties beneath my nightclothes. Luke should have noticed. Luke should have touched me to find out. But he was out cold from the whiskey and I had never felt so alone.

Norman made me feel warm and safe, and wanted. Maybe those were bad reasons for doing what I knew I was about to do—*if* he would have me—but I have truly never felt safer and more comfortable than I did embraced in the bodyguard's strong muscular limbs.

His lips brushed my forehead, moved softly down to my temple and to my eyelid. They rested there struggling to go no farther. I reached up to feel my breast pressed against his abdomen, my ear next to his heart. I felt the rapid beats;

heard the quick breathing in my ear. My own pulse raced and my breath grew tremulous. As my arms circled his neck his hands came down under my arms, sliding smoothly to my narrow waist. I envisioned him following every curve and arc of my body with pencil on paper and found the idea of his sketching me, nude from memory, intoxicating. Every movement of his fingers was the tracing of the pencil or a piece of smudgy charcoal rendering my body in a dance of light and shadow.

"I refuse to love you, Lucy," he said very firmly into my ear. "If we do this...can you...live with that?"

I could live with whatever he desired if he stopped this yearning, if he would just satisfy my need for him, it was burning so painfully.

He flattened his palm against the small of my back forcing me to arch, my pelvis pressing forward and my legs supporting me on tiptoes. I felt his hardness, and melted into him, the powerful muscles of his chest crushing me just as he had crushed the sketchpad, and the drawing of me against his heart.

I tilted my head upward. I wanted to feel his lips on mine. He groaned and turned his head away. I kissed his chin and the side of his square jaw, felt the stubble rasp against my tender skin. I rubbed my fingers against his cheek, controlling his body with my own, trying to reach his lips again with mine.

"No kissing," he growled. "You can't make me love you."

But I wanted him to love me. Everything else was falling away. All thoughts of Luke had diminished in comparison to Norman's masculine presence. Every cell in my brain knew this was wrong, that I must fight this yearning desire, which was only physical. That was what he was telling me. We lusted after each other, but I didn't care. I had no presence of mind left. All I wanted was what my body wanted. And my body wanted him.

I felt weak and angry, not just at myself, and at Luke, but

at him. How had I gotten myself into this situation? And yet I knew in the next minute, unless Norman bodily thrust me out of his room and into the dark hallway, I was going to his bed. He growled. It was an expression of rage as much as desire. He was fighting the yearning to force himself between my legs, knowing that he would be betraying his boss and his best friend. Dammit. How had I let it come to this? This whole sordid situation was my fault and yet I hardly cared. That was how much I wanted him. He was losing the battle, the last chance to force me out of his room had passed and now his mouth was tearing at the silk around my breasts.

He lifted me into his arms and carried me over to the rumpled bed, and dropped me roughly on the sheets. Then he was on top of me, my robe already on the floor as he worked at removing the rest of the flimsy silk that covered my body. He laid his cheek against my chest and I heard him sigh, then he raised himself and entered me and I almost cried. The pleasure was incredibly complete.

"Lucy," he whispered.

I opened my eyes and gazed into the warmth of his, then his lips came down on mine so soft and loving and tender, and we were lost in the wonder of our bodies.

***

When it was over, I found my head nestled in the hollow of his shoulder. It was strange to find myself in Norman's arms, in Norman's bed, and yes it was scary. I dared not look into my lover's eyes. I know what I had asked of him, what I had maneuvered him into doing was wrong. I had gone to his room without this intention. It was just when I saw that drawing of me I lost my mind. And my will. I hoped he could forgive me.

I felt Norman's lips on my cheek. It was a very soft kiss. Then he rolled away and reached for a package of cigarettes that were on the nightstand. I knew he smoked, but only rarely. And only when he was stressed.

That was what I did to him.

He lit the cigarette and propped himself up slightly on the pillows. We stayed silent. He inhaled the smoke and I studied the orange glow as he sucked and then I watched it vanish. He blew the smoke away from me. He did not ask if I minded. He knew I did. This was my punishment and I accepted it.

I felt a bitter hollow emptiness as I watched him smoke. It was no more than I deserved. I wanted nothing more than to feel his arms around me again and feel that sweet tender kiss.

There were tears pressing against my eyes and I knew I had to get out of there before they spilled.

Oh, what were we going to do? I had messed up everything. Luke would never forgive me. Why should he? And Norman? I had made him commit a betrayal that he had once sworn to me he would never commit.

I rose and grabbed my nightgown and dragged it on. It no longer felt sexy. It felt dirty. I picked up the robe and fastened it tightly. Would he even look at me as I left? How was I going to face him ever again? And what was I going to tell Luke?

How could I have been so selfish? Luke was in trouble. He was mourning Arianna. That was the whole issue. He wanted her, not me.

Still, how could I crumble to my feelings without thinking? Now I had ruined both relationships with the two men I cared about most in the world. The tears had their way. I rubbed away the wetness and ran for the door. Before I got there, I heard the creak of the bed and Norman's body leaving the mattress.

He had snuffed out the cigarette and now his arms were around me. I cried into his chest.

He cupped my face in both of his hands and raised my lips to meet his.

His breath when we stopped kissing came haltingly. He smelled strongly of smoke, but how could I mind? There was nothing about him that I could possibly mind. He kissed my eyelids until I stopped crying. Then he lifted me into his arms and sat down on the bed with me in his lap. He was still naked and beautiful but I felt safe again.

"My sweet, Lucy," he whispered. "Please, don't cry."

"I can't help it," I moaned. "I've messed everything up. I am so sorry, Norman. I should have left when you told me to."

He planted his lips on my temple. "It takes two to tango, honey."

"You didn't want to tango."

"Well, there's some debate over that."

I laughed through the remainder of my tears.

"I really did mess up," I said, glassy-eyed. "And you probably think I'm a slut."

He held my hand and stroked my palm with his thumb. "Do you think *I'm* a slut?" I laughed despite myself. "Nothing is further from the truth," he assured me.

"Oh, why did I come to your room? Why did I have to look at your sketches?"

"I'm that good of an artist, am I?" He chuckled to cajole me out of my dark mood. I felt the corners of my mouth twitch in amusement. He could always make me smile.

I draped my arm around his neck and kissed the side of his head. "I feel so guilty."

He nodded. "So do I."

"You're so different from Luke," I said.

He shrugged. "I should be. He's a billionaire. I'm not."

"I really don't care about that."

"I know you don't."

"I have to tell him."

Norman was silent for a moment before he said, "No, you don't."

I looked at him.

"He's got too many problems to deal with right now. He doesn't need this. Not now." He stood up, sliding me off his lap to my feet. "Besides. This thing?" He shot a look at the bed. "It's not going to happen again."

"Norman—"

He cut me off. "It doesn't matter how I feel about you, Lucy. It *can't* happen again."

"But I don't think I love Luke. And I'm pretty sure he doesn't love me."

"You're still his girl."

I wanted to break it off with Luke but I knew Norman was right. How could I do that to him in the midst of all this tragedy and mystery?

"Tomorrow morning you might change your mind," he said.

I shook my head. What I was more worried about was that *he* might change *his*.

CHAPTER 16

Had I really done that last night in Norman's room? Or was it all a blissful dream? It was morning. Luke was up with a blinding headache from all the whiskey he'd imbibed. He tossed two Tylenol down his throat, chased them with three gulps from a bottle of water, and groaned. "Serves me right," he said. "You okay?"

Not really, but I nodded. Guilt weighed heavily on me. Why had I laid this burden on Norman? But what was done was done. Was he right about keeping our tryst from Luke? Luke seemed oblivious to anything other than his own personal concerns. Arianna was the only thought on his mind.

Norman knocked on the door and we avoided each other's eyes. The three of us went downstairs to find breakfast. Rosa and Sophia fed us fresh bread rolls with homemade preserves, farm cheese and hot coffee. Everything must have been delicious but I barely tasted it. Luke was moody. Did he notice the tension between Norman and me?

He reiterated what we had discussed after our encounter with Giovanni the previous evening and how the requisition form might trigger Arianna's memory. Then we set the plan into motion. Surely Arianna would recognize her own signature? I was dressed in a blue and white striped, flouncy skirt and cropped white cotton top. I pulled a floppy brimmed sunhat onto my head and topped the guise off with sunglasses as we left the hotel after breakfast into bright sunlight. The requisition form with Arianna's signature was snug in my bag.

Norman kept a lookout from a safe distance and Luke sent Franco (who had been waiting for us outside the hotel) to learn when Giovanni was expected to leave for his appointment that morning. Franco returned to inform us that there had been a change of plans, that Giovanni had left him a note to go to the market in his 'sister's' place because she was feeling a little under the weather. Did Giovanni intend to keep his appointment? "Yes," Franco said. "He is already gone. Apparently, according to Grandfather he left at the cracking of dawn."

Did he mean the *crack* of dawn? I stifled a smile. "So, now what?" I asked.

Luke mused over the situation. "Franco, do you know where Giovanni went? The address I mean."

"*Si*," he said. "He is meeting with one of his wine suppliers, in town."

"Do you know who his wine supplier is?"

"*Si*. He is a man called Ippolito Vecchi. He has a warehouse in Bagnoregio. I will show you, yes? I must go to the market for Signor Zia anyways so it will not be much out of my way. Now, if you are ready we must go, or my grandfather will have my head for neglecting my chores."

"I think *you* should go," Norman suggested to Luke. "Lucy and I will wait for an opportunity for her to speak to Arianna."

"It should be me," Luke argued.

"You frightened her last night. If she really doesn't know who you are, you will just make things worse. I still think we should stick with our original plan and send Lucy."

All this time Franco was fidgeting to leave. How much did he understand of our conversation? Was he even paying attention? Was he aware that his grandfather and Giovanni Zia were involved in a smuggling racket?

"We don't want to lose Giovanni's trail," Norman said. "We know Arianna was working on something important, so important that she was willing to risk being here herself—and getting caught or killed. If we can find out, then we'll know what we're up against."

"Don't worry, Luke," I said. It took everything I had to avoid glancing over at Norman and to keep my eyes focused. From now until forever I would feel self-conscious in his company. But for the moment I must keep my distress from Luke. "Nothing will happen to her here. And if Giovanni is in Bagnoregio and you've got your eye on him, then maybe we can get Arianna out of his house."

"No. Arianna is my.... my responsibility. Lucy you stay with me. Norman, you follow Giovanni. Go with Franco."

Was Franco surprised at the change in travel companion? It seemed not. He started toward the bridge with Norman. For my part, I was torn, but nonetheless relieved to see their backs. With Norman gone I could stop being reminded of my guilt.

Luke and I returned to the vicinity of the tavern. It was closed and we travelled from the front to the rear of the building. We looked up and saw that the building had two stories. Below was the tavern. So was upstairs the living quarters where Giovanni was keeping Arianna?

There were very few windows. Here, I thought it would be advantageous to have had Norman with us. He could pass through locked doors. I had never asked him how he did it; I just assumed he had been trained in some kind of covert operations while in the army and could pick a lock, electronic or otherwise. It was one of the things I found intriguing about him.

It seemed Luke had this same skill. When our pounding on the door brought no results, Luke started to check out the windows. They were old with crumbling mortar and calking. He could probably smash in the glass but that might bring unwanted attention our way. It was true that there were very few tourists, but that didn't mean there was nobody on the streets at all. A pair of tourists came wandering down the cobblestone road, smiling. They were boisterous in their greeting. Americans, I presumed. They passed by. A local woman with a shawl over her head to protect her from the sun swiftly skirted us without so much as a nod. Was she, too, partner to the exploits of the village men?

While I kept watch for other passersby, Luke managed to open the back door to the tavern.

Everything was dark inside. I removed my sunhat and let it slide down my back, held around my neck by the chinstrap. My sunglasses I shoved over my hair.

The back door opened straight onto the kitchen. It had a smell of old food and grease, and wine. It was scrubbed and as clean as it could be. All the burners were cold on the stove and the sink was empty of dishes.

We left the lights off. There was enough illumination from the few windows to show the way. Inside the public area, chairs were turned upside down onto tables and the few wooden booths at the back were vacant. The air had a sticky feel and I wanted to leave, but we had to learn where Giovanni was keeping Arianna. Not a sound came from the kitchen or the bar.

We backtracked, and I followed Luke to a set of stairs that came off the rear of the kitchen. We did not see them at first because they were hidden behind a sort of partition that was half pantry, half coatroom. Shelves of olives, pasta, canned tomatoes; anchovies and olive oil were stacked from floor to ceiling. On the other side of the small space were hooks on the walls with coats and wet weather gear. Here it had a smell of rain and damp wood.

The stairs creaked when we stepped on them. Luke signaled that he would go first. I tried to walk as lightly as possible but still the steps squeaked.

At the top we paused. There was no door blocking the entrance. Luke walked in, called softly. "Arianna."

The air was stuffy up here but the smells were different. There was a fresh scent of flowers and I soon found the source. A short, ceramic vase held an assortment of summer blooms, mostly roses.

"Arianna?"

We walked into the living area. It was small with a sofa and a love seat and a wooden chest that served as a coffee table where the vase of roses sat. The furniture was dated like something out of the 1950s. A bright, locally woven rug sprawled on the wooden floor. Further on we found the kitchen. Breakfast things were in the sink like they had been left in a hurry. A half drunk cup of coffee stood on the soiled table. The chairs were pulled out. Giovanni had been suddenly called away.

"I don't think she's here, Luke," I said.

He frowned. "Find the bedroom. Maybe she's there." He was searching, hoping there were two bedrooms.

There wasn't.

I found the bathroom and a couple of closets while he opened the door to the bedroom. The bed was unmade, the coverings tossed any which way. "Arianna," Luke shouted. "Where are you?"

"Try calling her Justina," I suggested.

"Justina!"

No reply.

"Justina," I called. "Is anyone here?"

Luke went to a closet shielded by a curtain and drew it apart. There were clothes on wire hangers, men's and women's. He ripped angrily away at the peasant-style blouses and skirts hanging there. Then he found what he was looking for, a pale peach Chanel suit. "She was here," he said.

Yes, that was obvious. "But she's not here now. Where do you think he might have taken her?"

"Dammit," he said. "I should have dragged her away with us last night. Giovanni be damned."

"Come on, Luke. Let's get out of here." I extended a

hand to him. He ignored it. He searched the apartment from end to end.

"Luke! We should get out of here in case someone comes back."

"I *want* someone to come back. I want to beat the crap out of the bastard holding Arianna against her will."

Someone did come back. We heard noises in the kitchen below us. Luke lunged forward, ready to barge downstairs and confront them. "No, Luke," I whispered. "Maybe we can find out where they took her if we hide and listen."

The voices were in a mixture of Italian and English. How many people were present? Certainly more than two. One of them was vaguely familiar.

Luke was creeping down the stairs, when the third step suddenly squeaked. We froze. The breath caught in my throat.

There was silence down in the kitchen. They had been opening the refrigerator. Had the noise of the refrigerator door masked the squeak? I identified the clinks of bottles and glasses, then the splashing of liquid.

A pause came as though the people were drinking, and then someone said, "They've taken her to a safer place..." Were they talking about Arianna? My comprehension came in bits and pieces. Was my Italian better than I thought? I recognized certain words and was able to get the gist of what was being said. "And now that billionaire archaeologist and his bodyguard are snooping about." I caught this much because I knew the Italian words for 'billionaire,' 'archaeologist' and 'bodyguard' but the rest was gibberish to me. Between the English and Italian, I could only roughly translate what I thought they said. Then I caught this:

"*Non preoccuparti.*" Do not worry. The voice was distinctly female, but not Arianna's. Was it the voice I heard earlier, the one that sounded familiar? I glanced at Luke. All of his attention was focused on the activity in the kitchen downstairs.

"They're going to go wait inside the tavern," Luke

whispered to me. "They are talking about the Gorgon heads. Let's go."

Luke glanced back at me, reached for my hand and led me quietly down the remainder of the stairs. Thankfully, they only creaked once more, and by that time, the newcomers were safely inside the tavern on the other side of the swinging door.

Luke led me to the exit. "Wait here for a second."

Did he want to see how many people there were? I had heard at least three voices, maybe four. Was that the reason he had changed his mind about confronting them?

There was a small, greasy porthole in the swinging door between the tavern and the kitchen. Luke crept over to this and peered through the window.

A strange look suddenly overtook his expression. I could only see it in profile. Was it surprise? Certainly confusion.

What was wrong? I dared not make a sound in case I drew attention to our presence. Luke returned and, without a word, gestured me out the exit. The last thing I noticed as I stepped into the fresh air was the smell. Out here was the scent of sunbaked stone and herbs. Inside just as we left, I could swear I detected a whiff of lemon blossoms.

Was I imagining things and was it just the fragrance of a cut lemon? Why wouldn't they have lemons in their kitchen? Citrus was used to garnish all kinds of Italian cuisine and drinks.

Luke walked rapidly, deep in thought, and I hurried to keep pace with his long stride.

"Did you see who it was?" I asked. "Do you think they have Arianna?"

I was troubled by his frown and his silence. Had he seen something to tell him that she was in danger?

I remembered what Norman had said the other night. Arianna worked for an underground organization, an organization that she had founded. Was the abduction part of her plan or were those locals holding her against her will? I wanted to reassure Luke that she was safe, but by the look on his face I knew the timing was rotten.

He turned to me. "Giovanni must have gone early. I was watching from our balcony this morning and never saw anyone leave."

"'Justina'"—I made air quotes—"Was supposed to be in bed all day."

"Apparently Franco was lying about her feeling under the weather."

"Or he was told that by Giovanni. Or maybe, Landolfo, his grandfather. Who did you see in the tavern, Luke? Was it Giovanni? Had he returned with a gang of thugs?" Then I remembered the feminine voice. "Who was the woman? Do they have a woman in their gang, too?"

Luke headed in the opposite direction of the hotel. He aimed for the bridge. Funny how this morning when Norman planned to escort me across the bridge to follow Arianna to the market (when she was *going* to the market), it never occurred to me, once, to be afraid. Now I stood nervously at the edge of the cliff where the path from the Civita ended and the overpass began, all of my questions forgotten.

Already, Luke was several paces ahead of me. What had Norman taught me when the fear threatened?

"Lucy," Luke said, turning around. "What's the matter?"

"Nothing." I took a deep breath, and power-walked to him. Should I grab onto his arm? Things had changed, and I found my hands hanging slack to my sides. This man was my lover. At least he *was* up until a few days ago. We hadn't made love since Arianna's plane crashed.

I was selfish. Missing the affection he was now unable to give me. So I had turned to Norman. How could I be so insensitive? Arianna was his ex-wife. And he was worried about her. So worried that he had forgotten about *me*.

He stretched out his hand. I took it. "There was a woman in the tavern," he said. "She had her back to me. Her face was hidden and she was wearing a red coat."

Why did that spark something in my memory? "And the man she was talking to, who was it? Their voices sounded familiar."

"Yes, well, *his* would. I saw *his* face. It was Bruno D'Agostino."

"Really?"

Luke nodded. He frowned and pulled at the fashionable stubble on his square, handsome chin. "He had another man with him—a rough-looking guy, local I think—or I would have gone in and confronted him."

"I'm glad you didn't. If he's involved in this—" And then it occurred to me that of course he was. He was at the other end of the Pompeii connection. "Luke, if D'Agostino is helping Arianna to rescue artifacts, then isn't he one of the good guys?"

"If he was one of the good guys he would have told me what he was doing. Arianna and I have no secrets."

I paused, disturbed by his last statement. No secrets? Then where did that leave me? Luke and I had nothing *but* secrets.

"You're not sure?"

He scowled. "Of course, I'm not sure. He could be working for the terrorists. Do you think I would have just left without demanding some answers from him if I was sure?"

"Sorry," I said. "I was just asking."

His grip had loosened on my hand and I really just wanted him to let go. I wanted him to tell me the truth.

Now I was angry. How dare he drag me into his shadowy world and not expect me to ask questions? And who was he to tell me if I should become involved or not? He had too many unspoken agendas and it was time he gave up some of them.

I dropped his hand. We were almost at the end of the footbridge. "Are you still in love with her?" I demanded. I struggled not to sound so angry. After what I had done last night, what right had I? But the truth was, I needed to know.

He glared at me. Then his eyes softened. It dawned on him what this situation must be like for me. Not knowing where I stood.

He cleared his throat. "Even though she and I are separated it doesn't mean I don't care what happens to her."

"That's not what I asked you."

"What are you saying, Lucy?"

"I thought I was perfectly clear. Are you still in love with her?"

He dropped his gaze to the gorge below the bridge, sighed. "How can you ask me that, especially at a time like this? Her life is in danger. I'm just doing what any man would do if someone he cared about was threatened."

"Most people would go to the police," I said.

"I promised her a long time ago that I would steer clear of the police. It would expose her organization."

"Then you'd just let her die? Or whatever they plan to do to her?"

"That's harsh, Lucy."

It was. I shook my head, hoping the shaking would knock some clarity into my thoughts. "This is so complicated."

"It is." He took my hand again and kissed my fingers. A tide of guilt washed over me. I wanted to pull away but if I did I would have to explain. "Let me apologize," he said. "This was not the weekend getaway I had envisioned for us."

A wave of compassion filled my heart. I pulled his knuckles up to my cheek. This was a lousy time to wage my personal battles. They would have to wait. "I want to help," I said. "Please trust me, and let me help…. Sometimes it helps to have another point of view. Who else did you see in there?" My eyes darted back in the direction of Giovanni Zia's tavern.

He smiled and lowered his arm. "You're bright as a penny."

"You should probably stop comparing me to pennies. They're worthless now."

"I mean you're smart. I can't pull a fast one over you."

"I know what you meant. I'm still waiting for an answer. Who did you see in the tavern?"

"All right." He paused. "I saw Arianna."

My eyes jerked open, wide. I swallowed, in total disbelief. "You mean she doesn't have amnesia?"

"Apparently not."

"So the whole 'not recognizing us' was just an act?" His shoulders lifted in a shrug. So that was why he had hurried me out without waiting around to confront D'Agostino. He didn't want to blow her cover.

"When were you going to tell me?"

"Soon as we joined Norman in Bagnoregio."

"And you think this is smart? For her to keep silent? Someone tried to kill her. Won't they try to kill her again?" I paused. "Luke, do you have any idea what's really going on?"

He chuckled. That was the first time I had heard him laugh in days. I guess now that he knew Arianna was physically safe and actually somewhat in control of the situation he could relax. "I have no idea what's really going on, darling. I've tried to stay out of Arianna's business. I hate what she's doing. I think it's dangerous and doubly so for a woman. She won't listen to me. She never listens to me. She has her own mind and her own agenda. She's so strong-willed it drives me crazy."

And that's why you fell in love with her in the first place.

"Is that why you two decided to get a divorce? Because of her involvement with ISORE?"

"The bloody organization didn't exist until she invented it."

"But she's saving the world's heritage for posterity. If she didn't rescue these artifacts they would be gone forever. Either blown up or sold on the black market, never to be seen by human eyes again. Isn't that a cause worth fighting for?"

"Not at the risk of one's life."

You mean her *life.*

That was how much she meant to him.

"So what are you going to do?" I asked.

"I'm going to find a way to get her to talk to me. So I can discover exactly what the deal is. I want to know who the bad guys are."

Why? So that you can blow their brains out? And get her out of harm's way? It was just like Luke to act the hero. But was that what Arianna wanted from him?

"I need to know exactly what side D'Agostino is on," he said.

My phone suddenly rang.

"Are you expecting a call?" he asked.

"Only my sister. But I can't imagine why she would call at this time of day."

"Go ahead and take it."

I dug for the cellphone in my handbag and fetched it out, glanced at the caller ID. I frowned. Whose number was this?

"Hello?" I said, motioning to Luke to excuse me while I took the call.

It was the constable that had questioned me in the Spanish Quarter when we'd gone in search of Sulla Kharim's hotel.

"I'm sorry, Ms. Racine," he said. "But Signor Kharim just died."

CHAPTER
17

Oh my God. How could I forget about Dr. Kharim? He'd texted me to come to see him at the hospital and with all that had happened, I forgot.

"How?" I demanded. "How did he die?"

"Heart failure." A pause, then the constable asked, "Do you know if he had any next of kin?"

"I told you he was a casual acquaintance. I only just met him a few days ago at a museum function."

The police officer thanked me, told me that he needed me to visit the police station tomorrow for a few more questions, gave me the address and a contact number, and hung up. I stared at Luke. "Dr. Kharim is dead."

"Yes," a voice said from behind us. "And that's why I need your help, Luke."

A shockwave scurried up my spine. We swung around simultaneously and came face to face with Arianna. Luke's eyes widened. I felt my heart leap as he dropped my hand and lunged towards her. She held him off stiffly, hands raised. "Don't make a scene," she warned. "The cliffs have eyes."

She was dressed in the peasant garb, white embroidered blouse and long black skirt with a shawl covering her hair.

Her gaze glanced off mine. Did she recognize me? She shot a quick backward glance over her shoulder and gestured to us to follow her off the footbridge and onto the road. "Is there somewhere we can go to talk?" she asked, without looking at him.

When Luke suggested the hotel she shook her head. "That's too close to home. Do you have a car?"

"Over there." Luke motioned. We went to the rented Mercedes where it was parked on the side of the road. Luke got into the driver's seat. Arianna sat next to him. I had no choice but to take the backseat.

She immediately removed the shawl that was over her head and let down her hair from its messy bun. She combed out her glossy blonde locks with her fingers and tied the lot into a ponytail. I could see she was removing her long peasant skirt by the way she was wriggling in the front seat, and assumed she had something more contemporary on underneath. This was a distinctly different Arianna Chase than I had ever known. Did she even know who *I* was?

She and Luke were silent for most of the drive. He seemed to understand where it was she wanted to go. Didn't they say that couples, who were meant for each other could read each other's thoughts? We were headed for the lake. A small town, Bolsena, sloped from Mount Volsini, not too far away from Bagnoregio. This little community was a magnet for archaeologists and historians because of the ruins of ancient human settlements in the vicinity and an Etruscan necropolis. There were catacombs and ancient walls too. An enthusiast's dream. But it wasn't the archaeology we were here to discuss. It was because of the secluded locale that Arianna had chosen it.

Luke parked on a side street near the lakeshore where a strip of restaurants stood. There was almost no traffic. The wind off the lake catching in the trees and shrubbery and the scream of shorebirds sounded unusually loud. We sat down at a sidewalk café. A waiter came to take our order. There was no one within earshot and Arianna finally turned to where I sat across the table from her and studied me.

Her silence was unnerving. What was she expecting? I was trying to think of what to say to her. Nothing came to mind. Finally, I extended an arm. I said, "Dr. Chase. I'm—"

"I know who you are." Her bluewater eyes pierced me. She ignored my outstretched hand. "You are Lucy Racine. Museum Illustrator."

"Yes," I said, surprised. I lowered my arm awkwardly and went silent.

She returned her attention to Luke. "I'm assuming you've told her why I'm here?"

Luke nodded. "I've held my tongue from questioning you, Arianna. But now I want the truth. What exactly happened after the plane crashed?"

At first Arianna looked unwilling. Was my trustworthiness in question? Some sort of unspoken exchange passed between them, and it was clear that Luke expected an answer.

What followed was an account of how she had boarded the charter flight in Florence with two other passengers—her assistant Sherry Louie and the Swedish curator. Arianna had been sitting in the rear of the plane, needing the privacy to work on her speech when the engine failed. The pilot responded by attempting to steer the flight path into the least populated area.

By some miracle she survived the crash. Why was she spared? Only providence knew. The Pelican case containing the Gorgon heads was intact. All other passengers died. She somehow managed to crawl out of the wreckage to wander around the bottom of the gorge. Giovanni—who indeed was a smalltime criminal and an opportunist—happened to notice the plane crash first. He descended the slope to see what cargo he could salvage. He found the yellow Pelican case but not much else. The remainder of the luggage had been incinerated, including the small suitcase that had held her evening clothes for the gala.

Then he saw Arianna who was dazed and bewildered.

He solicited help from Franco's grandfather and together they rigged a rope to help her up the steep incline. Giovanni swore his accomplice to silence in exchange for a cut of the potential earnings from his newfound treasure, the Gorgon heads. They took her to his tavern where she had been ever since. An elderly woman came to clean her up. She lent her some clothes. The woman was nervous, uncomfortable in her presence, but offered no explanation.

Was this woman Landolfo's wife, Rosa? She had been nothing but kind and hospitable to us, although reserved and standoffish. Now I understood why.

"I remember nothing beyond that," Arianna said. At the time she had no idea who she was or why she was on that flight. When Giovanni figured out she had amnesia, he decided to take advantage. Had he recognized her? Did he know she was the head of the organization that was trying to intercept illicit smuggling operations out of the Middle East? That much was unclear. "All I knew for certain was that he'd told everyone I was his sister, Justina. I was from a small town in the north."

Everyone believed him, as did she. Even as early as last night when Luke went to the tavern searching for her, she had no idea who she was.

So, was the kindly old man from the souvenir stall party to the abduction? Landolfo's livelihood was at risk. Perhaps that was all it took to convince a man to abet a criminal. I was not allowed too much time to puzzle over his actions. Arianna was still talking even as the waiter brought us coffee.

Luke sighed a breath of pure relief that the worst the scoundrels had done was told Arianna a few lies. "So when did you get your memory back?"

"It began early this morning," she said, "before Giovanni was awake. Before dawn."

She awoke, caught a glimpse of her soiled peach Chanel suit hanging in the opened closet in the moonlight, and everything came back to her. "I imagine he thought he could

clean up that suit and sell it."
"I went through his apartment from end to end. There was only one bedroom. Where did he sleep?"
Arianna gave Luke a weary look. "On the sofa."
Silenced temporarily, Luke then asked, "Why didn't you make your exit then? You said he left before dawn. You were alone. You could have escaped."
"He had the Gorgon heads. I was sure of it. I had to stay to find out where they were stashed."
So, she decided to pretend she still had amnesia. Until she knew the extent of the tavern owner's involvement she was taking no chances. After Giovanni left for his alleged meeting with the wine supplier, Arianna escaped the tavern only to run into D'Agostino, a woman named Alessandra and one of his thugs. Arianna pretended not to recognize him. The woman was a stranger. They cornered Arianna near the souvenir stand and D'Agostino asked her questions, drilled her until she knew her answers were a matter of life or death.
A matter of life or death. I cringed at the words. The phrase reminded me of Sulla Kharim. Arianna caught the subtle movement as I shrank back into my chair, and stared. She was about to ignore me; thought better of it and asked, "What's wrong? Why are you reacting like that?"
I was at a loss. I was startled, and also frightened so I said the only thing that came to my mind. The truth. "That's what Dr. Kharim said to me before he died."
Silence. Then, "Ah yes. Kharim. They finally got to him."
I nodded.
"Who is this Kharim fellow?" Luke demanded. "And who are *'they'*?" His query went from me to his ex-wife. "I recognize the name. I know he was a colleague of yours, but apparently he was more than that. He was trying to contact me, but we never connected. What's he got to do with you, Arianna?"
Arianna raised her coffee cup and tested it. It was too hot and she set it down. Luke's remained untouched as he waited

for an answer.

"He was my contact in Aleppo. And he was murdered by the same people who tried to kill *me*." She turned her full attention my way. "How did you know him?"

Her blue eyes were piercing. Intent. She wanted answers and I wasn't sure I had any. "I didn't," I stuttered. "Not really. He came up to me at the museum gala and asked me to get a message to Luke. But then... then the news about you was announced and we forgot all about him... until a day ago, and... by that time it was too late. Someone had got to him." I faltered at my repetition of her words, flashed a nervous glance for confirmation at Luke. I was hoping it would take that burning gaze off of me. It was making me self-conscious where I had nothing to be self-conscious about. "The police want me to return to Naples tomorrow for questioning. I don't have any choice but to go."

Arianna ignored my digression "*How* was he killed?"

Talking to her was making my heart-rate soar. Why did she have this affect on me? No wonder I could never ask for a raise. "I think he was shot... originally. But they must have managed to resuscitate him... in the ambulance. He later died of heart failure."

"It was not heart failure," she said, shaking her head. "He was murdered in the hospital. They must have pulled his life support, then plugged it back in when he was dead."

The irony was killing me. The gist of those words was the same as what Kharim had implied about Arianna's ill-fated flight. The accident—and the death—was deliberate.

"Who are your suspects?" Luke asked.

"I only have one," she answered. "And he has fingers as long as Europe, stretching from the Middle East."

Who was this person? She gave no name. As far as she could determine, she was the target of the sabotage. However she hadn't reached this conclusion until early this morning. Many people were involved. There was a chain of criminals with its roots in Syria leading all the way to Naples.

The truth was she had suspected D'Agostino for a while,

although he was only a pawn in a much larger game. He had married a Syrian woman in Palmyra. Her name was Amira. Amira returned to her hometown with their son and daughter to visit her family a few months ago. But then the war took a turn for the worst. The borders were blockaded. It was Kharim who informed Arianna that things had gotten so bad. He was refused reentry into his own country. To what extent was D'Agostino's wife, Amira, involved? Kharim suspected her of fencing the goods.

"Her father, Ahmed al-Hadad is curator of ancient ruins in Palmyra," Arianna said. "Kharim believed that Amira was the Syrian contact. She has knowledge of her father's activities and easy access. He is in charge of a convoy of trucks filled with Palmyra's treasures that has caught the eye of the militants. The convoy's destination is Italy. At the moment they are hidden, waiting for word when it will be safe to leave. Because I have been out of commission, they are in limbo. The extremists are on the lookout. They want the goods and they want to sell them on the black market. They are worth, in total, almost a billion in American dollars. D'Agostino is their stooge."

"Are you sure?" Luke asked.

"One hundred percent. Why else would D'Agostino corner me like that? So I played the fool. Acted as though I didn't know who I was other than Giovanni's ignorant peasant sister—*when* he informed me that *that* was who I was, of course."

She stared him down. "One way or the other the militants are holding the family hostage. The city is poised to be taken. D'Agostino has no choice but to do whatever they ask if he ever wants to see Amira again."

Luke shook his head. I could see he was having trouble absorbing her news. His friend Bruno D'Agostino had signed off on the murder of Arianna to fence a smuggling racket. But there could be no good end to this. They would continue to insist on greater and greater payments. How many more lives would D'Agostino stand by and watch lost?

"I saw you sitting in the tavern this morning with them," Luke said.

Arianna nodded. "Yes. They forced me to return. I wasn't supposed to leave the tavern."

"How did you get away?"

"They left the tavern to go to Landolfo's souvenir stall. There was something that interested them inside the shop. I did not wait around to find out what it was. While they were gone I made my escape."

"You've got to leave here," Luke said. "I'll summon my Lear jet to take you home, back to Toronto."

"I'm not ready to go home… I have much unfinished business to complete." Her eyes left his face and drifted towards the scene across the street. The shimmering blue lake lay calm in contrast to the tension at our outdoor table. "Where is Depardieu?" she asked.

"Tracking Giovanni Zia at a wine supplier's in Bagnoregio," Luke answered.

"There is no wine supplier in Bagnoregio. I'll bet you anything he went to Naples."

"*Naples?* What for?"

"To finish the job he failed to do in the Spanish Quarter."

"No," I exclaimed. I had remained silent for most of Arianna's explanation but the insinuation woke me up. "Are you saying that Giovanni Zia shot Sulla Kharim at his boarding house in the Spanish Quarter?"

Arianna nodded. "I am saying exactly that. Or he got one of his thugs to do it. He left incredibly early this morning, long before daylight. He left orders with that boy to do the marketing for me. I should have escaped the tavern earlier. Then D'Agostino and his gang wouldn't have caught me. But I wanted to snoop around the place first."

"Did you learn anything?"

"No, but I did hear mention of my Gorgon sisters. They've stashed them somewhere."

"We know where those are," Luke said. "Landolfo has

them, locked away behind a chain-link gate in the back of his souvenir shop."

She nodded. "Well, I heard Giovanni talking to Landolfo. I went to search the village, that's why the getup." She meant the peasant skirt and blouse that lay in a bundle on the floor of Luke's rental car. As I had guessed, underneath the skirt was a more contemporary ensemble—a pair of long shorts and a short-sleeved top stolen from a laundry line. Did the borrowed outfit belong to Franco's mother Sophia?

"I figured if I put on my power suit I would have been seen. Traveling about as a local makes one much less conspicuous. But D'Agostino saw me in the peasant garb when I wandered over to the shop. I figured since he had recognized me instantly and showed no surprise at my appearance that he was involved. Well, you can imagine what he did when he saw me. He escorted me back to the tavern to wait for Giovanni. Little did he know; Giovanni had no intention of returning soon. So when they left to dig out the Gorgon heads, I slipped away and down the footbridge in your wake."

I knew Luke too well to question what was churning in his brain. He had been vaguely absorbing Arianna's story, but what really stuck in his mind was D'Agostino's culpability. "I find it hard to believe that Bruno would condone murder," he said. "Bruno D'Agostino and I are friends."

"I know, Luke. That's why I need your help. And I need Depardieu. Where's your phone; call him. Tell him to meet us here. And then call your pilot; we need to get to Naples."

"Why? What's in Naples?"

"D'Agostino."

"But he's *here*. I mean he's in the Civita di Bagnoregio. I just saw him with you at the tavern."

"He'll be on his way back to Naples by now. Once he has the Gorgon heads, he has no reason to stay. I don't know if you realize how valuable those heads are. For decades experts have debated over whether there are actually three

Gorgon sisters or only one—Medusa. Now I have proof. There are indeed three. Stheno and Euryale are not clones of Medusa when her head is lopped off. They were unique individuals. Sisters. That's why the militants covet this piece. They can sell it to fund their war. And you can bet Giovanni's going to be furious when he sees that he's been swindled. He'll demand payment. And I don't want to be around when those two confront.

"Now here's the deal. I want them back. The three heads together are worth several million dollars. But that's not the point. The point is: tonight I'm expecting a delivery of a very large fresco from my underground runners. And it's going to be delivered by helicopter. The fresco is the bodies of the Gorgon sisters. It is intact. The heads are broken into three pieces, but glued together that single piece is worth a cool fortune. D'Agostino needs it. If he returns the piece to the terrorists they will allow his wife to see him." She paused, looked from one to the other of us. "Now, do you see what's at stake?"

"You're going up against terrorists? My God, Arianna. You were almost killed. Is it worth your life for the rescue of a few artifacts?"

"This is world history we're talking about, Luke. The history of Palmyra goes back to biblical times. I can't just stand by and watch them demolish it."

CHAPTER
18

Luke got hold of Norman. The meeting with the wine supplier was a ruse to put them off Giovanni's trail. Norman drove to Bolsena to join us, and we ditched the cars on a side street to be retrieved at some later date. Luke summoned his helicopter to pick us up in a field near the lake.

Arianna decided we should kill two birds with one stone. I would show up at the police station as requested, albeit one day earlier. Luke and Norman would steal the Gorgon heads from D'Agostino and Arianna would drive down to Pompeii to receive the delivery of the fresco with the Gorgon bodies.

"I don't need to show up at the police station until tomorrow," I objected. "I'd like to help find the artifacts."

"There is nothing for you to do," Arianna said. "You will be safe and out of the way with the police."

Safe? Or just out of the way? There was no changing Arianna's mind. She was shouting over the sound of the chopper's engines. She sat next to Luke. I faced her, seated beside Norman. It was clear who was the boss here. As usual I was relegated to the backseat.

Norman cupped my hand. My hand was lying on my lap, palm-down. He withdrew his before anyone other than myself had noticed. Last night's revelation vanished from my thoughts. All I could focus on was how to prove my value to this team. As I watched Arianna show Luke the layout of the museum on her computer tablet I found myself in awe of her. How had she appropriated the schematics? She had means and methods, never to be revealed. And why did that matter? The only thing of importance was that she possessed blueprints of the museum in astonishing detail.

Where would Bruno D'Agostino hide the Gorgon heads before returning them to the militants in Syria? The National Archaeological Museum was enormous. They must have subbasement after subbasement of artifacts in storage.

The plan was for Luke and Norman to steal the Gorgon heads, and join Arianna in Pompeii. There, she intended to meet the shipment of the fresco bodies. Her runner would then take the valuable cargo to Positano and to Luke's yacht, where Emily and Luke's crew would receive the artifacts and store them in the yacht's hold.

"It should be simple," she said. "If we can figure out where D'Agostino has hidden the heads.... D'Agostino doesn't know that you suspect him Luke, so go to his office, take him out for dinner or something. Keep him occupied. And you, Depardieu, go search the office. And anywhere else you think he might hide them."

Luke shook his head. "It's going to take more than one person. It's going to take an army to search that museum."

"We don't have an army," Arianna said.

"Let me help," I offered. "I have an instinct for these things."

Arianna looked at me skeptically. "These people are dangerous. Anyone could be working for the militants. They have people in Europe—even in that museum. And I don't just mean D'Agostino."

"So much the better," I argued. "They won't know me. Who am I? Nobody."

I was not expecting encouragement from either Luke or Norman. If I was to convince Arianna of my worth I would have to do it myself.

Support came from an unexpected quarter. Norman said, "Lucy's right. She could search that museum less conspicuously than we could. She's loads smaller and slimmer than Luke and me, and has a much better chance of evading surveillance. And she does have an instinct."

I glanced sideways at him. *Thank you.*

Arianna continued to hesitate. She studied her digital blueprint. She was compelled to admit that searching the entire museum was virtually impossible.

Luke shrugged. "Norman's got a point. Lucy will not attract a lot of undue attention."

Should I be insulted or pleased by that remark? I decided to let it slide. So what if Luke no longer thought I was a striking beauty. The truth is, I never was. He just made me feel like I was because he had chosen me out of the myriad beauties available to him. My greatest desire was to be in on this mission, to prove my value and convince Arianna that I would be an asset to her organization.

By the time we landed at the Naples heliport she agreed. It was late afternoon. The sun was angling, making it difficult to see. At this time of day the museum was closed to the public. But some of the museum staff might be working after hours. D'Agostino would most likely be there.

"I can't come with you," Arianna said. "He'll recognize me. I have to get to Pompeii and meet that shipment before it gets dark."

We went to the car rental kiosk at Naples's busy heliport. Arianna objected to landing in Pompeii by helicopter even though the site had a convenient helipad. Luke's AugustaWestland AW 109 twin engine, luxury six-seater would draw too much attention to itself—and to her. If anyone was watching, she must avoid being seen. "I'll rent a Ford Focus or something similar that will blend in."

Luke rented a BMW sedan and had Norman drive us to the National Archaeological Museum in Naples. I was once again relegated to the backseat.

The distance took longer to cover than we would have

liked because of the crazy rush hour traffic. If D'Agostino had already left, so much the better. Luke was on his phone once more, trying to locate him.

"Bruno," Luke said gaily into the phone. "*Ciao*, my old friend, *come va*? Are you at the museum? I'm in the neighborhood and I was wondering if you'd like to go out for a drink, or even dinner?" He paused, smiling. "You have a prior engagement? That's too bad. Would have been nice to get together. Another time. *Arrivederci, il mio amico*." He clicked off his phone and said to Norman, "Coast is clear."

We finally arrived at the museum and found parking a few blocks away. How were we to get into the museum without setting off the alarms? It would have been easier had D'Agostino agreed to see Luke.

But luck was with us. Out of the front door, D'Agostino's secretary was just leaving. Luke ordered us around the corner of the building to a side door. "Wait there," he said. "Keep back, out of sight of the security cameras. I'll find a way to let you in."

He left us. We watched as he greeted the secretary. I caught Norman's amused look as Luke approached the well-dressed woman and made some excuse to go inside. I believe his plan was to tell her that he had forgotten something in D'Agostino's office the other day. By Norman's look of confidence and because I knew Luke the way I did, I had no problem believing that Dr. Trevanian, intrepid billionaire archaeologist, would find a way to get inside. I shook my head in mock disbelief as she let him back indoors. They were gone a long time. Had Luke managed to do more than just seduce the secretary into giving him access? Surely he wouldn't do more than that even if she wanted him to? Now my mind was going where it had no right to go. I shut it off. I waited, sliding back against the wall of the building to the side door following Norman's example to avoid being spotted by the cameras, only glancing at the time on my phone once.

Finally, the side door moved. It opened silently and

slightly. Luke whispered, "Okay get in here. I only have a few minutes before she'll wonder where I am. I told her I had to visit the little boy's room."

We slipped inside and stood in a dark hallway with stairs leading up. "No cameras in here. I checked. I'll need you to wait here and let me in this same door after I leave with her through the main entrance. Shouldn't take long. See you in ten. Fifteen at the most."

It was more like twenty. I guess the lovely *signorina* wanted Luke to escort her home. I squashed the sarcasm.

A cautious rapping came at the side entrance. Norman pushed the lever and opened the door. "She's gone, finally," Luke said. "Thought I was going to have to wine and dine her." He sent a glance upwards. "All quiet upstairs?"

We both nodded. He left us to go up and check on security.

"Hey," he said, from the top of the stairs. "All's clear. Let's go." He waved us up and Norman gestured me ahead of him.

We walked down several corridors. Luke explained to us the security situation. He had managed to show some interest, and his famous charm had done the rest. But the security guards at the door and the secretary had been more than willing to provide the information he needed. "So, there are four night guards at the front entrance. They take shifts doing rounds every hour. We can do this, but we have to keep out of their sight."

"What about cameras?" I asked. "Do they have surveillance cameras in the galleries?"

Both the men's brows shot up. Yes. I was smart. That was only common sense. After all I did work in a very large museum. And we had surveillance cameras everywhere.

"There are ways to get around that," Norman said. He explained to me how to keep out of their field of view. "So stay to the side of the camera or under it, and keep as close to the wall as possible. You're slim as a rail; you should have no problem. And if we get into real trouble I have this." He showed me a laser pen that would cause a flare or bloom in the camera, thereby obscuring the image, and our identities. He also had a baseball cap wired with IR LEDs. It created a similar effect.

"But we'll avoid the galleries," Luke said. "There's no reason D'Agostino would hide the Gorgon frescoes there. I think our best bet is his office and then some of the storage units downstairs."

"I guess it will be fastest if we split up." Norman clapped the LED wired baseball cap onto my head. "Those lights will blind the cameras if you need it. But better to stay out of their field of vision. The last thing we want to do is attract their attention with a bloom. Do you know what to do?"

I nodded.

Luke had his own laser pen, and Norman had his. "Okay, I'm going to take the office. Norman you take the storage rooms. And Lucy, since you're the smallest and least detectable, maybe you should take a quick scan of some of the galleries where you think the goods will blend in. But don't go in. Stay in the doorway out of sight of the cameras. If you see something that might fit the bill, call one of us to check." He tapped the phone in his breast pocket. "Stay in touch. Set your cell to vibrate and switch off the sound. If you get into trouble, contact one of us immediately."

I was left alone and scared. They actually trusted me to do this by myself. I stayed against the wall as Norman had instructed, even though he said they wouldn't waste money by installing surveillance in the hallways.

A few minutes later, I still hadn't moved. I really must be useless. All I had to do was slip into the Roman exhibits and have a quick look around. But I was afraid that I would be seen in the cameras. Without Norman and Luke's experience I worried over the cameras' exact locations. As I was debating with myself, something sidled up beside me. I jumped.

"Lucy, it's only me." Norman grabbed my hand and

squeezed it. He pressed his spine against the wall beside me.

"Are you sure you want to do this?"

He was the one who had drilled me on the qualifications for membership into ISORE. My thoughts were once again painfully ironic. I think I had already failed all ten of their requirements. Or were there more?

"Why did you come back?" I whispered.

"I had a feeling you might need me."

I squeezed his hand in return. "Thank you."

His forehead knotted in concern. He could detect my indecisiveness. I tried to control my erratic breathing and swore my heartbeats could be heard. "Maybe you should wait for us outside."

I glared at him, more disappointed in him than I was in myself.

"Or maybe you shouldn't," he said after receiving the nasty look I gave him. Amusement jerked at the corners of his mouth. Then his voice turned dead serious. "But you can't stay here."

I released his hand. "I'll be all right. I'm going in there." I pointed towards the Roman galleries.

I started to move, fast. When I glanced back he had vanished. It dawned on me then that I knew exactly where D'Agostino might have stashed the Gorgon heads. I kept walking until I reached the sign that said: The Chamber of Secrets.

I slipped inside and kept to the wall. I could see the cameras now that I understood what I was looking for. I stayed under them and beside them. No alarm bells sounded so I knew I was still safe. I was almost to the exhibit that had caught my eye when I stopped.

There was the goat and satyr having sex. And there was the Roman silver dinner set. I looked around further without moving from my spot. I found exactly what I was searching for. Dare I move closer to be sure? Among the stone penises and phallic lamps two pieces did not quite match the erotic items displayed here. The way the two heads were positioned, however, I guess you could call it erotic. The open mouths of the Gorgons were positioned over two stone penises.

Did D'Agostino think no one would notice? Well, I supposed they might not since everything in this room was of a sexual and even a pornographic nature.

How did Luke and Norman plan to open the case and steal the frescoes without setting off every alarm in the building?

I pulled my phone out of my bag and pressed Norman's number. At the time I didn't think it strange that I was calling Norman instead of Luke. And when I realized that it was Norman who answered—my voice dried up.

"Lucy?" he said. "What's wrong? Are you okay? I'm coming up. Where are you?"

"I'm in The Chamber of Secrets," I said. "Norman, I've found them!"

"Fantastic. Does Luke know?"

"Not yet. I... I called you first."

Why had I called him first? I think we both knew.

"Call him now. I'll be there as fast as I can."

I went to tap on Luke's number. He answered on the second ring. He was overjoyed that it had been so easy. But now came the hard part: how to get the Gorgon heads out of the display case and safely away to our rendezvous point in Pompeii?

Both men appeared at the doorway almost simultaneously. The three of us remained just under the security camera. There were numerous other cameras inside the gallery. So far we had not been sighted, but it was only a matter of time.

I pointed to the case with the Gorgon sisters. "How are you going to disarm the alarm system?" I asked.

"I'll have to find the power box. It's probably in the basement."

Luke shook his head. "No time for that."

"We have to try," Norman said. "Otherwise we'll have

to smash it in. And that will set off every alarm in the building."

"Wait," I said. This was an old museum and many of the display cases here were old-fashioned. Were they even wired to the main alarm system? "That exhibit is locked with a key. D'Agostino must have chosen that case for convenience. Those phallic pieces aren't particularly valuable because there are so many of them. It doesn't require high tech security. Who's going to steal some stone penises?" I cleared my throat and suppressed a smile. "He could just open it if he needed to get those heads out quickly. I don't think that exhibit is wired into the system."

Both Luke and Norman stared at me. I was full of surprises. Like I said, I worked in a museum. I had seen a few things about how museums operated.

"She's right," Norman agreed. "I just have to pick that lock without being detected by surveillance."

We all backed out of the gallery so that Norman could study the visible cameras. "Do you have the plans that show the camera angles?" he asked Luke.

Luke pulled out his phone and displayed the plan he had downloaded from Arianna's computer. "Okay, I'm going in," Norman said.

He slipped through the door. It was impossible to avoid all of the cameras. He used the laser to temporarily disable some of them. Luke followed him, doing the same while I waited at the door. There were three entrances to this gallery. I stood at the one closest to the display holding the coveted pieces. When Norman reached the glass cabinet, his back was to me. How was he picking the lock? It took a few minutes. Luke fidgeted behind him, but Norman was the expert, which was why Luke allowed him to be the one to break into the exhibit.

They hauled out the goods and placed them into a hard grey Pelican case. I was right. No alarm system in that display.

But as soon as we took a step outside the gallery, alarms

rang in every direction. Norman was the strongest of us. He was carrying the stolen artifacts. He was the last to step out, and froze at the sudden cacophony. All hell had broken loose. "Give the frescoes to Lucy!" Luke shouted. "Lucy run. Get outside to the car and take off. Don't wait for us. We'll hold them off here."

How could I leave them? I had no choice. We had to get the goods to Pompeii and to safety. Luke and Norman could handle whatever security guards were in the museum and then they would be out of there and in my wake as fast as could be. Before the police arrived. That's what I hoped.

I raced down the corridor, my arms loaded. Voices bombarded me from all directions. I dived down a stairwell. The guards were already at the gallery and I could hear the thud of blows. I stumbled down the stairs, losing the LED wired cap on the way. The frescoes were impossibly heavy. I had to stop to catch my breath before I reached the landing.

There was a door. Fortunately it led to the outside. I burst into the open air.

CHAPTER
19

Oh, where had we parked the car! I stood shivering. I turned down the road where I hoped it was, lugging my load. It was quite dark outside now. Streetlights illuminated the landscape of concrete, glass and stone buildings. Shadowy trees left sharp outlines against the sky.

As I paused to get my bearings, a car pulled up and parked. It was an expensive car, a sporty black Lamborghini with the top down. A man leaned out from the driver's side, and I quickly turned away and started walking. I was in no shape or mood for idle chatter. If he asked for directions I would be tongue-tied for sure.

"Ms. Racine?" he said.

My body went limp as I recognized the voice. I stopped and turned to confirm my hunch, and stood paralyzed. Numerous niceties struggled on my tongue to divert suspicion from myself, but nothing came out. I had jumped out of the frying pan into the fire.

"Dr. D'Agostino," I said, forcing charm and calm into my manner. "How nice to see you." After everything Arianna had told us about the man I was amazed I could behave so coolly. I shifted the weight of the Pelican case, which threatened to break my arms, and tried to appear

inconspicuous and innocent.
  I was about two blocks away from the museum. There was no reason for him to think I was involved with the burglary in progress. He was not terribly nervous. The alarms were inaudible from this distance because they were located inside the building.
  "Can I give you a lift somewhere?" he asked. "You look lost."
  "Oh, I'm not lost," I insisted.
  "But surely with that heavy load you need a ride?" His eyes were locked onto my Pelican case. Pelican cases were designed to transport costly breakable objects. They can take being dropped. Even survive a plane crash.
  "It's not all that heavy."
  "Where is your car?"
  "It's—" My eyes danced frantically in multiple directions. *Just lie for heaven's sake!*
  Impatience suddenly overwhelmed him. He opened the car door, blocking my path, and stepped out. "Get in the car."
  I thought to run but I knew I wouldn't get far with this heavy burden. When I looked back at him I saw he had a gun. "Don't make me hurt you, Ms. Racine. I really don't want to." The Italian friendliness was gone. He was grim and spoke in good English. He grabbed the Pelican case from me and smiled. He tested the weight and I knew I was in trouble. "So you found them. Where are your lover and his watchdog?"
  When I refused to answer he hoisted the case over the console to the floor of the front passenger side. There was no one on the dark street where the black Lamborghini was parked. He forced me to walk around the vehicle, gun nestled in my side and opened the front passenger door. He nudged me inside. I had no choice but to comply. He could shoot me from any angle because the top of the sports car was down. He slammed the passenger door shut, came round, gun still aimed at me, and slid into the driver's seat.
  I was frantic. What was happening at the museum?

Would Luke and Norman get away from the police? I was hoping to see them loping down the pavement towards me. Only two boys on motor scooters, Vespas, were rolling down the road. I was about to give up all hope when the boys slowed, and then stopped by the side of the car. "Is that you, *signorina?*" a familiar voice asked. "Is that you, Miss Lucy?" I felt the nose of the gun in my side. I forced my voice to sound cheerful even as I addressed the boy. It was Franco from the Civita, and with him was his cousin Giorgio.

"Hello Franco," I said lightly, my fear, I hoped, evident to them but not to my captor. If I could stall, they might catch on and notice that I was in this car against my will. It would be even better if I could stall long enough for Luke and Norman to come racing down the street to my aid. "And you too, Giorgio. What are you doing in Naples?"

"Giorgio got the day off and I finished my chores early so we decided to come to the big city for a few days. Sometimes we like to get away from the countryside," Franco said.

"*Si.*" Giorgio agreed. "Are you here sightseeing?"

The gun jabbed me in the side and D'Agostino spoke across me from the driver's seat. It was dark enough that the boys were unable to see what was going on behind me inside the car. "We must go. Say goodbye to your friends."

"You have a very beautiful car, *signore*," Giorgio complimented D'Agostino.

"*Grazie.*"

D'Agostino refused to be deterred. He turned back to the wheel the next instant, while my brain frantically churned. Outwardly I was calm, but inwardly I was panicking. How could I get a message to them to tell Luke and Norman where I was? There was no opportunity to pass them a note or tell them anything. The gun urged me to cut the visit short. I hoped my chattering to the two local boys detracted from the actions of my hands. I slipped my cellphone out of my pocket and hid it between the car door and my torso. I quickly tapped out one word: *Help!*

Then I stuck the phone into the boys' faces.

"*Arrivederci, amici,*" I shouted as the Lamborghini pulled away from the curb. Unfortunately the jolt of our departure jerked the phone out of my hands before I could press SEND. The phone went crashing to the pavement. There went my best hope to call Luke and Norman to save me. I only hoped the boys could read enough English to know I was in trouble.

D'Agostino yanked me back into the seat from where I was leaning forward and hanging my head over the door. He instructed me to fasten my seatbelt because we were going for a fast ride. He drove in silence for a few moments, the gun still in his grip. The scenery washed by, buildings and cars and pedestrians. Here was a stoplight and if I could just get out and run—

But no. His gun jabbed me in warning. His eyes turned to me. "Tell me where Arianna Chase is," he ordered.

"I don't know where she is," I said, frightened.

His eyes darted to the road, then he glanced back at me. "I think you do."

I shrugged, trying to keep my pounding heart from leaping straight out of my throat. I kept silent.

"She is expecting a delivery. Am I right?"

Speech was impossible even if I tried. My throat was so dry. The silence loomed.

"By the way you are fidgeting, I can tell I am right. I knew I should have locked her up. Amnesia indeed! I knew she was faking! But Giovanni insisted she had no idea who she was." He scowled. "Where is the drop? On the grounds of Pompeii?"

The light changed and he stepped on the gas. I was hoping to get an opportunity to escape when his vision returned to the road. No such luck. He was quick and he was desperate. I had no doubt that he knew how to use that firearm.

"Answer me. Is the drop at Pompeii?"

The historic site of Pompeii had been closed off to the

public for the past two months for reconstructive work to make it safer for tourists. There would be no one there to see a helicopter deliver a cargo of valuable frescoes.

"I don't know," I answered.

He shot me a sideways glare. He was lucky in that the next few lights were green. I don't know how long it took to get out of the city but I wasn't saying another word. He went silent. I knew his distraction was temporary. If I tried to leap out of the car at any of the points where he was forced to decelerate he would shoot me.

By the time I sorted out all of my panicky thoughts, he turned south onto the motorway and sped into the night along the A3 *autostrade*. Outside the city limits the darkness was not so sharp in contrast to the streetlights. It was really only dusk. In the near distance I made out the hump of Mount Vesuvius. We would have to pass the famous volcano before we reached Pompeii. I forced my gaze to return to my captor. How was I going to get out of this car?

"Don't look at me like that, Ms. Racine," he said. "I am not a bad man. I am only in a bad situation."

"Is that why you are kidnapping me?" I accused him.

"I am not kidnapping you. All I want is what is in that Pelican case. From the weight of it I know you have found the Gorgon heads.... I will let you go after I have seen the goods safely to its destination."

I glanced down at the Pelican case full of frescoes. My eyes slowly moved up to D'Agostino's face. "Let me go now," I begged. "What do you need *me* for?"

"You have seen me."

Scary things were starting to stir in my mind. By the way he said that, it sounded like he needed to get rid of me. I had to get out of this car or I would never see Luke and Norman again.... And I could not die without telling both of them how I felt.

"It is not what you think," he said.

"What *do* I think?" I whispered.

"I do not wish you to think badly of me. So I will tell

you my story. Then you will understand why I must do what I must do." He redirected his full attention to the road and accelerated. We were going at a fast clip, far faster than I felt comfortable with. He dogged the car ahead of us, sped up then swerved around it, and left it in his dust. When the vehicle was far behind us he slowed to a more reasonable speed and said, "How much do you know of antiquities trafficking in the Middle East?"

"I know that Syria's heritage is at great risk because of civil war."

A small movement of D'Agostino's head signified agreement. "It is worse than that."

I nodded. "Peoples' lives are at stake."

"Yes. The rebels and even locals have resorted to looting antiquities in exchange for money. They need to live on something. And innocents are being killed in the crossfire." He went silent for a moment. "But it is the extremists that have turned the country into an apocalypse. Militants have taken over the war with no regard for human life."

I was well aware of the situation and I nodded vigorously this time. "I understand."

"No," he said. "I think you do not. None of you do. You archaeologists and historians, you museum people only care about history…. The loss of valuable objects… I cannot seem to get the gravity of the situation across to anyone. People are *dying*."

This was a story I was already familiar with. Images of war-torn villages and towns were plastered all over the media, communities rendered to rubble. I had to convince him somehow that people were aware and that they cared. "I know," I said, "and western governments are doing all they can to help civilians."

"They are not doing enough. So I have taken the situation into my own hands." He glared at me before shifting his eyes ahead. "Let me tell you why I have done so."

His hands tightened on the wheel. Every muscle in his

body went taut under the fine fabric of his expensive suit. A thin sheen of sweat covered his face. The line of his mouth was straight although a muscle convulsed somewhere in his jaw. He did not speak for a moment and then his voice came filled with hate. Last week he had learned that Islamic extremists had captured his wife, but worse they were in possession of his children. She was not a criminal working for the militants of her own free will—as Arianna thought. She was fencing antiquities for the extremists to prevent her children from being murdered.

"Her father, Ahmed al-Hadad is curator of ancient ruins in Palmyra," he said. "He was informed that his family—*my* wife and children—will be tortured and executed if he does not surrender a convoy of trucks filled with Palmyra's treasures to the militants. The convoy is on the road to Turkey. The extremists want the goods and they want to sell them on the black market. They are worth, in total, billions of American dollars. Amira, my beautiful wife—and myself—are their tools. We are helpless, so we obey them—because they hold our children's lives in their hands."

"Why didn't you tell this to Luke?" I asked, gasping in horror.

"Do you think he would help me? It was too late for me to appeal to ISORE for help; their leader was already a victim. So I turned a blind eye after those villains sabotaged that plane. Luke's... wife... Arianna Chase was on that flight."

There it was again. The word. *Wife.* I knew they were once married. I knew they were not yet divorced. But they had not lived together in years. Why did no one use the term ex?

I ignored the troubling thought. Now was not the time. "But *you* didn't do it."

"Of course not. I am no murderer.... But I could not stop *them*, and I did not try. Even when I suspected sabotage I failed to speak. After that, do you really believe Luke Trevanian would help me?"

I paused to gulp. "Yes... Yes, I do. I think he *will* help you."

He scoffed. "Even if he was willing. How? How could he help me? He would have to break the law. He would have to cave in and hand me the artifacts so that I can give them to the militants. Do you think he would do that? He won't even support his wife's efforts to *save* the artifacts. He has rejected her organization ISORE. What is any of this to him? A multibillionaire? Bah! He will not help me any more than *she* would.... The militants are holding my family hostage, *signorina*. The city is poised to be taken. I have no choice but to do whatever they ask if I ever want to see my loved ones again. So do not judge me too harshly. It is a horrible position to find one's self in. A position in which you cannot say how you would behave unless you actually found yourself having to choose between your children's lives and that of an acquaintance!"

I shook my head. Bruno D'Agostino had turned a blind eye to the attempted murder of Arianna to buy a little more time for his wife and kids. But even if he complied and returned the Gorgon heads with the bodies, there could be no good end to this. They would simply demand further and costlier payments. How many more lives could he stand by and watch destroyed in order to save his own family? These people were terrorists. That was the only reason Arianna and Luke would refuse to help him.

But surely, somewhere inside them, they had compassion? Surely, D'Agostino did not know them as well as I did?

"So you see, Ms. Racine. I cannot ask for outside help. The police, the government, they will not help me. Only I can help my family—if I comply with what they ask. Those devils will torture my little ones and then kill them." He shot me an edgy glance. "What would *you* do?"

"I agree with you," I said. "We must give your wife's captors what they want. I'm sure Arianna will understand if you explain it to her."

"No. Not that one," he said. "How many times must I repeat it? She is cold, that one. She cares only for the objects. The antiquities. The history. She will not capitulate to terrorists. Even Sulla Kharim would not capitulate to terrorists and he is Syrian. No, so he had to be eliminated before he could expose me."

D'Agostino killed Kharim? I shivered. His logic made no sense. Arianna already knew of his Syrian connections. I decided that this was not the line of questioning that would serve me best. I tilted my head slightly his way.

"If it involves the life of your children, she will help you. I know she will."

"I cannot take the chance. I won't. I must deliver these Gorgon heads and retrieve the fresco of the bodies. And remove any obstacles that get in my way. You—"

What did he plan to do with me? He was probably right and Arianna would not cooperate with terrorists, not even to save the lives of innocent children. Because, dammit all, it was war. And innocent kids were dying in the Middle East everyday.

How to get out of here? How to warn them that D'Agostino was Sulla Kharim's killer, and that he would stoop to murder to save his family? I looked down at the floor of the Lamborghini. There was only one thing that would make him stop the car.

Adrenaline soared in my system. I had to use it for something. I had learned since coming on this Italian expedition that I possessed strengths I never knew I had. Even physical strength. It only took a lapse of mind and a force of will to act. I bent down and quicker than he could grab for his gun, I heaved the Pelican case out of the speeding Lamborghini and heard it thump onto the road. *Oh, please, please, the artifacts won't be smashed to pieces.* But lives were at stake.

D'Agostino swore at me in Italian and slammed on the brakes. The speeding Lamborghini had sent the Pelican case flying backwards at least fifty feet. He catapulted out of the car and ran towards the discarded artifacts.

All his thought was on the Gorgon heads. As soon as he was a safe distance away, I scrambled over the console into the driver's seat, and shifted into DRIVE. The sounds of my speedy reaction threw his gaze my way. With a vicious curse, he realized too late his mistake. He had left me alone in an idling car. Panic had made him negligent and now he was paying for it. He abandoned the Pelican case. I stomped on the gas pedal. The car shot forward with him racing, screaming after me. I could not waste anymore time. I no longer had the luxury of compassion. The precious cargo may be lost, but I had to make it to Pompeii. The steep mound of Mount Vesuvius loomed over me.

It must be true what they say. That adrenaline gives a person the strength of ten people—or more. I was testimony to the fact. Hadn't I just heaved thirty pounds of fresco out the window? Now it was his turn to be pumped full of the hormone. He was fast. The pounding of his footsteps sounded too close. Before I could get the car clear away I heard a tremendous thud. He had leaped, grabbed onto the backseat of the open top, and now sat in a crouching position with his feet braced on the bumper. I stepped on the accelerator and plunged the Lamborghini into the blackening night.

The scenery flashed by. I could not identify what it was, only washes of grey and black and faint lights in the distance. There were trees, surely, and a cloudless sky, spangled with stars.

D'Agostino clung for dear life as I powered the vehicle in leaps and swerves attempting to jolt him off. He clung like a spider to a web refusing to be jerked loose in a relentless storm. I knew if I didn't lose him soon my nerve would fail. I would tire from driving at this speed. I glanced at the speedometer and saw that I was far beyond 160kph. I dared not go faster for fear of losing control of the car.

In the rearview mirror D'Agostino's hulking body slowly dragged itself forward against the stiff wind. My own hands were cold but whether that was because of the wind or my terror, heaven only knew. The only saving grace was that there was little traffic now, and I realized we were no longer on the main motorway. Somehow, in my frantic dance with the steering wheel I had swung us off the main drag and we were plowing steadily upward into an ever deeper and darker abyss. Behind us a single light followed. It fell back until it disappeared.

The ribbon of road wound up a graduated incline. I zigzagged at the highest speed I dared without flipping the car. At the top loomed the wide pyramidal summit of Mount Vesuvius.

CHAPTER 20

How could I have made such a wrong turn? Now I really had to shake him off and get back on the *autostrade* or I was doomed.

But the sharp curves in the road were forcing me to slow down and at each turn, D'Agostino crawled closer to me.

Finally, still fighting a wall of wind, he climbed over the top of the seat and slumped into the passenger seat beside me, panting. He was short of breath and barely able to speak. "Stop the car!" he snarled in a hoarse rasp.

In response to his demand I jammed my foot on the accelerator. That startled him, almost threw him out the side of the vehicle face-forward. With one hand he grabbed onto the top of the car door and yanked the seatbelt on with the other. Now I would never be able to shake him.

"What is your plan, *signorina*?" he asked. "This road leads to the volcano."

What about the gun in the side compartment of the driver's door? That was the only place he could have lodged it. If he'd had it on his person he would have used it by now. No. It was there in the side compartment. It must be. I only need grab it. Then I would be in charge.

But when push came to shove could I shoot a man?

Therein lay the quandary.

I was driving too fast to take my hand off the wheel for long. I had only a split second to do it. If only I knew the exact location of the gun!

When I finally gathered the nerve to try, and took my eyes off the road for a microsecond, D'Agostino's hand came slamming down on my driving wrist. The car swerved wildly as I recoiled from the pain, jolting my foot off the gas. His other arm crossed into the driver's side, blocking my view. He snagged the wheel. *Oh God, we were going to crash.* I stomped on the brake.

It was just as well that we screeched to a stop. From here the road narrowed into a footpath barely wide enough for a small car. The Lamborghini might have fit, but the end of the road would have been the same. There was nothing up there except for the volcano's crater. We were at an altitude of 1200 meters he told me. On this side of the crater no tourist facilities existed as they did on the other side. Even had there been any, they were all closed. The Volcano National Park was shut after sundown. I was alone. No one would think to look for me here.

"Get out of the car," D'Agostino ordered. "And behave. Or you will regret it."

"Please, Dr. D'Agostino," I whispered. "Killing me won't help you get your family back."

"Who said I was going to kill you? I am not a murderer. I told you."

"But you admitted to the death of Sulla Kharim."

"Did I? Then you misunderstood. I merely turned a blind eye when he was murdered."

"It's the same as killing."

He stared at me beneath that starry sky. I saw no compassion. He was still fired up after the terror of having me hijack his car and nearly killing him while trying to jerk him off the trunk of the vehicle. The rage still burned.

"Get out before I change my mind." He leaped out of the car and rushed to the driver's side as I frantically fished for the gun in the depths of the door compartment. He swept open the door just as I felt my fingers curl over the handle of the revolver. The motion of the swinging door yanked it out of my hands. As we scrambled wildly to see who could retrieve it first, he won. He gripped it, sending it upward to point the nozzle in my face.

I got out of the car.

The wind slapped my face. Chills rippled along my arms. The air was colder up here and more volatile. My skirt beat about my legs. The cropped jean jacket I wore overtop flapped at my chest. My hands were stiff from gripping the steering wheel and I flexed them to bring back mobility. My lips were dry, cracked. I desperately needed a drink.

"There's some rope in the trunk. Fetch it out," he commanded.

Despite my cramping fingers, I removed the rope and dropped it at his feet. I was hoping he would have to bend down to pick it up. Then I could kick him. Or run. But he merely ordered me to lift the tangled coil and drape it over his shoulder. At least he did not ask me to carry it.

I shuddered as my mind went over the possibilities he intended for that rope.

"Now walk," he said.

His gun pointed in the direction of the summit. The path here was unpaved, covered in slippery rubble, and lined with rickety wooden rails. False security, I thought.

Three minutes later we were at the top.

What was he going to do? Was he going to shoot me and leave me for dead at the bottom of the crater? Or was he going to strand me here to find my way down in the dark and cold in the middle of the night?

It was worse.

"You're going down there," he said.

"No. No, I'll die down there."

"You'll die up here if you don't do as you're told."

"Please, Dr. D'Agostino. Don't do this."

"You're in no danger, Ms. Racine," he said. "I only want

you out of the way. But if you push me you will give me no choice."

"That was an idea. Could I push him into the crater? He had said it was a thousand meter drop.

"There's a solid ledge there in the crater about fifteen feet down. If you look you can see it. I'm going to lower you down there. If you remain against the wall of the crater and not try to escape you will live."

"No, please. I'm terrified of heights."

"Then you'll feel safer down there."

There was a short section of metal rail on this rim of the crater. On the opposite side where the tour groups normally went half of the crater's edge was railed off to prevent tourists from falling in. But here, the railing was sparse and incomplete. I had been so preoccupied that I had no occasion to look. But we were over 1200 meters in the air.

"Tie the end of this rope to that railing there. Do a good job or it won't be my fault if you go plunging down into the bottom of the crater."

His command had a nightmarish quality to it. Was he actually going to force me to do this? If I refused, what would he do? In the moonlight his face was gleaming with sweat and emotion. The designer suit he wore seemed incongruous with his sinister intent. His jacket and slacks flapped in the breeze. His tie was disheveled, as was his hair. The worry lines in his forehead took on a deep craggy appearance. His face was grim and he had a vise lock on his firearm. If I annoyed him, I believed he could kill me with just the slightest provocation.

I went to the rail, and with nimble fingers tied a tight knot to one of the spindles. The stiffness in my hands had eased. I knew the twists and turns of a good knot like I knew my own name. One thing I had learned living aboard Luke's yacht was how to secure a mooring line with nautical expertise.

"Now fix a loop under your arms and make it strong. Your life is in *your* hands."

I gulped. We were really doing this. Despite the flailing panic my mind circled the options. If I kicked him, struggled with him I would end up in that crater anyways—but dead. This way if I could make it through the night without going stark raving mad, someone would see me down below in the morning. Tourists groups began soon after dawn.

I tied the loop firmly under my arms.

"Now climb over the rail and into the crater."

"What if there's no ledge?"

"There is. Now go. I'm running out of time. If you make me wait any longer I will push you."

Would he really push me, and leave me dangling on twenty feet of rope? I started the climb down. The crater wall was steeply sloped—but it *was* sloped. That was better than a sheer drop. It meant I had a chance of climbing out of here. After a few minutes of nerve-shattering descent I felt unyielding ground.

I was on the ledge. The surface was soft but firm. There were patches of vegetation growing out of the earth, unidentifiable in the inadequate light. It was miserably barren here and I was trapped. I raised my eyes seeking mercy, compassion, empathy, anything. It was inhuman to leave a person stranded like this at the bottom of a crater. Oh yeah, I wasn't exactly at the bottom. It could be so much worse. He had left me on a ledge, where people could see me when light came. I rolled my eyes up helplessly. Surely there was some humanity left in this wretched shell of a man. Was there even an ounce of hope that D'Agostino would have a change of heart, and haul me back to the top?

It really wasn't that far up. If he left the rope I could climb out. But he had no intention of allowing me to get out that easily. I heard him grunt, then cuss, as he tried to untie the rope. Thanks to Luke's sailing crew I had learned well. He'd need a knife to undo that knot.

"Step out of the loop," he shouted.

"No!" How could he force me?

"I can see you down there, Ms. Racine. If you try to run

you will fall into the depths of the crater, down one thousand feet to the bottom. Is that what you want?"

I saw the gleam of his gun as he pointed it at me. "Untie the rope and step out of it."

The loop was loose enough for me to wriggle out of it. My fingers fumbled with the scratchy, hairy noose. Oh, if only I hadn't lost my phone, I could have called Norman to come and save me.

It was as though D'Agostino had read my deepest desire. "There is no signal down there, Ms. Racine. So if you have a cellphone you will not be able to call for help."

I obeyed him. The rope began a slow ascent up the slope. I had a fleeting idea to jump up and grab the frayed, dangling end and yank it out of his hands, thereby jerking him forward and into the crater. But no luck. He was standing behind the section of metal railing. It was low but he was a short man. The rail bar came up to his waist. On anyone taller it might have been the impetus that would send him over the side. But this man was stout and firmly rooted to the ground by his own excess weight. He would not fall in, and the desperate action would only enrage him further. Even a man who had no intent to kill could lose control in a moment of passion.

The length of rope sailed up and out of my sight. I tilted my head skyward. About three feet of it hung into the crater as though to taunt me.

And then there was silence.

For a long time I heard nothing. No traffic, no birds, no insects. Only the wind. But at least down here I was sheltered from its bitterness.

My arms wrapped around my chest in an effort to control my trembling. If I stayed down here I would freeze or go insane. I rubbed my hands together in an effort to draw some warmth and to get the circulation going. Remaining inactive was not an option. I had to come up with a plan of escape.

Arms outstretched, knees braced, I clawed my way forward. My nails filled with grime. My hands buried into soft, loose soil, ever yielding as I tried to climb up without benefit of a rope. The slope was not gradual enough. The incline was sharp, vertical in spots. I slipped repeatedly on the falling rubble and dirt. This succeeded only in making me dirtier than I already was.

The panic began to close in on me. How steep was the drop on the open side of this ledge? Steam rose from somewhere in the black hole, followed by a nauseating smell of sulfur. Was this volcano active? Impossible. Otherwise it wouldn't be open to tourists. Would it? Surely the authorities would not endanger tourists by allowing them to climb to the top of the volcano if there were any threat of an eruption? But then this was Europe. Their laws and safety standards differed from ours in Canada and the United States.

I craned my neck as far as I could in the direction of the drop without stepping closer to the edge. How wide was this ledge? Dare I look? It was dark down there and the only light came from above in the starry, moonlit sky. *Be grateful for that.* It could have been overcast, and then I would have been lost in the blackness of the crater. Or worse, it could be raining.

My only hope was out of my reach. Despairingly I stared up at the rail outlined in black against the grey sky. If only I could get that rope to slither down to me. I began to search for rocks that I could throw. Surely I could throw a rock fifteen feet? I'd just have to be careful of my aim so that any ricochets didn't bounce back down on me and hit me. I explored the ground but not too far. I found a few rocks and piled them near the base of my rail sighting. Then I started to pitch the rocks at the base of the rail hoping to shake loose the rope, and start some momentum going to send the length down to me.

I knew the top end was still firmly fastened to the railing. D'Agostino had been swearing in disgust when he couldn't get it untied. Clearly he had not brought a knife with him, but then why would he? What would the director of a museum need with a knife?

My thoughts were blathering, verging on incoherent. Aim. Throw. *Damn.*

The rocks mostly missed their target. When they hit, they *pinged* sharply, and bounced back and over my head. I had to duck and dodge to avoid getting hit. It wasn't working. The rope moved maybe a couple of inches, no more. It had not reached the critical mass needed to start the entire coil tumbling.

I was out of rocks and didn't dare search for more. I had no idea how far this ledge ran or how wide. I slumped down with my back to the wall and stared unhappily into nothingness. The smell of sulfur from some active parts of the volcano fouled the air.

Then I heard a sound. A shot in the dark. A bang, like a firecracker. But no one would be setting off fireworks here. My heart ticked over, hammering in my chest. I leaped to my feet, turned to look. That was a *gunshot.* I know it was. Silence for long interminable minutes. Then a voice? It was faint. Did D'Agostino have a change of heart? Why had he fired his gun? I strained my neck trying to see.

I could see nothing.

Now there was silence again.

"Where is she, you piece of shit?" It was Norman's voice.

I wished I could see what was happening. Had Norman intercepted D'Agostino on his return down the footpath? Did Norman have a gun? I was sure he had. But so did D'Agostino. Who was the better shot? I would place my money on Norman.

I could see two figures up there. One tall and powerful, the bodyguard. The other was D'Agostino, shortish and portly. The museum director was no match for Norman Depardieu, but D'Agostino had a gun and that gave him the advantage. And even though I was fairly certain that Norman also had a gun (it was part of his job to carry one), he would resist using it until he knew where I was.

How had Norman found me? What did it matter! I was

just overjoyed that he had. "Norman," I shouted. "I'm down here!"

He glanced below and that was his mistake. D'Agostino took the opportunity to kick his tall opponent in the gut, setting him off balance. His weight sent him over the side of the low railing, while quick reflexes allowed him to twist his torso and grab the base of the rail as he fell. Had he overshot he would have gone straight over and maybe down past the ledge and into the crater. He would have been killed, and it would have been my fault. Horror caused me to freeze as Norman dangled there. D'Agostino in a rage for being delayed one more time kicked Norman's hands causing him to let go.

CHAPTER 21

The slope only minimally slowed his fall. He tumbled down just past me and I ran to grab him before he slipped off the ledge. "Shit," he muttered, when he realized one leg was half-hanging off the edge into empty space.

I grabbed his arms in a frantic attempt to pull him to safety.

"It's okay, sweetheart," he said. "That's not doing anything. I can get up."

He crawled to his knees and I threw my arms around his neck. "Baby," he said. "If we don't move away from this bluff we're both going down into the abyss."

How could he be so cavalier; he was almost killed!

I let go and back-stepped toward the wall of the crater. He followed me, and then looked up. "*Merde*, that is quite a climb without a rope. And practically vertical at that."

"I am so sorry, Norman," I sobbed. "I almost killed you. If I hadn't shouted, you wouldn't have looked down and then you wouldn't have been caught off-guard."

"That's why you should never take a woman into the field with you," he said, chuckling.

"How can you laugh? That crater is a thousand feet deep."

"I've fallen into deeper."

"Seriously?"

"Seriously." He curled his arms around me and drew me in close. "Not the most romantic place you could have chosen for a secret tryst."

I knew what he was doing. He was trying to take my mind off what I had done. It wasn't working. "I am so sorry."

"Don't be. I am not dead. Or maimed. And only a little beaten up. I don't think I look any worse than you do."

"I look bad?" I dropped my arms from his shoulders and patted the dust from my clothes.

"Actually, you look fantastic. I've never been so happy to see anything in my life.... Oh Lucy," he whispered, hugging me close. "I thought I'd lost you."

I folded my arms around his neck and he lowered his head to meet my lips.

He raised his face. "Don't ever do that again."

I managed a smile. "The kiss or the disappearing act."

"The disappearing act. And yes, the kiss too. That probably should be tabled until we sort out what's what."

"How did you know where to find me?"

"Those boys from the village. They suspected some mischief. Giorgio followed you and Franco stayed behind when he saw Luke and me escape through a side door of the museum. He followed us to our car and showed us this." It was my phone with the message frozen on the screen where I had left it, typed but unsent. "Giorgio was on your tail and texted his cousin when he reached the city outskirts. He followed until the Lamborghini turned onto the mountain road. He said he knew something was wrong when he saw the erratic, high speed the car was racing. And that it was headed for the volcano. Franco described the make of the vehicle. We knew it was D'Agostino's. So we borrowed Franco's Vespa and tied it to the roof of our car. I took it up to the volcano after Luke dropped me off. He's gone to Pompeii to make sure D'Agostino doesn't intercept the delivery and injure Arianna."

I did not ask why it wasn't Luke who had come to rescue me.

"What happened?" I asked. I pointed upwards. No movement or sound came from above. Loose flurries of wind occasionally found its way down, but other than that the humming of the wind was our only companion from above. D'Agostino had long since vanished. "Did you ambush him before he could leave?"

"I did indeed, but I wasn't counting on him having a gun."

"Where's yours?"

"Probably at the bottom of that crater." He gently untangled me from the stranglehold I had on his neck. "I left the Vespa a distance back from where D'Agostino parked his fancy ride. I saw him coming down the mountainside; he didn't see me. I hid behind his car and when he approached I jumped him. Then I forced him at gunpoint to take me to you. He led me up there." His hand gestured to the railing above us. "Unfortunately being as tall as I am I have a high center of gravity which made it easy for the jerk to trip me over that shallow rail by my own weight. I should have known better."

"But I distracted you."

"Still, I know better. I've been trained not to be distracted." He paused, struggling with his next words. "Oh, hell," he said.

"What is it?" I started to run my hands over his shoulders and arms. The hard cords of his muscles filled the palms of my hands. "Did you hurt yourself when you fell?"

"No." He stared at me and shook his head, seizing my wrists to stop their caressing movement. It occurred to me then that perhaps it was the predicament we were in. I struggled to make out his expression in the shadow of the crater wall. It was clear by the tone of his voice that he was frustrated. "Well, maybe," he spat. "I feel like cussing every swear word I know." And there were a lot. He cursed under his breath, "I am in big trouble." Then got control of himself, and released my wrists.

We were both in big trouble, in more ways than one. I tried to see into his eyes, wanted to make him elaborate, when my gaze moved past his shoulder to the ground beyond. I was tense but I was no longer frightened. Norman was with me and he would think of a way out, although his mood was disconcerting.

The gleam of gunmetal shone in the semi-dark. I went to fetch the unwieldy firearm and handed it to him grip-end forward. He slipped it into his back pocket. I tried to lighten a situation that was nowhere near light. "Don't worry. We'll get out of here. Tomorrow morning when the tourists arrive they'll see us, and call for help."

"I don't mean that. And FYI, I fully intend to get us out of here long before that. I want to stop that SOB from getting the Gorgon frescoes and all that money."

"Norman." I grabbed his arm to still it. I felt his muscles flex in resistance. "D'Agostino's wife and children have been abducted by terrorists. They're threatening to torture and kill them. That's why he's working for them. They're holding him hostage."

"Wow. That sucks."

"It does. It doesn't absolve him for doing this to us, but it makes it easier to understand."

"Did he hurt you?"

"No, but I think I scared the crap out of him." Then I proceeded to tell Norman about the car chase up the mountainside.

"Holy crow. You did that?" He laughed.

It was amazing what you could do when motivated.

He took my hand, and slid down to sit in the dirt against the crater wall. I slumped beside him, and he turned and gave me a tender look. "When I said I was in trouble, I meant you."

He cupped my chin and drew my face gently towards his. He kissed my lips lingeringly, and I found myself exalting in the fact that he found me so irresistible. I remembered him telling me that he refused to love me. That was why the night I went to his bed he objected to kissing me. That seemed like an eon ago now, like a dream. Had it really happened? It was so surreal. And so impossibly romantic. *Oh my God.* I almost brought my hands to my lips to cover my gasp. He *loved* me.

"Lucy, we can't keep doing this. It's interfering with my work."

I turned to take in his face, his whole body, as much as I could see of it in this tight position. Did I feel the same? Had fate intervened? Was everything that had occurred up to that point meant to happen? He had sketched a picture of me. Why had he done that if not because... I shook the thought out of my mind. I was getting ahead of myself. But... if I had guessed correctly... The thought occurred to me again. He loved me.

"How did you do it before?" I asked contritely.

A pause. "I never did it before."

He'd never fallen in love before?

I lowered my eyes, and felt pressure forming behind my eyelids. I was exhausted and charged up at the same time. I had almost killed myself and another person in a high-speed chase. I had been threatened with a gun and forced to climb down inside a crater. I had almost caused Norman's death. And now this. It was one thing if he was telling me he didn't love me. *That* I could take. But he seemed to be doing the opposite. He was breaking it off with me before it could even really start—because he *did*. That made zero sense.

Well... I stiffened my back and let go of his hand. We weren't really together, were we? You couldn't really lose something you never had.

I swallowed. He never wanted this. I had forced it on him.

"I've made you sad," he said.

"You've made me confused."

He glanced sideways at me. Then silence, and I suddenly

realized how truly dark and desolate it was down here. I should have been hungry and thirsty and just plain physically debilitated. But his presence was consuming all of my thought and feelings, and I was ignoring everything else. I listened to him breathe. I heard my own breaths in the quietness. I said softly, "This doesn't have to do with Luke anymore, does it."

He sighed. It sounded like the wind; it was so forlorn. "Oh, it does. But please try to understand."

I stood up and brushed the loose soil off my skirt.

He stood up too, and now I had to arch my neck to look up at him. We were at an impasse, as we seemed to be with all things. At least he was somewhat willing to talk, but he did choose his times. And this was a bad one. I let out a long exhalation of air to match his. My lips were dry and I was tiring of this. I could see that he was too. Nothing could be resolved down here and it was dumb to even try.

"I understand perfectly," I said. "You want to go off on dangerous adventures, saving precious relics, and you don't want a helpless woman tagging along (I made certain the sarcasm was obvious).... Because... (Suddenly, I had no room for sarcasm because what I was about to say was true) because I might make you look away at the wrong moment and then you'll fall and be killed. Fine. I don't want you to be killed either."

I spun away from him and shot a steep look up the wall of the crater to the top. I stiffened my back. It was a struggle to contain the inexplicable anger. "You said you could get us out of here. Then, let's get out of here."

Quiet breathing before he spoke. "You are so cute when you're mad at me."

He was trying to cajole me into good humor again. It was completely ineffective. "I am not mad at you," I said. "Only disappointed." I added, rather unfairly, turning my sight up at him so that I could really see his face. "You really *aren't* all that brave are you?"

He scowled. "What do you mean?"

"You know exactly what I mean. I am not going to help you. If this is what you want. Then you're on your own. I refuse to make it easy for you."

Silence while he pondered my last statement. "And what about you. Have you told Luke?" he asked.

"What should I tell him? You just informed me that there's nothing going on between us. I made a mistake—one *stupid* night." I closed my mouth, and struggled to resist the urge to respond to any further comments.

We probably should have just left it at that. But would he let me have the final word?

"Now, you just want to hurt me," he accused.

I glared at him. "It's okay for you to hurt me. But not okay for me to hurt you. Well that is just *so* fair, isn't it?"

"Dammit, Lucy, I never asked to fall in love with you."

He had finally admitted it. The feelings I was experiencing were mixed: frustration, desire, tenderness and pure unadulterated rage. "So, it's *my* fault." I scowled, then let the tears fall. "Well, maybe you're right. It *is* my fault. You were always a perfect gentleman.... I'm sorry, Norman."

He cupped the back of my head and laid it against his chest. If only the world would stop and we could keep this moment. But things were against us.

"Let's not fight about this, Lucy. This was all sort of sudden. For you, I mean. I've known how I felt about you for a long time. I had no intent to betray Luke. And I wouldn't have. I was fine just staying on the sidelines and watching. I am not proud of having lost control." He waited a few seconds before he resumed. "And you? I don't think you've made up your mind."

His words were gentle, self-blaming and not unkind. He was not accusing me of anything. Although, if anyone was to blame it was me. The sigh that left my lungs spoke for both of us.

Nothing could be decided down here. I mopped my face on his shirt. I was getting him wet. These tears were probably the result of fatigue and reaction, emotional exhaustion as much as anything else. He stroked my hair and kissed me lightly on the top of the head.

No doubt I *was* exhausted and I told him so. I begged him to ignore the tears. D'Agostino had put me through the wringer. I was unaccustomed to being used that way.

"It's okay, Lucy," he said. "I don't mind. As long as I'm not the cause of your tears."

He wasn't. Nonetheless I had better toughen up—and fast. It wasn't over yet.

CHAPTER

22

Norman was mentally calculating the distance to the surface of the crater. "Can't be more than fifteen feet," he said. "How tall are you, Lucy?"

"Five feet, six inches," I answered. My eyes were dry and I felt better. Why crying made you feel better was beyond me. It had something to do with hormones, but now was an inconvenient time to figure it out.

Norman was six foot five. I knew that because I had once asked Luke who was also tall (six four I believe).

"That's about a yard of rope hanging down. Looks like it's still fastened to the rail."

"It is," I assured him. "I tied it there myself. It's a secure knot. Luke's yacht crew taught me how."

"D'Agostino made you tie that rope and climb down here on your own?" He cursed. I realized that the image of Jesus Christ carrying his own cross had flashed into Norman's mind. Or maybe he had likened it to digging your own grave. When Norman was angry, you knew it. His eyes rolled like he was possessed.

"The man was under duress," I said, trying to soften the effect. "And if we don't hurry and find a way out of here we won't be able to help Arianna—or him."

"I will not help that son-of-a—*Fils de pute!*" he swore under his breath.

If we stayed down here much longer I will have learned definitively the entire vocabulary of swear words in French.

He got himself under control and mentally recalculated how far he would have to jump from the ledge to reach the top of the crater. He leaped about three feet off the ground but that wasn't nearly high enough to catch the rope. The third and fourth time he tried only succeeded in knocking a pile of dirt and rubble down on us. It was a good thing the ledge we stood on was solid. But that last attempt had me worried. I swore the ground beneath our feet had shifted.

I grabbed his arm. "Stop that, Norman. You might collapse the ledge and send us down *there*." I shot a glance over my shoulder to the black abyss. The smell of sulfur seemed to have subsided or maybe it was just that we had habituated to the stink. I thumped the loose soil off his chest for something to do.

He stood rocking from one foot to the other in the same spot. Had there been more space on this ledge he would have been pacing. His fingertips drummed on the thighs of his pants, then he looked up. He threw himself at the side of the slope and tried to claw his way up but his efforts resulted in the same outcome as mine. The slope broke away and followed in a river of dirt and rubble.

He shook the filth off and grumbled.

"I have an idea," he said. "What kind of shoes are you wearing?"

They were three-inch high sandals and I had regretted wearing them ever since I landed inside this crater. My feet were filthy and the shoes were ruined. They were not among the gifts Luke had purchased for me. They were my own and had a special place in my heart.

He studied them. "Take them off."

"Why?"

"I want you to climb up onto my shoulders, and I don't want those heels stabbing into me."

He faced the wall and tested the ground for stability, and then semi-squatted. "Okay. All aboard. Get up."

My feet sank into the loose dirt as I removed my shoes. "Those are coming with us," I warned. "They cost me a bundle."

He stuck his hands back and took my sandals, and shoved them toe-first into the pockets on either side of his thin leather jacket. "Okay, now up."

He got back into position and I admired his tight backside (what was wrong with me!) I leaped onto his back and wrapped my arms around his neck and my legs around his waist. It took a few minutes for me to wrestle my legs to a kneeling position so that I could climb up onto his shoulders. "You're going to have to stand up, Lucy," he grunted. "Surely, you were some kind of cheerleader in high-school or college." One hand went to my thigh and gave a firm squeeze. "You've got the legs for it."

I wasn't the only one having lewd thoughts—although I ignored the sexual innuendo. My to-do list stopped at sex in a crater. And he was right. I *was* a cheerleader way back when, a damn good one at that. And if he was teasing me, then he was about to find out exactly how good. It was just that it had been over ten years since I'd done any major moves.

The vertigo wasn't a problem then. I don't know what happened.

I counted to three and leaped. I landed in a squatting position on his shoulders. I heard a muffled grunt from him, as he slowly straightened, careful not to upset my balance. He inhaled a deep breath and flexed his shoulders. His hands got a grip on my ankles. The guys in the cheerleading squad had a long way to go to match Norman's broad shoulders. I had a solid perch and was perfectly balanced. I steadied my knees, braced for the rise and stood up. *Oh my God*, I did it!

The rope was just out of my reach. I would have to stand on tiptoes.

I gathered my breath for the next task.

"How we doin', honey?" he asked.

"I might have to jump. Are you ready for that?"
"You bet."
"You'll have to catch me."
"No problem."

Norman was not a male cheerleader. It was essential that I trusted male cheerleaders in school to catch me in mid air. This was different; could he do it? I found my lips curling in satisfaction. Of course he could. Norman could do anything.

"Ready?" I said.
"Shoot."

I leaped into the air and snatched at the rope with both hands. It came plummeting down in an erratic series of angry thuds. To avoid getting hit, I spun as I fell. Norman caught me in his arms my skirt flying over my chest, my bare legs cupped in his hands.

"Gotcha, gorgeous."

He held me suspended off the ground. He was trying to keep things light as we should, but it was a night full of emotion and tension. I kissed him on the lips. I couldn't help it. I felt his mouth move and open to receive more of mine. We did that for a minute. It was stupid but I was in no hurry to get out. I also knew if we kept this up, I'd have my underwear off and him inside me before I could say No.

"What are you thinking, Lucy?" he asked.
"Nothing. Put me down."

He lowered me to my feet. And I slapped the dirt that had come down with me. What was wrong with me? This was a most inopportune moment for playing out my erotic fantasies. Did I want to get out of this hellhole or not?

Norman tugged on the rope. It remained firmly fastened to the rail spindle at the crater's rim. "Feels solid. You did a good job."

"Of course, I did," I said.

He grinned. "I meant getting the rope down…. Yeah, and the knot too."

"I knew what you meant." I felt a bit high after the excitement of actually succeeding at something that Norman couldn't achieve alone.

If this ledge was wider I could have given it a running start, leaped up onto his back and scrambled up the rope in two minutes flat. It was narrow, too narrow. So it was back to the cautious climbing.

Now that I knew I could do it, the second time around was a breeze. I was on his shoulders and up the rope before I could even exhale.

Norman came up after me. Clearly he was practiced at climbing ropes. When he reached the bottom of the rail I stuck out a hand to help him up.

"Really, Lucy? If I grab onto your hand I'll just pull you back down there—Move back. I might hurt you when I swing myself up."

So much for my being chivalrous. He landed beside me and we stared at each other, laughed. We were a mess. And not out of the fire yet. The laughter was as much from relief as from anything else. It felt good to breathe fresh air again. The air in the crater had stunk of sulfur.

"Shoes, please," I said as we stood together in the stiffening breeze.

He dug into his jacket pockets and drew them out. I brushed off my feet the best I could and snapped the straps on. I hoped we had a short walk.

"Are you cold?" Despite the fact that it was the peak of summer—and in the city it was quite warm even at night—the evening temperatures at higher elevations were considerably colder. He shrugged off his jacket and draped it over my shoulders. It was enormous on me but I was grateful for the warmth. It also smelled pleasantly of him and that made me feel secure. I slid my arms into the sleeves and rolled the cuffs up until I could feel my hands again.

"Shall we?" he asked and jutted out an elbow. I looped my arm through his and we started down the rubble path. It was slippery and my shoes were inadequate for the hike. It was not like it was my choice to be on this volcano. I never had a choice of footwear. But at least it was all downhill from here—literally.

A sudden whiff of sulfur rose from the crater into my nostrils. "I wonder when that volcano is set to explode," I said. "It's active you know."

Norman nodded. "It's supposed to blow every twenty years but hasn't shown much activity in over seventy."

"Well, I hope it holds off a little longer. Until we get off this smokestack."

"Don't worry, it will. The whole thing's monitored by scientists. They'll know within days when it's likely to blow. Long enough to stop the tourists and evacuate the towns."

Despite everything that had happened I felt strangely elated. I guess that's what getting out of a deadly situation will do for you. The relief is so intense it feels like an orgasm. But I could see by the change in Norman's expression that the reality of the situation was sinking in again. "What do you think D'Agostino is going to do?" I asked. "He told me he didn't kill any of those people. So I believe Arianna is safe."

"Believe him if you like," Norman said. "But the sooner we get to Pompeii the better."

"Luke is there, isn't he?"

He nodded. "But I don't know how many more men the bastard has radicalized."

"Radicalized? That's rather a harsh term. D'Agostino is not a terrorist. He's just a desperate man trying to save his family."

"We'll see."

"Where are we going?" I asked.

Norman motioned to a Vespa by the side of the road. It was smaller than a motorcycle but larger than your average scooter. Could it even seat two? I saw there was only one helmet. I voiced my concern.

He handed me the helmet. "Don't worry, Lucy. I'm not leaving you here. One way or another we're both getting on Franco's little lifesaver of a transport even if you have to sit on my lap."

CHAPTER
23

Mount Vesuvius is a force of nature. If it were to erupt today it could destroy entire cities. Not to mention the millions of lives that would be lost. But that has never stopped people from living in the Red Zone in the shadow of the mountain. As we ripped through the night—and no, I did not have to sit on Norman's lap—I saw what might be best described as a 'squatter' crisis. Seven hundred thousand people live illegally on the volcano's slopes and hold their lives in their own hands. Unfettered urbanization has marginalized the poor. Rampant development has pushed these helpless people past the vineyards and farm country, into the foothills and up the mountainside. Hazardous loopholes allow developers to build wherever there is a piece of land to build on. Politicians turn a blind eye. As long as Vesuvius keeps her lid on, residents will live oblivious to the danger.

It may be true that scientists are monitoring the volcano's activity, but just how accurate are computers? And do they even have publicized evacuation routes? In the chaos of structures capturing my view, I thought no. I looked out and away, past Norman's bunched shoulders. The squatter villages are an eye-opener. All over the world people live this way with politicians complicit. Politicians understand the danger of living in eruption zones. They know the consequences. But are they prepared to crack down on safety standards? No. Not until they are forced to deal with the terrible human consequences. History recalls that the consequences can be devastating. For God's sake, Pompeii isn't famous for nothing.

The distraction in my thoughts was good. It was making the time fly fast.

The road Norman chose for our descent was a shortcut and bypassed the secluded, long winding road I had taken on my mad ascent up to the peak. It was why I had noticed none of these crowds of shacks earlier. That, and the fact that I had been racing for my life. With a mad man after me, why would I have noticed the shanties, even had I taken this route?

On this side of the volcano the density of low-income housing was obvious. Crooked, gabled roofs and drooping laundry lines cut through the scenery. Here and there sprawled the junk of abandoned rusted vehicles. The shoddy houses, rapidly constructed of cheap materials made shadowy ghosts against the glowing night sky. Curls of grey smoke rose from chimney tops; the harsh carbon smell burned my throat. Many in the squatter neighborhoods had no electricity. They cooked with wood stoves. Those with electric lights used them sparingly at nightfall.

I shifted on the seat behind Norman. I laced my fingers about him tighter. His hard body and animal warmth made me feel safe. It was a tight squeeze, but it was the most exhilarating ride I had experienced in a lifetime. We turned onto the *autostrade* and aimed for Pompeii.

There was very little traffic. It must be late. I had no idea what time it was because I never wore a watch and now my phone was lost.

If only I could read stars or the moon. *Can one even tell time that way?*

When we arrived it was very quiet. The ruins of Pompeii

have been restored for tourist visitors but as I said, the grounds are shut down for repairs. No sign of people anywhere. Only a few lights. When the site was opened for night viewing the entire ruined city was illuminated. Lighting was minimal now, simply for safety, in case anyone happened on the grounds after curfew.

The place had an air of mystery, as well it should. Where were Arianna and Luke, and D'Agostino? Ghosts walked here. Re-emerging from the darkness of centuries, stone arches and pillars reached for the sky, a vast canvas that glowed with stars.

We stopped at the closest entrance and left the Vespa by a stone wall. If we should stumble into anything suspicious it was dangerous to announce our presence on a motor scooter. Besides, the roads inside the ancient city were bad. No smooth ride there. We'd be bounced and jostled by cobblestone pavers. There were spots where no vehicle short of a bike could get through.

As we reached a strange thoroughfare Norman stopped. Springing up from the sunken road were bridges of steppingstones. Why? To carry pedestrians to opposite sidewalks of course. But more—

"I guess you know what those are for?" Norman said.

The answer dawned on me with sudden clarity. Those steppingstones were so that people could avoid the sewage floating down streets in ancient times. Despite our desperate task a peculiar calmness overcame me. I could discuss history and archaeology with Norman forever. Was that odd? Of course it was. Luke was the archaeologist. And I had never discussed history or archaeology with him—unless you included the smuggling. A racket he seemed forever destined to be involved.

Norman took my hand, bade me follow him. We were on the edge of the city where former brothels, and ancient narrow lanes, workshops and utility rooms flanked the road. We remained outside the houses. They contained furniture and ornaments, kitchenware and bronze and terracotta lamps.

The most valuable objects had been moved to the museum in Naples. One of the most peculiar things was the abundance of graffiti. Not modern vandalism but ancient Roman electoral inscriptions, risqué jokes, gossip and rumors, about famous persons or politicians. Some of the graffiti concerned women's special endowments, and what visitors thought of their visits to the brothels. Seriously. Did people ever change?

The Amphitheatre was located in the eastern part of town. This was where we headed.

"It's the most likely spot for a helicopter to land," Norman said.

No doubt. We entered through a gate and climbed the steps of the stone Amphitheatre. Moonlight shone brilliantly, casting shadows down one side. From this vantage we had an excellent view.

In the center of the large open arena sat a black helicopter. It was stationary. The rotors lay inert. Part of the grounds around the chopper was covered in grass. This area appeared darker than the irregular patches of pale, sandy soil on the outskirts. Dark weeds sprouted along the cracked stones of the Amphitheatre. Several people were standing there on the gravel. A human figure sprawled at their feet. Male or female? It was impossible to guess. The helicopter pilot maybe? I was positive it was neither Luke nor Arianna as they were unmistakable. I made out their distinctive forms. They were hard to miss despite the low light level and hazy darkness. They were both tall and proud and beautiful no matter the situation. Bruno D'Agostino held them at gunpoint.

"Stay here, Lucy," Norman said. "Keep out of sight. I'm going down. I owe that joker a little something."

"What are you going to do?" I asked.

"Get his gun away from him."

"How?"

"Stop asking questions and let me do my job."

His sharp tone hurt. He was under stress so I kept my

feelings to myself. He felt bad for snapping at me, and pulled me towards him with one hand. He planted a kiss on my forehead. Then rested his chin on the crown of my head. When he spoke his tone was firm but imploring. "Stay here. *Please.*"

He removed his gun from his back pocket. I waited a few minutes, indecisive and anxious. Then I decided to go with my gut.

My shoes made a *clackety-clack* sound. This style of footwear was meant to draw attention to the wearer. Nothing I could do about it, but stay low like Norman had advised. And hope that no one would see me. Could I obey orders? Not on your life. So I followed. But it was hard to stay low while tailing him. These steps were open and without rails. It was also a challenge to move soundlessly. I stripped off my sandals and went barefoot on the cool stone. I bit my lip once to cut off a yelp as I stepped on a pebble; then resumed my descent.

I trailed at a safe distance.

Norman started down a second, and then a third set of stone stairs. At the moment D'Agostino's back was to him. The man was totally unaware of our presence, but that could soon change. All it would take was one false move to attract his notice, and I had no idea how Norman planned to cross that open expanse of arena undetected.

Fortunately, he was dressed in dark clothing and training shoes. Not me. I had a powder blue, short, jean jacket on over a white crop top, and a blue and white skirt that flapped in the breeze. Norman was at the bottom of the steps now, and sidled face-out against the wall of the first tier of bleachers, eyes focused ahead. I descended unseen, halfway down the stairs behind him.

He moved on. When I surmised he was far enough for me to resume my tracking of him undetected, I continued. He was in shadow. I figured if I stayed far enough behind against the wall, the shadows would hide me.

The sound of a kicked stone caught my ear. Norman

stopped about seven yards from where I waited. Had I promised to stay behind? Um. No. He would be angry if he turned and saw me. I stayed still as a mouse. He was just short of a black archway. That must be the former entrance for the gladiators. He paused to listen. His gun was clasped in both hands as he aimed it inside the arch to have a look. I imagine he saw very little in the gloom. His actions verified this notion. He slipped the gun into his right hand, dug in his left pocket for his phone. Eyes still on the archway, he flashed the light of his phone inside. Saw nothing.

I waited until he had passed to the other side of the arch and was moving slowly along the wall. Then I slung my sandals into one hand, and ran across the cool grass until I had almost reached the arch.

From here I decided it would be safe to wear my shoes. I snapped the straps on over my heels. Then glanced up to see how much distance Norman had gained on me. D'Agostino and his hostages were only about twenty paces from where he stood.

I started to pass the archway in his wake. He stopped and turned to look back. I ducked into the arch. My heart jumped. Something hard pressed around my waist and a hand covered my mouth before I could scream. *Norman!* But only a grunt escaped from my throat. Oh, if only I had done as he had asked and stayed up in the stands where I was safe.

I heard a sharp exhalation of air and a cuss in Italian, as my teeth sank into the hand muffling my lips. "*Gesù.* Try that again, *bitch,* and you are dead."

I gulped. He had removed his hand from my mouth when I bit him. Now that hand had a vice grip on my arm and a gun was shoved into my side.

"Walk!"

He forced me outside the archway into the arena. He made no pretense of stealth or quiet. Norman was close enough now to ambush D'Agostino. He was buried in shadow and perfectly camouflaged. I on the other hand might as well have been standing in a spotlight. My pale clothing glowed. We stood in the moonlight. I arched my neck to look up and back. The man holding me captive was none other than Giovanni Zia.

Both Luke and Arianna saw me. Their heads jerked ever so slightly my way. This attracted Norman's attention. His head turned. Was it disappointment, anger or surprise in his expression? He was practiced when it came to controlling facial muscles. But when he saw me with the gun to my side, I felt his horror. I had committed a fatal error and if I got us all killed—well that didn't even bear thinking about.

"Drop the gun, *signore*," Giovanni said.

Norman scowled.

"You do not wish to see the pretty lady's dress all spattered with blood, no?"

There were only two of them, and I knew the calculations that were spinning in Norman's head. The risk was too high. I would be killed if Norman tried anything.

Norman dropped his gun.

"Kick it to me.... Slowly. I will shoot her if you do anything stupid."

Norman booted the gun towards us and it landed near my feet.

"Pick it up *signorina* and give it to me. Carefully."

I crouched down. I felt Norman's eyes on my every movement. Giovanni had his gaze fastened on Norman.

My fingers curled around the barrel of the gun, and I rose and handed it to him. He stuffed it into his back pocket.

"Now walk over to your friends. Both of you."

I was about to obey when a gunshot blasted the air. Strange—how people turn to look even when they know better. Something about the suddenness making the response involuntary. Norman was a quick thinker. As well, he was quick on his feet. For some reason I already knew his intent. Giovanni's hold had loosened on me when he turned to seek out the source of the gunshot. I ducked. At that moment Norman rushed Giovanni who was off-guard. I rolled out of the way. Norman tackled the Italian thug to the ground and I scrambled towards the fallen gun. Giovanni still had Norman's weapon in his pocket. Rising, shaking, I pointed the gun at Giovanni.

A voice boomed out of the darkness. It was D'Agostino. "Stop, Ms. Racine or I will shoot." His aim was on Arianna. He knew if the gun were aimed on Luke, Luke would not hesitate to rush him. But with the weapon threatening his ex-wife, D'Agostino had leverage.

"Lucy." Another voice came from behind Giovanni and Norman. Both had stopped wrestling the other when I retrieved the Italian's revolver. The voice was incredibly familiar. "It's alright. Take the other weapon from Giovanni and hand it to Depardieu. On your feet, thug," she said to the Italian. "Slowly. If *she* doesn't shoot you, I will."

I saw only a flash of color behind the two men. Red. She was wearing a red coat. And now I knew who she was.

"Lucy. We're running out of time. That pilot over there needs medical attention."

"Marissa?" I gasped. But how could it be possible? I had seen her dead.

"Yes. It is I. You are surprised. I understand. I will explain later. But first do as I say."

I went behind Giovanni. I stole the gun out of his pocket. Norman had risen, too, and I thrust the other weapon at him. On that instant when Norman's attention had been diverted, Giovanni bolted, only to be shot by Marissa.

He fell facedown and groaned.

"Don't move, either of you!" D'Agostino shouted from the center of the arena. "I will kill them both."

We had forgotten about D'Agostino. He still had his firearm fixed on Arianna.

Marissa said, "Bruno D'Agostino. I am placing you under arrest for the smuggling of Syrian artifacts, kidnapping and assault—" She shot a brief glance at the sprawled pilot. "—And if that poor fellow is dead, then murder."

"He is not dead," D'Agostino wailed. "I am not a murderer. But you—you have betrayed me." I realized now that hers was the voice I had heard inside the tavern earlier that day when D'Agostino and his company had caught Arianna wandering about the village in search of the Gorgon heads. Had she gone undercover as one of his accomplices? The answer would have to wait. D'Agostino was still armed and dangerous.

"Drop the gun."

The duress was too much for the former director of the Naples National Archaeological Museum. I say former director because he was going to prison. He released the weapon and it tumbled out of his claw-like fingers. Luke caught it on the rebound while Marissa who was really the Interpol agent, Alessandra Piero, tossed a pair of handcuffs to Norman. She indicated the inert Giovanni. Norman cuffed him while I remained frozen, the gun still double-fisted between my clenched fingers. Piero kept her revolver focused on D'Agostino. When she reached him she ordered him to lie facedown on the ground, then she tossed a second pair of handcuffs to Arianna to cuff D'Agostino.

"I'm sorry it had to come to this, Bruno," Arianna said.

The man moaned.

"Lucy." Norman drew my attention back to him. He extended his free hand. He did not chastise me for following.

During all of this chaos I stood paralyzed, unable to move or act. My heart still thudded. My palms were moist with sweat, my head pounded.

"The gun, Lucy. Give it to me."

My hands were frozen on the revolver's grip. My fingers refused to obey. The firearm remained pointed at Giovanni Zia.

"He can't hurt you now," Norman said.

Giovanni lay on his stomach with his hands cuffed behind his back as a pool of dark blood eased its way out from beneath him. He bled into the sand and grit and tuffs of trampled grass.

"Please, sweetheart. Pass me the gun."

Norman gently wrestled it out of my grip and enfolded

me in one arm. He kissed the top of my head totally oblivious of whether or not Luke watched. I imagined not. Too many things seized his attention: Arianna, Bruno D'Agostino's betrayal, and the miraculous reappearance of Marissa AKA Alessandra Piero.

I relaxed into Norman's strong, muscular chest, tears of exhaustion threatening once more.

"Are you okay, Lucy?" he whispered.

I nodded.

"Can you walk?"

I nodded again.

I had not proven myself to be terribly useful in the situation. I had probably once again failed at any test that would allow me admission into Arianna's covert organization.

"Then let's go," he said.

It was not far. His grip on me remained strong until we reached the others. Luke looked up then. If he was disturbed by the fact that his bodyguard had his arms around his girlfriend he gave no sign of it. He came towards us and Norman dropped his arm instantly. He was suddenly reminded that I was not his to hold.

Luke gently enfolded me in a brief hug. "You okay?"

"Yes."

He turned back to Marissa who was calling for an ambulance. Norman observed her as well. Her sudden and unexpected appearance had the effect of a ghost haunting our memories.

Pleasure, chills and curiosity assailed me simultaneously.

When she ended her call, Luke demanded, "Where the hell did you come from? I thought you were dead."

CHAPTER

24

"I am not deceased as you can see."

"Marissa," I interrupted. I ran and threw my arms around her. "I am so happy to see you."

"You must call me Alessandra now, Lucy. Marissa Leone is dead." She gently disentangled me. I caught a whiff of lemon blossoms as she turned to Arianna. "Did he have the goods on him?"

She was referring to the Gorgon heads. Arianna nodded. "They are somewhat damaged, but we can attempt a repair job."

That too was my fault. I had heaved the treasure out of the Lamborghini and onto the road in an attempt to make off with D'Agostino's car. As I watched the two efficient women interact I realized that they were part of a team. Was Alessandra Piero part of ISORE all along? Even when she was undercover as Marissa Leone? What was her role in all of this? My thoughts had a desperation about them, but I knew any explanation would have to wait. There were two injured men to attend to—and D'Agostino to deliver to the police.

***

On our return to the city Luke rented the entire upper floor of the Palazzo Caracciollo Naples Hotel. Luke's fame, reputation and influence came in handy, and management bent over backwards to accommodate our needs. After hot showers and a change of clothing purchased in the hotel boutiques, we planned to gather together in the lounge for drinks. It was well after midnight. The bar was still open.

The idea of sharing a room with Luke felt oddly wrong. I was agonizing over how to tell him that I wanted my own space when he made the decision for me. He booked individual rooms for each of us. Was he having second thoughts? Certainly during this trip to Naples our relationship was practically nonexistent. We had no time to spend alone. And then I remembered what he had once told me. Everyone needed his or her personal space. Sex was one thing while sleep was another. The two did not necessarily mix.

Nevertheless, I was grateful. I had no idea how I would broach the subject of our relationship. Whether we still had one. He was obsessed with Arianna, even now that he knew she was safe. For my part it seemed she had never needed his help or protection.

And then there was Norman. What was I going to do about him?

We had no chance to talk.

I went downstairs dressed in an outfit Luke bought for me from one of the hotel's ritzy shops: a white linen dress, shaped to my body with a tulip skirt. It was simple and elegant but I knew it would pale in comparison to anything Arianna wore. Why must I insist on competing with her? In the looks department I could never win.

My friends were seated on plush red sofas, Luke across from Arianna and Alessandra beside her, with Norman next to Luke. I stood in the doorway opposite the men. What should I do? Again I felt out of place. These were a group of people whose lives were bound up in adventure, excitement and real purpose. They were politically involved in issues that mattered. Things I only read about in the newspapers.

The one person who was looking at me was Norman. Luke only had eyes for Arianna.

Maybe I *had* no place among this crowd. What could I offer them? But my curiosity got the best of me. I crushed the urge to hightail it out of there and catch the next flight home. And by home, I meant Toronto. After all, what *did* happen to Marissa, I mean Alessandra? I had gotten to know her in our time in Positano. We had joined forces to search for the Black Madonna and the killer of our friend Tommy Buchanan. And then she disappeared. If nothing else I was entitled to hear her explanation.

She must have noticed the direction of Norman's attention because she turned her head. She rose, and smiled at me. "Lucy. Hope you're rested? We've been waiting for you. Luke and Norman have been chomping at the bit—to use your English term—for me to tell my story, but I insisted we wait for you. After all you were a big part of it. Come and sit. Someone go order her a drink." As she spoke I noticed the Italian intonation. When I had known her aboard Luke's yacht she had used an American accent.

"What would you like, Lucy?" Norman asked me. He rose to signal the cocktail waiter.

I glanced around. Luke was drinking scotch. Norman of course did not imbibe. He had a frosted glass of club soda with lime and mint on the glass table in front of him. Piero was drinking a Campari and soda with a lemon slice. Arianna had a glass of white wine. Expensive I had no doubt. I needed something stronger.

"A martini, please," I said. "Vodka and two olives. And make it a double." I was feeling rather James Bondish.

Norman's eyes twinkled, though his lips remained unmoving. He gave the waiter the order in Italian and offered me his seat beside Luke. I sat down.

Luke absently placed his hand on my knee and gave it a squeeze. I stole a quick peek to determine Arianna's reaction. None.

"So what happened to you?" Luke asked Piero. "Last

time I heard, you were dead." His approach was direct and indelicate. He must be tired. A subtle grumpiness seemed to override his trademark charisma. He glanced sideways at me, as I was the original bearer of that horrible news.

The last time I had seen Alessandra she was lying on a subterranean cave floor with her neck twisted at an impossible angle. I had touched her throat and found no pulse. Or I had felt her throat in the wrong place. Whatever. She was alive. Obviously.

"I was unconscious. Not killed. Your captain, Leo Spatz, knocked me out when I found his stash of illicit goods and recognized him. He was Tommy's murderer. He realized I knew of his evil act when he saw that I was familiar with his tattoo. He left me for dead. But the cool air in the cave helped me to regain consciousness. When I found myself alone and with no possibility of getting help, I managed to crawl away. I left through the tunnel, got in touch with my people at Interpol and was fixed up at a nearby hospital in secret. It took me weeks before I was ready to go back into service. And when I did, I went once more undercover."

"It was you," I said, suddenly. "You've been following us!"

The corners of her red mouth twitched.

"You came to my room in Bagnoregio! And again at the Civita!"

She nodded. "I wanted to make sure you were safe, Lucy. After all I'd put you through."

"Mostly you just gave me a scare when I thought Spatz had killed you."

"I apologize for that too. And I apologize for the secrecy, but I wanted to get you alone, to speak with you in private. Always you were accompanied by these two watchdogs. Every time I thought I had the chance to talk to you on your own, one or the other of them would appear—especially that one." She pointed a finger at Norman. Well, he was a bodyguard after all. She knew that. "I was suspicious about these two." Her eyes darted from one to the

other of the two men. "I suspected a connection with Arianna's mishap. It was hard to trust them."
"But now you do?"
"Yes. Arianna has assured me that Dr. Trevanian can be trusted as can his bodyguard, Norman Depardieu."
She was a little curt with them. Just how much *did* she trust them? I glanced from Luke to Norman and felt an upwelling of affection and gratitude. I would trust each one of them with my life—and *have*. I wanted to tell her so.
"So, you're working with her?"
"I am. When I learned of Arianna's plane crash I immediately went searching for her and hooked up with D'Agostino. Remember—I have strong connections in the museum community, plus links to organized crime. A few years back I was in Syria involved in a search for contraband firearms and chemical weapons. I used those connections to seek out D'Agostino's wife. My Intel allowed me to gain D'Agostino's trust. He thought I was on his side. We knew D'Agostino and his wife were fencing the goods on this side. The big unknown was identifying which crooked dealers were purchasing the stolen antiquities in North America."
Luke's eyes widened. This was obviously news. But something else had occurred to him. "Wait a minute. Let's rewind a bit… A while back you were working for *me*. You came aboard my yacht—what—to spy on me and my team?"
"Tommy Buchanan was working for Arianna. We were trying to determine how the artifacts were being smuggled out of the country."
"And you suspected me?" Luke was livid.
"If not you," Arianna cut in. "It was someone aboard your boat." Her eyes flitted ever so briefly in Norman's direction, but he stifled any reaction. "I suspected everyone, in fact. Turns out I was correct."
Luke frowned. "We were searching for the church's icon, not illicit Middle Eastern relics."
"I know, but it was the only lead we had."
"You thought someone was using me?"

"Maybe using you. Most certainly using your boat."

Because they *were*," Piero interrupted. "At least that was the intention. Wasn't the Black Madonna hidden in a secret hold aboard your yacht? Weren't they planning to smuggle it to North America and sell it on the black market?"

"But that's besides the point," Arianna concluded. "We were after Spatz, only we didn't know it at first. He was using your boat."

"Is that why you wanted it as part of the divorce settlement?" Luke demanded. "Surely, you could have trusted me, Arianna. And told me of your suspicions. We were married for almost a decade."

"Yes. Which was exactly why I couldn't. You were violently opposed to ISORE. How could I bring you into my confidence?"

"*Violently?* That's a bit strong."

"Wrong choice of word." She shrugged. "But you know what I mean." Silence dragged for a few awkward moments. We were becoming uncomfortable witnessing this marital spat. Arianna was first to catch on. She broke the silence.

She returned to topic. "I wanted your yacht, yes—because then I would be in control. And I could keep an eye on Spatz … The Black Madonna was only one of the things he was after. We're pretty certain Syrian rebels paid him to smuggle stolen goods across the Atlantic to North America. And had been doing so for years. From there the contraband was divided amongst major cities with connections to the underworld. Toronto, New York, Boston, Chicago. Unfortunately our investigation came to a dead end. He was shot by one of Positano's over-enthusiastic, small town police officers over a piddly religious icon. And now he's dead…. Spatz would have been more useful to us alive than dead. He had information we needed."

"That piddly religious icon—as you call it—was worth eleven million dollars on the underground. Furthermore, it was a rare Black Madonna and was considered priceless to the church that lost it." Luke paused. His eyes suddenly widened. "Wasn't it *you* who recommended Spatz to me in the first place?"

"It was Marco Ferri who referred *him* to me. And we all know how that turned out. But that's in the past.

"We have more serious rescue operations that need our attention. And that escapade of yours in Positano has only hardened my conviction to the cause. We need you, Luke."

Arianna swung her head in the other direction. "And *you* Depardieu. We need your skills and expertise to help us salvage some of the world's most ancient and most precious history." She returned her gaze to Luke. "You have the brains and the wherewithal. I've seen you do it. If nothing else came out of that foolish escapade with the Black Madonna, it did prove your value. I'm asking you one more time, Luke. Join us."

When my drink came, the others had finished theirs. Except for Luke who had also ordered another scotch. Everyone was worn out from the excitement in the Pompeii amphitheater. Arianna insisted Luke mull over her proposition. They would discuss it some more in the morning.

I needed to approach Arianna about D'Agostino and his wife. Could the head of ISORE forgive what he had done? I still believed his wife and children were innocent victims. They were caught in an impossible situation. They could be saved with her help.

Piero and Arianna rose. The former smiled at me and said, "We'll talk tomorrow, Lucy. We all need to sleep—especially you. I heard about the horrible ordeal you suffered up on Vesuvius."

A weak nod. Beginning to fade. The martini was going to my head. Under the effects of exhaustion and an empty stomach, the liquor was affecting me faster than normal.

The two women vacated the lounge. Luke got to his feet, too. He said, "I forgot; there was something I wanted to ask Arianna." He tossed back the remainder of his scotch (that amount of pure whiskey would have knocked me out flat) and excused himself to follow his ex-wife, somewhat unsteadily, into the corridor.

CHAPTER
25

Luke was gone. I was alone with Norman. I sipped the last of my martini, pinching the toothpick with the olives between my fingers. Norman downed the dregs of his club soda until there was only a wedge of lime, a sprig of mint, and some melting fragments of cracked ice remaining at the bottom of his glass.

Under the effects of the booze and fatigue I felt bold and surreal. Norman sat kitty-corner to me in an armchair. With a questioning glance across the coffee table, he shoved a ceramic dish of mixed nuts at me. "Did you get anything to eat, Lucy?"

Those smoked almonds looked delicious. I plucked one from the bowl and placed it on my tongue as I waved the olives around on their toothpick. *Ahh. So tired.* Semi-sprawled on the sofa, I shifted myself closer to Norman's armchair and kicked off my right stiletto. My bare foot landed on his thigh, making him flinch.

"What are you doing?"

"Nothing."

He grinned. He lifted my heel and began to knead the ball of my foot with his free hand.

"Are you drunk after only one cocktail?" Norman asked,

massaging my toes.
    I yawned with delight. I stripped the olives from the toothpick. Then popped them into my mouth and chewed them sensuously. "Oh, maybe. Ooh, that feels *so* good."
    He slid his hands up my calf to my thigh. His magic fingers mesmerized me, watching the movement of his hands as much as relishing the sensation on my skin. I was lost in the wondrous feeling of arousal, and now his thumbs were teasing between my legs, when a voice said, "What the hell?"
    It was Luke. He had returned, and he was frowning.
    Norman dropped my leg to the floor with a thud. I winced.
    I stared at Luke, flustered, but not so flustered that I was tongue-tied. He and I had been drinking. We shared that cloud of euphoria that came with physical exhaustion, adrenaline, and over-excitement, exacerbated by booze.
    "You weren't here and I needed a foot massage." The toothpick fell into my empty cocktail glass with a thin *ping*. The lie had come out easier than I had expected. If the truth be known I was verging on inebriation when I suddenly ceased to care. "I didn't know if you were coming back."
    "That looked more like a leg massage." He observed my bare leg, the one minus the stiletto. I had the presence of mind to toe the floor searching for it. Luke came to me. He found the shoe. He got down on one knee and slipped it onto my foot like he was Prince Charming placing the glass slipper on Cinderella's delicate foot. Surprisingly, he sounded unperturbed, maybe a little tipsy. We were all dancing on the same intoxicated cloud. Except for Norman. Norman abstained from alcohol. Norman was exempt. He was not on this fat, mesmerizing, puffy cloud with us. I suddenly felt overwhelmed with self-consciousness, and wished he were. I vaguely felt his eyes watching every move made by his boss.
    Luke wobbled to his feet and extended a hand. "Come on Lucy, time for bed."
    I was nervous now, the heady feeling slipping away. He

wanted me to go to his bed? He had booked me my own room. Was he asking for sex tonight? I shot an anxious glance at Norman. He caught it briefly and looked away—as if to say, it was my decision. How, after everything that had happened with Norman, could I bring myself to return to Luke's bed?

The effects of the martini vanished.

"Luke, I'm really wasted."

"So am I. Come on. Let's go or do you need me to pick you up?"

My answer came hastily. "I can walk."

Outside his room, he tapped the magnetic keycard and held the door open for me. Norman had escorted us, as was his custom. "You can go, Depardieu."

I was a little concerned over the formality with which he addressed the bodyguard. Ordinarily they were so much chummier.

"Luke," I objected as the door swung shut behind us. "I really am exhausted. It's been a terrifying night. I'm all wired up. And so are you." I squeezed his hand. "You're very tense." *And maybe a little drunk?*

"All the more reason to hit the sheets. Get your clothes off."

This forceful demand was unlike Luke. He *was* drunk. Again.

"I think we should wait until tomorrow. We need to talk. I'm going to my room."

He grabbed me by the wrist and I squealed. I knew beneath the scotch-induced aggression Luke had no intention of harming me; he was not himself. We really needed to talk about what had happened in the lounge. I was certain he suspected something. And if he did, he was right. We were both culpable and by 'we' I meant Norman and myself. I owed Luke an explanation. If only he were sober.

"You should go to sleep. We'll talk in the morning."

"I don't want to talk." He still had my wrist in a vice grip. He yanked me toward him. I tripped over an area rug that was on the polished hardwood floor. I fell with a yelp and a thud, as he let go.

A frantic knock came at the door. "What's going on in there? Are you guys all right?" I heard the door latch click. How *does* he open locked doors? One day in the future I would have to find out. Norman swung open the door and stepped in.

I was just getting off the floor when Norman came rushing at Luke. I jammed myself between them before they could hurt each other.

"It's not what you think," I shouted.

Norman wanted to wrap his arms around me. I could see it in his eyes. Was it obvious to Luke, too? But Luke was in no condition to fight Norman. Norman was stone cold sober while Luke was raging hot with alcohol. How much had he drunk before I came downstairs to the lounge?

"Trevanian," Norman said. "I'm putting you to bed. Lucy, go to your room."

There was that formality again. I felt my stomach sink as I watched them. Luke flung Norman off him. He glared. "Where is my wife?"

That last remark shot home. This fit of anger had nothing to do with me.

"I'm assuming she's in bed, like the rest of us should be." Norman's voice was icy. I felt guilty about that too.

"Let me help you to bed, Luke," I said, my voice filled with compassion.

"I'm sorry, Lucy. Did I hurt you?"

"No. I tripped." I straightened my dress, mentally checked for bruises. I was fine. Just ready to scream if one more bad thing happened.

"It's okay, Norman. I'll get Luke to bed. He just needs to sleep it off. We'll be okay."

Norman's eyes narrowed at me.

I sent him a look of pleading. Luke was now cooperative as Norman assisted him to bed. He sat on the edge of the mattress while I removed his shoes and his shirt. "Stay with me, Lucy," he implored.

Luke glanced from Norman to myself. Did he know? More, did he care?

Luke lay down in his shorts. I covered him with the sheet.

I shot a backward glance at the bed. Luke was no longer conscious that he had company. Still, we spoke in whispers. "It's fine, Norman. That outburst had nothing to do with us."

He sighed. We made our way silently to the door. Luke was deep in dreamland now. It was safe to leave. He wouldn't know that I was gone. And Norman refused to allow me to be alone with him when he was in a foul mood.

"Does he often get like this?" I asked.

Norman shook his head. "Only when *she's* around." His eyes turned sideways at the exit.

I opened the door. I nudged him outside into the hallway. It was quiet. Everyone sane was fast asleep. He fumbled in his breast pocket and pulled out a package of cigarettes. He drew one out and searched for his lighter. I took the cigarette out of his fingers and shoved it back into the box. "You can't smoke inside the hotel."

"Oh, yeah. Right."

I handed him the cigarette box, and he returned it to his pocket.

He was stressed by the whole situation—especially by what had happened between us—and the tension it had caused for himself and Luke. I will never stop feeling guilty about that no matter the outcome. But one thing was certain. Things could not remain the way they were. It was that whole thing about unspilling milk. It could not. Be done.

"We have to tell him, Norman," I whispered, raising my voice only slightly despite the fact that we were alone and Luke had drifted into slumber. The emptiness of the corridor seemed to require that kind of respect. "It isn't fair to any of us."

He shook his head. "Not yet. Luke isn't himself. Not with *her* around."

"He still loves her, doesn't he?"

He shrugged.

"Is that why you two never got along?"

"Still don't... particularly. But I admire her. I admire what she's doing, trying to save the world's heritage. However, when it comes to Luke—" He hesitated. "—I wish she would disappear."

I glanced down at the floor. If my head didn't find a pillow soon I would pass out from fatigue.

"Lucy, you need to go to bed. You're dead on your feet." I still had the door propped open with my hip. Norman shoved the door wider to check on Luke. No movement. He snored quietly, something he only did when he'd drunk too much. Norman let the door slide shut. Now, I had no choice but to go to my room. I had left his magnetic keycard inside.

"You're a good friend, Norman. Luke's lucky to have you."

He ignored the compliment, gently prodded me in the arm and turned me towards my room. I obeyed, too weary to fight him. When we arrived at my door, he touched me lightly on the cheek.

"Sleep tight, princess," he said. He stuck out a hand for my keycard, opened my door, returned the keycard to me, and nudged me through. "I'm going outside for a smoke."

I stared at the shut door for three seconds after it closed. Then went to the bed, and fell on it without removing my dress.

CHAPTER
26

The Sandman was either ticked off at me or on vacation. Sleep evaded me. True I was exhausted to near delirium but my brain kept chattering, piecing together the events of the night, but more—obsessing on what had just occurred between me and Luke. Why was I such a coward? I slammed a fist down onto my pillow. The hell with sleep.

I rose and changed out of the wrinkled linen into a simple, beige shirtdress with wide pockets (another one of Luke's generous purchases), shoved my keycard inside one of the pockets and left the hotel room. I had no real plan. By now it was 2:47 am. The hotel was silent except for the night concierge and a few straggling partyers, trying to make it back to their rooms without puking up their dinners. What was I thinking? Not a smart idea to leave the hotel in the dead of night.

The smell of chlorine down one of the corridors led me to the outdoor pool. The liquid surface glowed aquamarine in the few floodlights that remained lit to prevent guests from accidentally stumbling into the water. Around the oval swimming pool sat recliners and beach chairs in neatly arranged rows. All of the daytime mess had been cleared by the evening shift, ready for the next morning. At the unmanned kiosk was a stack of stiff white towels.

I stole an overhead glimpse at the high windows of the towering hotel surrounding the swimming pool in a quadrangle of turquoise ceramic tile. Each curtained rectangle was dark. Everyone was asleep, as they should be. I was alone except for a warm, soft breeze that tickled my body with its gentle touch. A swim. Yeah, a swim was what I needed. I would wear out my body—and hence my brain—and then I'd be able to sleep.

But I had no swimsuit.

No matter. My red bra and matching panties could easily pass for a bikini. I peeled out of the shirtdress and dropped it on a lounger. The sandals were next. Then I moved to the edge of the pool and looked down.

My body arced into a clean albeit rather low dive. The water surged coolly over my skin and bubbles rose to the surface. I broke through to the top, invigorated, sweeping my hair from my face. A refreshing thrill surged through to my core. How was this going to help me sleep? I smirked. I was more awake than ever, but my muscles felt less tight. I dived to the bottom of the pool, flipped directions and glided elegantly to the surface.

I was about three quarters of the way back to my starting point when I saw him.

He stood by the pool's towel kiosk, one hip resting against it, a cigarette between thumb and middle finger. He had not changed clothes. He still wore pale chinos and a dark shirt. As he crossed his arms the knots of muscle in his biceps strained across his chest. He moved his hand up, popping the stub of a cigarette between his nicely shaped lips for a final puff. The tip glowed orange and snuffed out. He dropped the smoldering butt into an empty ashtray on the kiosk.

"*Merde.* What are you doing, Lucy?" His sultry French accent had my knees turning to jelly. Fortunately, he couldn't see my leg muscles convulsing. And I was in the shallows. Very little chance of drowning.

"What does it look like I'm doing?" I asked.

"Are you out of your mind? You're in your underwear."

My eyes dipped briefly to my bra. "How could you tell?"

"I've seen enough bras."

I swam up to meet Norman as he approached the edge of the pool. He squatted to get closer to my level. "I must say you look quite fetching in your red undies—against the turquoise water."

"Join me?"

He glanced swiftly upward in the direction of one of the windows. Luke's window?

"At least take off your shoes and dangle your feet. It's quite refreshing."

"The last thing I need to be is refreshed."

I treaded water until I bobbed just below him. His shoes were right at the edge so I untied them. "Off," I said. "It won't hurt you to soak your feet."

"If I take off my shoes, will you come out of the pool?"

I hesitated. "Okay. Yes."

He smiled. He backed up a few inches and removed his shoes and socks. Then he rolled up his chinos and came toward me. "Now, come here."

"Feet in the water. You promised."

"I promised no such thing. Y*ou,* however, did promise. You said if I took my shoes off, you would come out of the pool."

"Why do you want me out of the pool?"

"You're not in appropriate attire." Once again he glanced up and rotated his eyes at the surrounding hotel windows. There was no chance that Luke would awaken from his stupor.

He got down on one knee, his right foot forward, and bare toes curling over the smooth tiles of the pool edge. A hand extended and his fingers wiggled. "I don't want you cited for promiscuity and being a public nuisance."

I was hardly being promiscuous or a public nuisance. This was Italy for God's sake. After France, Italy had the most liberal morals on nudity.

"Grab on, I'll haul you up."

He missed the glint in my eye or else he would have pulled back. All night I had been trying to keep him from falling into volcano craters and now he was at my mercy.

He had as much as admitted that he had a high center of gravity. Let's just see exactly where that center of gravity was. I reached up to take his hand, at the same time I braced my feet against the wall of the pool and tugged with all my force. He came shooting head first like a cannonball, and I burst into uncontrollable giggles as I scooted away from the splash zone.

He plunged about three feet before rising to the surface, sputtering French invectives. I think he might have just called me a wily little bitch. I laughed and dived away from him. He was a strong swimmer and reached me in four strokes. He hooked me by the back of my bra. I suddenly felt it release. Oh my god! It started floating away on its foam cups and I frantically grabbed it to me. While I was occupied trying to cover my free-floating boobs, Norman dipped sharply downward into the depths taking my bottoms too. Holy shit. I scrambled to snatch back the panties but they were snagged around Norman's first two fingers like a flag waving in the breeze, only this was happening underwater. His other hand reached out and grabbed the bra from my loosened grasp. Norman had wrenched the red undergarments—my only protection—from curious eyes who might well be peeking through their darkened windows at us.

He burst through the surface, shaking his head like a dog.

"As I recall, you like skinny dipping," he teased.

It was not as if he had never seen me naked. And the whole idea of him getting an eyeful was sizzling to the point of torture. I was honest about how much I wanted him. *He* was the one to resist. So why this? Was he punishing me for enticing him back at his hotel room in Bagnoregio? If that were the case, this seemed like the wrong way to exact revenge.

"You pervert! Give those back," I yelled.

"Come and get them." He swam to the side of the pool and hauled his dripping muscles out. Water ran down his shirt plastering the light cotton against his rippling chest as he stood up. His pants puckered around his hips and thighs leaving nothing to the imagination.

I whistled. "Nice view."

He turned around.

"Even better," I teased. "Don't tell me you *don't* like this... Your body is doing the talking for you right now." My laugh echoed in the quiet night. Sooo.... Who's punishing who?"

He dangled my underwear on his fingertips. Then went over to where my dress lay and scooped that up, too.

"I'd say only one of us is in control of the situation. And if you don't keep your squeaky yelps down, you'll be doing a nudie show for the entire hotel. Here, you can have the sandals." He tossed them in my direction. They landed just short of the water. "No clothes. Just sandals. *Phew...*" He mock-wiped sweat from his brow. "That's *hot.*"

"Norman," I whispered harshly. "Stop being a jerk. Give me something to wear."

"I like you like this. I always have."

I tugged myself up against the side of the pool to cover myself from the view of the windows.

"It's all yours. You know it is. I'm not the one fighting."

His face suddenly turned serious like he remembered why he had to resist me. And why he opposed a break up with Luke. What that reason was he refused to share. Was it *only* because Luke was his dearest friend?

The truth was it disturbed Norman to have other people see me like this. It disturbed him even when I was with Luke. Until I broke it off with Luke—abstention or not on Luke's part—as far as Norman was concerned his boss and I remained an item until further notice.

Norman threw my bra and panties to me. They landed in

the water. I dived for them letting him get an eyeful of my rolling butt. I looked up and saw that yes, lights were beginning to switch on in some of the rooms. It was time to put this game to rest. I sidled up to the edge of the pool and dragged the wet things on. Fortunately from a distance, the red made my underthings look like swimwear.

I placed my palms on the tiles alongside the pool. When Norman saw me struggling to get out without benefit of the ladder, he moved in. He lifted me with hands cupped under my arms as though I were a child.

He set me on the tiles and went to grab some towels for both of us. He gently dabbed at my brow and cheeks before he dropped the white terrycloth into my hands. We mopped down in silence, he still clad in the sopping clothes. From his pockets, he gingerly plucked out his limp wallet, some keys, the hotel keycard, a lighter and a package of very soggy cigarettes. About the cigarettes, I was quite unapologetic.

Squeezing water out of my spongy padded bra, I toweled down as best I could. I had not thought through this escapade carefully. Now I would have to return to my room in damp, clinging underwear. Or maybe not. Some people were still doing the Peeping Tom thing from their lit windows, so I couldn't very well do a repeat of stripping down to my birthday suit. But I *could* put on the shirtdress and remove the offending underthings afterwards.

There were some deft moves I'd learned in my high school locker room to hide my prepubescent body prior to adolescence.

I whipped the bra through the right armhole of my dress and shimmied out of the panties without even having to lift my skirt.

Norman scowled at me as I shoved the clammy balls of red spandex into my handbag. "Great, you get to go commando. Which is stinking hot, by the way. While I get to walk through the lobby like I lost a fight in a barroom brawl, and got pushed into the pool."

"Because you *did*." I gave him my Cheshire cat grin.

He shook his head. "*Merde*, why do I bother with you?"

"Because you like me."

His scowl turned into a grimace, which with some effort could be mistaken for a smile.

He threw his towel on a nearby beach chair and collected his wet things. "You owe me a new wallet and a fresh pack of smokes." The latter he tossed into a nearby trash bin, along with his waterlogged lighter.

"It was worth it." I giggled.

We returned indoors. By now it was almost 4:00 am. We were due at the police station in less than five hours.

We wandered through the lobby. It was starting to see some early morning activity. People stared at Norman in his wet clothes, while I looked more or less normal. We went to the elevator to wait. "So, what was with the midnight stroll?" I asked. "You couldn't sleep either?"

He shook his head. "And after that little sideshow you gave in the pool, I am going to have more than visions of leaping sheep in my head."

CHAPTER
27

Norman escorted me to my room, which was next door to his. He didn't want to talk, but I did. He left me at my door and went to his, and took out his keycard. Little did he know that I had followed and now stood beside him.

I tapped his arm. He swung towards me. "Go to bed, Lucy."

"I'm hungry."

"Honestly. You want to eat?"

His keycard hovered over the locking mechanism. I snatched the card and tapped the lock. The door clicked open. I pushed the door wide, and stepped all the way into the room. He followed me, annoyed.

He sighed, plucked his cellphone off the nightstand, where thank goodness he had left it, otherwise it would have been submerged by my spontaneous decision to dunk him (then he would have been really ticked off at me) to check the time. He raised the receiver to the houseline and tapped for room service.

"What do you want?"

"Smoked salmon benedict."

He ordered two of those, coffee and water.

"And French fries."

"Seriously, Lucy. You want fries with that?"

"Yes."

Norman ordered me into his bathroom while he changed out of his damp pants and shirt. I will admit to sneaking a quick peek through the gap, while he was pulling up his khakis.

Breakfast came quickly and was wheeled in on a white cloth-covered trolley. The waiter laid the food out on the table by the French doors and removed the silver lids but not before dropping a starched linen napkin on my lap. When he left, Norman picked up my plate. "Okay. You're going back to your room."

"Why?"

"You know why. Now leave."

"Fine." I got to my feet and shoved the plate back at him, stomach complaining atrociously, and marched towards the door. I swung around. "Why are you such a jerk?"

He put the plate back down in the space opposite to his on the table. "Okay, you can eat with me."

"I don't want to eat with you. You are impossible. I don't even understand you."

He sat down and tucked into his food. The salmon benedict smelled delicious. And the fries even more so. Why was I having a craving for French fries?

His eyes turned towards mine. Damn him, I was salivating. He pinched a fry off the side plate and waved it at me. He popped it into his mouth. "Yum," he said.

"You are such a jerk."

He rose to his feet. "Duly noted. Come here. Sit down."

"No."

He came to me with another fry between his fingers. "Open up, please."

I scowled. "Now you sound like my dentist."

A glint of amusement appeared on his face. "Why? Does he have a sexy French accent too?"

Crap. I blushed big time. How did he know I found his accent knee-buckling hot?

Oh, screw this. I was starving. I snatched the French fry out of his fingers and shoved it into my mouth. Then I went to the table and sat down.

I dug in. I felt like I hadn't eaten for a week. A quiet chuckle came from Norman. "Guess you weren't kidding when you said you were hungry."

***

Norman yawned. I looked across the table at him. Now what would be perfect was if he would just let me crawl into bed with him.

He recognized the mischief in my eyes. "What other hijinks do you have up your sleeve," he demanded.

"None. I was just wondering if I could borrow a T-shirt to sleep in. I don't have a nightgown. All of my clothes are still in Bagnoregio."

"So are mine."

"I know you have a spare T-shirt. You were wearing it earlier when we were in the volcano."

He sighed. He was doing a lot of that tonight.

He got up and went to the armchair where his old clothes were piled, and disengaged the T-shirt. He shook it out. No dust came from it because he had been wearing a jacket overtop. I knew that, which was why I had asked for it.

He threw it at me. "Can I go to bed now?"

"In a minute. I want to ask you something." I turned my gaze to the connecting door that joined his room with mine. "Why are our rooms connected?"

Norman shrugged. "Ask Luke. He booked the rooms."

"Who is *his* room connected to?"

"What makes you think his room is connected to anybody's?"

"It is, isn't it?"

"I don't know."

"Yes, you do. Your room is connected to mine because *his* is connected to Arianna's suite. Am I correct?" When he remained silent I added, "What does it mean?"

He exhaled louder than I think he had expected to.

"Maybe he's thinking of getting back together with her," I prompted.

"He hasn't said so."

"Does he tell you everything?"

"Pretty much."

I touched his arm. "If he goes back to Arianna, then we can be together. Can't we?"

"I'm not doing that, Lucy."

"But I thought—" How could I possibly be wrong? After what had happened in Bagnoregio and everything else he had done to show me how he felt. No matter how hard he denied it, I knew he felt something. "Why not? What did I do?"

"*You* didn't do anything. It's what *I* did."

I paused. What could he possibly have done? I had been torturing myself with this question ever since our escapade with the Black Madonna in Positano. What was with him and his enigmatic silences? "You're a good man, Norman. I don't care what you say. You couldn't possibly have done anything that bad."

He gently took me by the shoulders and spun me ninety degrees towards the door. Oddly, it was the connecting door I now faced.

"You're a good man, Norman," I repeated.

"Keep thinking that," he said. "Now go to bed. I want to sleep."

I went to the connecting door and opened it. It was loose. The door on the other side was loose, too. I whirled to catch his glance. "Why is my door unlocked?"

His explanation explained nothing. Somehow he had unlocked it.

"Makes it easier for me to get to you if you need me." I made a slight move towards him. He put two fingers to my parted lips. "I don't mean that. I mean if someone tried to break into your room."

Because I had suffered a break-in once before.

I said nothing and passed through the double doors and

into my room, hands full of his soft shirt that smelled delectably of him.

I got ready for bed quickly. Norman had shut his door but I hadn't heard him lock it. I pushed it slightly to confirm that he hadn't. It moved. I left my side unlocked as well. Clad in his T-shirt I went to the queen sized bed and climbed in.

A quiet humming came from the air conditioning. The lights were out and the drapes drawn. Soon it would be light. Was there even any point in closing my eyes?

Everyone had secrets. This whole group of individuals whom I had grown to respect, value, and yep, maybe even love had dark mysteries hidden behind their every thought and action. I wanted so much to belong, to help, to be one of them. I lay on my back and stared at the ceiling. The person I was most curious about was Norman. His every word and behavior told me he had a bad case of hotmosis—and that I was the cause. Then why oh why wouldn't he give in to it? *Yes means yes.* I had done everything including throwing my naked body at him, but still he resisted.

A distinct creak caught my attention. A light tap came at the door between our two rooms. Then Norman's voice, soft and husky with French flavors. "Are you awake?"

I sat up in bed. He stood in the dark, his tall masculine presence overpowering my senses. I believe he was shirtless.

"Is something wrong?" I asked.

"*Zut—*"

That one French syllable turned me to jelly. A shiver of anxiety escaped down my arms.

"I wanted to apologize for what happened earlier. In the pool."

"You mean when you called me a wily little bitch?"

A barely perceptible laugh hung in the darkness. "You understood that?"

"*Si.*" We were in Italy after all. Shouldn't we be practicing our Italian? I had little of the lingo in my lexicon, so it was just as well that we kept it to Franglais.

"No. Well, yeah. That too. You're a darling. You don't have a bitchy bone in your body." And he should know. "I meant I shouldn't have played with you like that. Not in public." The shadow of his head hung low. "Not in private either. We have to stop it. I told you after that illicit tryst we had in Bagnoregio that that was not happening again. I meant it."

Was he ever going to tell me why? Because how was having hot sex with a man you had a bad case for wrong? Even a little bit.

"Good night, Lucy."

"Wait— I can't sleep. Stay with me for a while. I won't molest you. I promise."

A soft chuckle came from his direction. "You have me wrapped around your baby finger."

"I'd like to have you wrapped around more than that."

"Enough with the innuendo. If you want me to stay you have to stop it."

"Sorry. I will. Come and lie down beside me. I just want to feel you next to me. Then I can sleep. Look. You don't have to get under the covers. You sleep on top. I'll stay underneath."

"Worst idea. *Ever.*"

"Please."

He could never resist a 'please'. Not from me. I shifted over while remaining under the blanket. He lay down beside me and crossed his arms over his chest. "You look adorable in my T-shirt by the way."

I snuggled against him. I could see his silhouette. My imagination did the rest.

I looped my arm through his. What I really wanted was for him to wrap himself around me like a pretzel.

I kissed him on the edge of his jaw. Then tucked my head in the muscle of his shoulder. "You're doing a very poor job of not molesting me," he whispered.

"Good night, Norman," I said.

I fell asleep shortly before sunup.

CHAPTER
28

Next day I kept my appointment with the police. I had no chance to speak with Luke alone. God knows we needed to talk, but no one would give us a break.

What relevant information I possessed I gave to the authorities. After taking my statement concerning Sulla Kharim and then another statement over the events of last night, they released me. During my interrogation, Arianna, Luke and Norman had been questioned by other officers and also released. D'Agostino was treated in hospital. His wounds were minor. After that they moved him to the city jail until bail could be set. I found it difficult to hate him or to desire revenge. Sure he had forced me into a crater under gunpoint, but he never had any intention of killing me. He knew the tourists would find me the following day. I would have been rescued. All he had wanted was to keep his bargain with the terrorists so that his family could live another day. I understood what he was going through. Appreciated his sense of hopelessness. Unless we intervened, he was going to prison. And his family was going to die.

"Arianna," I said as we gathered in the lobby of the police station. "If you would just speak to him—"

She cut me off. "Lucy. You are a nice person. Too nice.

D'Agostino is a criminal. End of story."

"He is desperate. He would gladly trade places with his wife and kids if that would save them."

"It won't save them. The militants want him on the outside, fencing the goods so that they can get paid to finance their war. They are terrorists. The only way he can convince them of his loyalty is to hold his family hostage."

"But what if we could get his family out of there?"

"How? I don't have an army. My operatives are trained to protect themselves and to rescue objects. Not people."

"But we could do it."

"Why do you keep saying 'we'? You are not a member of this organization."

"But I would like to be."

She laughed. I guess it was the first she had heard of my ambition. Norman obviously had not let the news leak.

"What do you know about rescuing people?" she inquired.

"Nothing. But I could learn. Arianna, we can't just leave this alone. What use is saving objects, history, heritage, if there are no other generations to appreciate it? People are *dying*." I had used Bruno D'Agostino's own words, used the same inflection and emphasis. He had gotten to me. How could I let this go?

"Why do you care so much? These people are strangers. You only met D'Agostino a few days ago. Is your memory so short? Have you forgotten that he tried to do away with you by dumping you in the bottom of the crater on Mount Vesuvius?"

There was no point in rehashing this again. "He only wanted me out of the way. And just for that night. All he wanted were the frescoes. They are worth a truckload of firearms to the extremists."

Arianna's attention was suddenly drawn elsewhere. Her gaze shot above my head, somewhere on the wall. I followed her visual cues to a flat screen TV mounted in the police station's waiting area. She gently nudged me aside and stepped up closer to the screen. Luke's interest had been attracted as well, and he moved up beside her.

A news channel was on. It was in Italian. No translator was required because I could see from the images on the TV what it was about—another Syrian city in ruins.

"What are they saying?" I asked Norman who had made his way to my side.

"It's a warning that the images to follow are disturbing. *Le immagini sono inquieti.*"

Civilians had been hit with nerve gas; they were foaming at the mouth. Young children crying. Bodies sprawled on the streets.

"It's Palmyra," Arianna said.

The camera panned the scene where a video posted online showed the figure of a hooded militant, flaunting an Ak-47 semi-automatic assault rifle, gloating over his demolition of the city. The next part almost made me shut my eyes. Norman noticed me cringe and drew my head against his chest to block my view. Luke and Arianna stood in front, their backs to us, eyes fixated to the screen, Norman's instinct to protect me hidden from their view. Certainly, he himself was unaware of his own actions. I pulled my head away from his embracing arm, forced myself to watch.

The video was an execution, and Arianna flinched, although she made a heroic effort to conceal it. A gleaming saber came down on a man, who was forced to kneel, and his head was sliced off. Just before that part I *did* turn away, shutting my eyes.

"It's Bruno D'Agostino's father-in-law," Arianna whispered to Luke.

I was close enough behind them to capture their every word.

Luke nodded. He had met Amira and her father, Ahmed al-Hadad, the curator of ancient ruins in Palmyra a few years back. In those days the children were toddlers. Arianna on the other hand was a grad student conducting fieldwork in Syria under his supervision. The bond between teacher and student was immeasurable. Some ties could never be broken—not even by death.

Were those tears in her eyes? Arianna focused on the TV screen as the camera switched back to the militant leader claiming responsibility for the heinous execution. She raised a slender arm and pointed, her voice hard, determined. "Cham Nassar. You will pay for this."

She turned, and headed out of the police station. Luke, Norman and I tracked her to the pavement where Alessandra Piero waited. Piero had been consulting with the local police providing any evidence that was relevant to the events in the Amphitheatre. At the same time she covered any traces that might lead to the discovery of Arianna's illicit rescue organization.

"Did you see the news?" Arianna asked the Interpol agent.

Piero nodded, indicating her phone. "We must act soon. Those trucks of artifacts are hidden in a cave on the desert's edge. We have to get them out of Syria before Nassar sniffs out their location."

"There's been a delay," Arianna said. "The engine has blown on one of the trucks and it's blocking the other. They *can't* get out."

"Then *we* have to get them out."

The two women exchanged meaningful glances. They flashed quick looks around the surrounding buildings. "There's no privacy," Arianna decided. "Let's go to Luke's room to talk. It's the biggest one."

Luke had booked the penthouse suites. They overlooked the city and Mount Vesuvius on one side, and the sea on the other.

His suite had a massive living room. That fact had missed my notice last night. My mind—and body—was on more personal things.

Arianna went straight to the big screen TV and switched it on to search for the news. She found a station reporting the horrific crimes in war-torn Syria. A video captured from

YouTube played, showing a headless body strung up on a Greco-Roman column.

My eyes recoiled briefly before I forced them back. I must watch. If a sight such as this incapacitated me, what use was I in the rescue effort?

Arianna remained standing, sighed.

"He was the curator of ancient ruins in Palmyra, was he not?" Piero asked.

Arianna nodded. "Seventy-eight years old. My dear friend Ahmed al-Hadad protected the ancient ruins of that city for four decades. The extremists hated him. Cham Nassar despised him. Said he was not an Arab worthy of the name if he would not fight for Islam. Ahmed was a saint. Cham Nassar is a monster. He had that fine, gentle, wonderful man murdered!

"Alessandra. How many men do we have to rescue those trucks?"

"Not enough. We need *these* two." Piero raised her arms, and turned to Luke and Norman who were fascinated by the story on the oversized flat screen.

Each one of them, I knew, was worth five ordinary men. Arianna met Luke's eyes square on. "How much does D'Agostino mean to you?"

"We're friends. Or I should say we *were* friends. But after what he put Lucy through—"

She cut him off before he could finish. "Lucy—"

Whatever she meant to ask was irrelevant. I had made up my mind days ago. For years I had been feeling restless. I needed a purpose, something to give my life meaning. Was that why I impulsively went along with Luke when he uprooted my life and transported me across the Atlantic to Italy? At the time I gave it very little thought. I had interpreted my choice as a need for excitement, something to make me feel alive. But was that really the reason? Now that I muddled it over—no. I wanted to do something that mattered. I wanted to rescue Amira D'Agostino and her children. "Please, Arianna. Put me to work."

"It's a dangerous thing you're asking, Lucy. Do you understand what it means? I can't promise you anything. You will not be safe. There are no fancy hotels or expensive restaurants where we're going."

"I have never owned a Chanel suit," I answered.

Arianna tossed her head back and chuckled. "I like you. I like your guts. I am still a little concerned though. You have no training. But you did manage to find those Gorgon heads in a massive museum, and somehow you managed to get yourself out of that crater too. You will be a valuable asset, Lucy, if only for your ingenuity and ideas. But you will still need to be trained. You have to be able to protect yourself." She swung around to find Luke. "Your girlfriend is willing to help us, Luke. What about you?"

A strange recoil jerked in my stomach at Arianna's use of the term 'girlfriend'. How was I Luke's girlfriend? He had behaved excruciatingly un-boyfriend-like ever since the news of his ex's plane crash.

Luke frowned. Whether he disapproved of my vow of service or just thought I was compulsive and foolish remained to be seen. He seemed at a loss for words.

"Depardieu?" Arianna asked, seeking the bodyguard.

Norman had turned away while we were discussing ISORE's next move. He angled back now, dramatically, and studied Arianna. She almost always addressed him by his last name. It was a formality that emphasized the lack of an intimate connection between them. Would that ever change? What kind of history did they have together? Sometimes personalities simply clashed. Was this such a case?

She stared directly at him. He returned the stare. How could these two ever get along? They were so different and yet in many ways the same. Both were strong-willed, independent and single-minded. And yet when it came to the crunch they could cooperate. That was something Luke needed to learn. He was so used to running the show, he refused to forego the microphone and let another person have the stage.

Norman drew out his package of cigarettes. He shook one out. He, too, was intimately affected by the beheading of the Syrian curator. What connection he had with this well respected Arab I doubt I will ever know, but if Norman admired him and regretted his death, then he must be a truly admirable man indeed. "I'll be on the balcony," he said. "But you can count me in."

He left. Arianna faced Luke once more. "Your bodyguard is leaving you to work for *me*. What do you say? I need you, Luke."

One more thing about Luke Trevanian—he is stubborn. I can't always follow his lines of logic or his perception of the world or even his interpretation of human behavior, but one thing was certain. He tried to be on the side of right. In this case, his choice was a struggle. No one wanted to be manipulated by terrorists. And I also realized that his feelings for his ex-wife figured strongly in his decision-making.

He continued to resist. Maybe it was the hangover. It's hard to make decisions when you feel rotten. But Luke never mentioned the unpleasant incident in his room last night. Had it slipped his mind? Seemed to me, Arianna's wellbeing superseded any memory he had of it.

"What do you say, Luke? We could use your help. No—let me rephrase that. ISORE *desperately* needs your help."

"Fine." He released a sound like air escaping a balloon. "You need my money. Okay. You can have it."

She shook her head. "I need *you*. I need your resources, your contacts, and your connections. Your charm. At one time I could slide in and out of Syria as easily as I do in Europe. Things have changed. The borders are blocked. You can get us into the country. I know you can."

She scowled when he failed to respond. No amount of tenacity would make her wheedle with him or seduce him, or turn on her own charm. She was straight, forthright and undeceiving. "I won't lie to you, Luke. This task will be demanding. But that man—that monster Cham Nassar—is the worst enemy of archaeology. He will kill anyone who tries to save it. Our friend Ahmed dedicated his life to preserving historic ruins. He died for the cause. Did you know those Greco-Roman columns—where they strung up his headless body—were ruins that *he* restored? Nassar knows, and he's laughing at the irony. He is bent over double laughing at *us*. How can we let him get away with this? I won't let him. In Ahmed's name I am going to rescue those two army trucks filled with precious historic artifacts and bring them to safety. If it's the *last* thing I do."

Wow. The wonder and admiration I felt for this woman, the total and complete power she seemed have on the people around her. Only Luke was a holdout. But I could see by the tension in his muscles that it wouldn't last much longer.

"Okay—Okay, Arianna. You've broken me. I'm in. But we get D'Agostino's family out first. The artifacts are secondary."

"Agreed." Arianna seemed overjoyed, as overjoyed as someone with her personality could be. It appeared she was about to throw herself into her ex-husband's arms, but checked the impulse almost as soon as she felt it.

I was filled with pride, and something so big, it was indescribable. Arianna had accepted me into her rescue organization. That was the most amazing thing to happen to me in—*ever*.

Luke and Arianna focused on each other while Piero focused on them. I took the opportunity to slip away and joined Norman on the balcony.

He was half-finished a cigarette. I was out of his line of view, behind him. I watched him exhale, and then suck in some more smoke. I wished he would quit. But it wasn't my place to tell him so.

His handsome face was in three quarter profile. He was leaning against the balustrade, his powerful back slightly hunched, elbows braced on the coping, the cigarette clamped between right thumb and forefinger.

The tip of the cigarette blazed orange and then extinguished itself. He blew out a grey circle, smiled, turned fully, and faced me. "Hey." His smoky French accent was soft and reassuring. He crushed out the butt on the balustrade and dropped it below.

"You might hit somebody with that, down there," I chided, moving beside him. I stopped myself from looking for fear of the vertigo. Norman observed me. I made no effort to resist his gaze.

"It was out."

Filthy, dangerous habit. It could kill him. But how was that any of my business? As far as everyone was concerned I was still Luke's girlfriend. I needed to know though, whose girlfriend Norman thought I was.

"Why did you change your mind about working for Arianna?" The answer was irrelevant. What difference did it make? He was entitled to change his mind. I was happy he had. Yet I still wanted to know.

"Who's going to teach you how to handle a gun?" he said.

My lips twitched into a smile. "I'm glad you think I can handle one."

"You're going to have to learn, Lucy." His voice became serious. "This mission is no joke. Why do you think Luke and I have resisted for so long?"

"Don't try to scare me, Norman. I am not going to change my mind."

"I wasn't trying to change it. I'm just trying to protect you."

"Is that your job?" I asked softly.

Norman lowered his eyes. His fingers fumbled at his breast pocket for the cigarettes. I clamped a hand over his to make him stop. I forced him to look at me.

"I want to tell Luke. About us."

"I need a smoke," he said.

"You just had one."

"I need another one."

"Why does it make you so nervous? He has a right to know."

"Luke's decided to join up, hasn't he?" Norman inquired.

"Yes."

"We're going to have to live together in tight quarters when we get to Syria. You heard what Arianna said. No First Class hotels."

"So?"

"I don't think it's in the best interests of the mission."

"Luke only has eyes for Arianna."

"Try telling *him* that."

"You think he doesn't know?"

"I *know* he doesn't know."

"That's why we have to tell him. Well…. *I* have to tell him."

"I think we should wait until we get D'Agostino's family out to safety and those trucks full of artifacts into our hands. We need to have our minds on the job…. Dammit, Lucy. Do you see why I didn't want this to happen?"

Tears were pressing against my eyelids. *Damn you*, I thought. How could someone with such an amazing heart of gold be such a vicious heartbreaker?

His eyes took on a gentleness that made things worse. "Here—I have something for you." He removed the item out of his back pocket. It was a sheet of paper folded twice into a square. "I want you to have this." He handed it to me. "I don't need a reminder of how much—" His voice caught. He cleared his throat. "I'm reminded of that—everyday. Every. Single. Time. I look at you."

He didn't have to tell me what the paper was. I already knew. Slowly, I unfolded it. A teardrop escaped down my cheek.

"Lucy. Please don't."

The lovely sketch of me reflected back in all its sensuous splendor. It was so beautiful and so perfect, and while I wanted him to keep it, I knew why he was giving it to me. He could do others if he wanted to. After all he had drawn this one from memory and a little imagination. But he wanted me to know that my feelings were reciprocated despite the fact that our feelings for each other were forbidden.

"Lucy. I wouldn't have given it to you if I thought it would make you cry."

I sucked up a sniffle. "It's all your fault. Why do you have to be like this?"

"Like what?"

"I don't even have the words to describe what you are."

At that moment I saw a shadow emerge from the doorway. Norman's body blocked the intruder's view. I quickly refolded the drawing and shoved it into an exterior pocket of my handbag.

Luke stepped onto the balcony and approached. "Private party? Or can anyone join in?"

I scrubbed my jaw of salty tears, and forced myself to smile.

"Can I talk to you for a minute?"

"Sure," I said, swallowing back the emotion.

Norman took the cue to exit, although every nerve in my body willed him to stay.

Luke took my hand. He frowned slightly. Had he noticed the tears? I shoved the emotion to the back of my mind. "Are you sure about joining ISORE?"

I nodded. "I really think I can help."

"I have no doubt that you can. But you're not really cut out for it. You have no idea what you're in for. The living conditions—"

"I'll get use to it. Norman said he would train me."

"About Norman."

Here it was: my opportunity to get everything out in the open.

"There's something you need to know about him."

I stared. What could it possibly be? Why would he think that it would matter to me, unless... unless... he already knew about us?

"First I want to apologize for last night. I was drunk. I don't know how I got so inebriated. But it won't happen again. I'm sorry if I hurt you, Lucy."

"You didn't hurt me, Luke. It was an accident. I tripped on the rug and fell."

"Good. Not that you tripped, but that I didn't hurt you. I was worried that I'd—"

"You didn't."

"You don't have to work for Arianna, you know. I can fly you home on a moment's notice. I know this trip to Italy was miles from what you were expecting. It was hardly what *I* was expecting."

I reached up and hugged him around the neck. Why did I do that? I was suddenly filled with an uncontrollable affection for him. That was why it was so painful. I felt his arms come around me, and my sixth sense told me that Norman on the other side of the glass doors watched us. Was Arianna watching? Oh, how did she really feel about her ex?

I stepped back before things could get more intimate. I was one troubled and confused woman. Maybe Norman was right and we should put everything on the back burner. The important thing at the moment was rescuing D'Agostino's family.

"Luke, can you tell me something?" I asked.

"Sure, honey. What is it?"

"Why did you change your mind? About ISORE I mean?"

"I saw how Ahmed's death affected Arianna. She can be headstrong. I have to go to Syria to keep her from being killed."

And Norman had to go to keep *me* from being killed.

I sighed. I did not know how any of this was going to work out in the end. But it seemed, at the moment, we were all on the same page.

Now read on for a taste of the next exciting book in the Fresco Nights saga.

MIDNIGHT IN PALMIRA

CHAPTER
1

This was a predicament to beat all predicaments. How to appease my sister? She had no idea of my daredevil escapades in Positano and Pompeii. And she certainly would be alarmed to learn where those last two incidents had taken me.

Colleen's whiter-than-white teeth beamed from my phone's screen. She was ribbing me good-naturedly to give her all the dirt on my relationship with Luke Trevanian. Should I tell her the truth? That it wasn't the intrepid billionaire archaeologist I was gaga over, and that the reason for my current speech impediment and red face was, in fact, his bodyguard? I cleared my throat, sneaked a glance. As always, Norman's presence gave me a sensation of pleasure mixed with nervousness. He sat across from me in the VIP lounge at the Naples-Capodichino International Airport. Luke was busy somewhere with airport officials, using his influence to schedule a spur-of-the moment flight plan for his jet. We were waiting for Arianna Chase, our boss, and the head of the International Save Our Ruins Effort.

"I want the dirt. I know you, Lucy. Have you rubbed nubs, yet?"

I muffled a chuckle. It was usually me doing the smut

talk. Not that I had all that much to talk about. But more than *her*—since *she* had a husband, and was into her fifth month carrying my highly anticipated niece.

"Oh, come on. Humor me. I'm *married*. I'm not *dead*."

"Cliché." I groaned.

"All the more reason to humor me."

Fine. "He—*he* is amazing." Knew how to tickle all of my buttons. And *then* some. I sighed. Dare I share more? Colleen thought I was talking about Luke. I wasn't. My voice had gone very quiet. Had Norman heard me? He was acting blasé, reading something on his phone. As usual. I wanted desperately to tell my sister how I felt about Norman. But he was sitting right there, flashing the occasional sexy look my way. Okay, maybe he didn't mean for the glance to appear sexy. But damn it, it was.

"Where are you anyways?" she demanded when I stifled a moan. "Looks like some kind of fancy lounge. Flash your phone around so I can see."

"No. That would be rude."

"Rude? Rude to whom? Is lover-boy there? I can't see him." The guests of the VIP lounge were mostly rich people like Luke and Arianna. "Are you at an airport? It looks like you're at an airport lounge! A really fancy airport lounge! Lucy, where are you going?"

Think fast. "I'm in Naples. We're waiting for our flight." *True. All true.*

"What are you doing in Naples?" Colleen's pink-painted lips twisted with the query.

"There was a conference. ICOM."

She was familiar with the acronym. International Council of Museums. Her husband, the classics curator Shaun Templeton worked with me at my museum in Toronto. "Oh, right. So it's over? You're headed back?"

I mumbled something that could be a Yes or a No depending on one's interpretation. I felt rather hot and betrayed both by Norman's nearness and by my half-truths. I never lied to my sister. Well... *almost* never. I glanced up, semi-rose from my slouched position in the VIP armchair. Norman's eyes were fixed on something behind me. Curious, I turned to look.

Not surprisingly I saw one of the most sophisticated and attractive women I'd ever seen. No, it wasn't Arianna Chase—although she would qualify for the description. This woman was no one I had ever seen before, but clearly such was not the case for Norman. A confident smile appeared on her unblemished face. I switched to catch Norman's expression. He had a look of discomfort (anger?) and—what—disdain?

Getting flustered, I thought: Who the hell *was* she?

"Hey, I've got to go, Colleen. They're calling our flight." *Another half-truth. Crap. No. Another out-and-out lie.*

Norman had risen to his feet. He appeared more edgy than ever which only served to stir my interest. He looked as though he wanted to escape and would have taken off right then and there, had I not lurched out of my seat, both hands outstretched, and tackled his arm. "Where do you think *you're* going?"

"Let go. I need to visit the little boy's room."

Hardly. He was not getting off that easy. The woman's gaze was fixed on Norman and she was rapidly approaching. Too late. She was standing right in front of us.

He knew this woman. *Intimately.* I glanced from his face to hers and back again as they greeted each other.

"*Hé.*" Norman muttered. He had used a very colloquial French term, the equivalent of 'Yo' or 'Hey' in English.

"Well, hello, Norman Depardieu. You were the last person I was expecting to see. Fancy meeting you here." The woman's eyes flicked back and forth as she swiftly scanned the room. "Where's the boss?" She was clearly familiar with Norman's relationship with Luke.

There was no sign of the billionaire so she returned her gaze to Norman. Norman ignored the question. "So *chéri*, what brings you to Italy?" She moved forward to give him the European traditional kiss on each cheek, but he recoiled. The reaction was so obvious that my jaw dropped slightly. "Oh, come now. Surely we can be friends?" She flashed him a dazzling smile, a perfect cheekbone-to-cheekbone smile that was usually only seen on Miss America contestants. What was going on here? I wanted to ask but neither of them acknowledged my existence. Norman's response was almost a snarl.

"Fine. Have it your way." The stranger's long sultry lashes dipped toward me. I was still clinging possessively to Norman's arm.

She was about to introduce herself to me when Norman spoke up. "This is my wife."

My eyes popped out of my head—talk about gobsmacked—but I forced my metaphorical eyeballs to return to their metaphorical eye sockets.

An exquisitely dry smile. "Your wife?" Why did she sound incredulous? Why *couldn't* I be his wife? "And *I* am Gillian—" An announcement came over the PA system interrupting her. She returned my handshake, made a superficial apology. "That's my flight. Nice to meet you— Mrs. Depardieu." There was no missing the subtle sarcasm. "Wish I had more time to chat—" And then without further comment, she left with a click of stylish high-heels and a swivel of her classy, mauve pencil skirt.

Norman stared at her back like he couldn't believe his eyes. Who *was* Gillian and why did she have this effect on him? I realized I had looped one hand through his elbow, while the other still clutched my phone. I shoved the phone into my handbag. Had he just told that woman I was his *wife?*

The pallor of his skin deepened slightly as he caught my eye. He gave me that amused twinkle that was typical Norman. It was as though he had said aloud: *It had the desired effect. And now, may I have my arm back?* Oh yeah, he had a way of turning the tables on me. It should have been him who was mortified not me.

"Why did you want her to think I was your wife?" I demanded. Not that the idea was repulsive to me.

"It's not important."

Clearly it was.

"*Alors*, here come Luke and Arianna."

Switching to French was not going to pacify me. Believe me. Not this time. No one called me his wife without an explanation.

"Let it go, Lucy," he whispered as Luke waved. He gestured for us to follow them out a side door. Which I presumed led to the runway and the location of our private jet.

I should make it clear at this point that we were *not* returning to Positano, contrary to what I had allowed Colleen to presume.

Once aboard the aircraft I made sure I sat next to Norman. Luke seemed not to notice. He and Arianna, conspiring over an event we intended to crash in Aleppo, sat ahead of us. I was so obsessed with what had happened in the airport lounge that I paid no attention. Nor did the opulent amenities of Luke's Boeing 747-8 VIP private jet make much impression. I remember noticing the color palette: white, grey and taupe. Cool, elegant colors that reminded me of just how much this plane must cost. I was beginning to take for granted the comfort of the armchairs, leather sofas, marble bathroom with standup shower and dining room. But at the moment it all took a backseat to what was nagging at me.

"Wife?" I said.

He glanced around surreptitiously. Then let his lids lower until his irises embraced mine. "She was nobody I wanted to remember. My reference to you—in the way I referred to you—was to make certain she understood."

"I see." Although I did not.

There were very few times when Norman expressed anger. I knew that whoever Gillian was she was important. I patted him lightly on the hand. All right. I would let it go for now. He leaned over and let his lips brush the top of my hair.

This act was ostensibly to look out the window, which was to my left. He sat on my right, and needn't have been so cautious. No one was looking.

I turned to the window. It was going to be approximately a three-hour flight from Naples to Aleppo. The event we intended to crash was an award ceremony for the Syrian First Lady at the Hôtel Baron. Alessandra was meeting us there. Apparently she had news.

I made myself comfortable on the cushy, beige, leather armchair when my phone dinged. I realized I had not set the thing to 'airplane mode'. Before I did, I stole a quick glimpse at the text. *Argh.* Colleen. She had no patience when it came to her baby sister. Just wait until my poor niece was born. The little tyke was in for nonstop mothering for the rest of her life.

***

We dressed in the comfort of private chambers on the jet. I had brought a knee-length, black cocktail dress, nothing too attention-grabbing. Arianna had warned that we must not draw attention to ourselves. This event was a propaganda stunt created by the Syrian president's team to try to convince his countrymen that his government was good.

For our part the politics could either aid or thwart our purpose. We must avoid any entanglement with the civil war. We were here to get news of Bruno D'Agostino's family who had been coerced by threat of death to help the Islamic extremists in their black market trade of precious artifacts.

The Hôtel Baron had a checkered history. At one time it was the most luxurious hotel in Syria. It was certainly the oldest. It had hosted the likes of Lawrence of Arabia, famed mystery writer Agatha Christie, French president Charles de Gaulle, the American billionaire David Rockefeller, and President Theodore Roosevelt and First Lady Edith. Other notable guests were European royalty. During the Syrian civil war, the hotel was bombed five times. Most of the rebels had been chased out of Aleppo, although cells still existed, and distant mortar fire was testimony to this fact. But the current president's wife wanted to make a grand gesture and encourage refugees to return.

And this was how she planned to do it? I gazed around at the opulence that had been restored. The hotel was small by any measure as it was built at the turn of the last century. But to show her respect for history, the character of the architecture was retained. A great ballroom had been added on an additional floor, and this was where the event was taking place.

I noticed that the Syrian president was not present at the event. However security was impeccable and soldiers with automatic weapons stood guard at every entryway. I realized as I stood anonymously amongst the one hundred or so guests that this had become a way of life for Syrians.

Arianna, with Luke's help, was on the guest list; the rest of us came as entourage.

"There's Piero," Norman said.

Alessandra Piero, the former Interpol agent, was dressed appropriately in a mid-calf sheath dress with a jacket to cover her shoulders. Arianna, gorgeous and stylish in grey and black with a cashmere pashmina over her arms, greeted her. She sent a look our way. This meant that whatever Intel Alessandra had was to be relayed to Norman and myself. Luke and Arianna must appear completely engaged in this event. They could not be seen to be speaking to anyone less than members of the royal family and their A-list guests.

I glanced over Alessandra's shoulder as she approached. The long, rectangular windows behind her were dressed in dusty rose velvet. Crystal chandeliers hung from the vaulted ceiling. The floors were of polished marble and mosaic. Rumor had it that the First Lady had donated millions of dollars renovating this hotel. This floor alone cost millions.

Hence the celebration and the award. Which just happened to be a pendant made of gold. It was not yet safe to reopen the hotel to the public. "But," she said. "One day soon it will be. And we will be ready to bring prosperity back to

Syria. The renovation of this hotel is symbolic of the future."

The president's men gave the signal to applaud and the media that were permitted to cover the event began to snap photos. "The First Lady of Hell," Alessandra said under her breath. I glanced up in surprise. Alessandra normally kept her opinions to herself.

Mrs. President was quite beautiful in her own right. In fact everyone present fell into that category to some degree. She was dressed in a semi-formal royal blue dress with a white and blue scarf around her neck. Ironically, she did not cover her head or arms as most local women did. The contrast to the ragged, dirty inhabitants that I had witnessed on the drive into town was startling. No wonder the people had rebelled.

And this. This grand gesture was not going to cut it.

"Any sightings of the family?" Norman asked Alessandra. His voice was barely audible.

The ex-Interpol agent nodded. "Good news. Amira D'Agostino is alive. She has been seen."

"Where?" Norman asked.

Before Alessandra could answer, movement caught my eye. A woman had walked past near the center of the ballroom. I recognized the pencil skirt. The mauve color. It was not a shade that most people could pull off. I recognized the shapely hips and killer legs in high heels. I forgot to excuse myself, and both Norman and Alessandra noticed as I jerked around to see if it was really her—the woman from the airport.

Norman grabbed my arm when he saw her, too. I knew he saw her, although he denied it when I asked him.

"I didn't see anyone in a mauve pencil skirt," he said. "What *is* a pencil skirt?"

Alessandra's eyes flickered from mine to his. "It's a tight, straight skirt meant to enhance the female form," she answered disdainfully.

I saw her. I know I saw her.

The formal part of the afternoon was ending. The First

Lady was lauded with praises for her generosity and charitable work. She tossed her expensively tinted blonde hair. The master of ceremonies likened her to a Syrian 'Princess Diana.'

I heard Norman snort. It was not loud and I was certain it was inaudible to everyone around us. But I had heard it. I was beginning to see what all the fuss was about. Mrs. President could go back to her billion-dollar palace in Damascus with her personal assistants and bodyguards. But her people were stuck here. In war torn Aleppo. I almost laughed at the fact that she had poured so much money into refurbishing this hotel. Her final words came over the microphone as she took her bows—and her leave of her guests. "The war in Aleppo is over," she said.

"Liar," Norman whispered under his breath.

I went to one of the windows and glanced out. This hotel and the streets outside were not of the same world.

Thank you for reading *Pompeii at Dusk*, Book Two of the Fresco Nights Saga. If you enjoyed this book and the series, please leave a review on Amazon. It will help spread the word. The fun doesn't end here! Book Three is now available.

Fresco Nights
(Fresco Nights Saga Book One) – Deborah L. Cannon

Billionaire archaeologist Luke Trevanian and his sexy bodyguard Norman Depardieu seduce museum illustrator Lucy Racine into their shadowy world. Is it the end of her routine life? Yes! These are two mysterious men with dark pasts. She is attracted to both. They have the bodies of athletes, the charm of gentlemen and the alluring ways of con artists. Are they also a pair of crooks smuggling priceless artifacts? Lucy refuses to believe it until Luke whisks her off on his mega yacht to Italy's romantic Amalfi Coast. Their purpose is to dig up Italian frescos. Instead she digs up his past. That past involves a Black Madonna worth millions of dollars on the black market. Art thieves and Interpol are racing to get their hands on it. Will Luke's name be cleared of the theft? Can Lucy love a man with a shady past, whose ex-wife just happens to be her boss? Or is it the bodyguard she loves? Sometimes the heart doesn't know what it wants. In the heat of the night and the cold of murder, Lucy must decide what she wants.

Pompeii at Dusk
(Fresco Nights Saga Book Two) – Deborah L. Cannon

At a fancy museum gala in Naples, Lucy Racine and boyfriend billionaire archaeologist Luke Trevanian get bad news. The guest speaker has been killed in a plane crash on the cliffside of a small Italian village. The crash victim is not only Lucy's boss but also Luke's ex-wife Arianna Chase! Luke insists that Arianna is still alive. New information suggests the plane was sabotaged because of a stolen Medusa. Arianna is not dead after all. She is the prisoner of a local smuggler. Now Luke is hell-bent on rescuing his ex. Is he still in love with her? Her suspicious behavior points Lucy to a smuggling racket that trades antiquities for guns. An underground network running from Syria to Pompeii leads straight to Luke's ex-wife. Confronted with the truth about Arianna's shadowy activities, Lucy turns to Norman. He is the only person she trusts, and the man she secretly loves. In this second installment of the Fresco Nights saga Lucy's life is about to change when she uncovers a terrorist plot with roots deep in the Middle East.

Midnight in Palmyra
(Fresco Nights Saga Book Three) – Deborah L. Cannon

Lucy Racine and her partners in crime, billionaire archaeologist Luke Trevanian and his bodyguard are recruited into a secret organization. What is ISORE? The International Save Our Ruins Effort. What is their mission? To save a woman curator and her two children from terrorists, and to intercept a convoy of artifacts from Syria bound for Europe's black market. The terrorists are relentless. They kill the woman curator. Now her children's lives are at stake. Lucy works in close quarters with Luke and Norman to plan the children's release. Can Lucy hide her desire for the bodyguard? He has sworn to protect her. He is devastated when she is kidnapped. Now Lucy's skills for survival are tested to the brink. The threat to her life exposes the heart-wrenching rivalry between her two heroes. But true confessions must wait until Lucy escapes the terrorists, and the team moves in to reclaim Palmyra's historical ruins and the lost children.

Baghdad before Dawn
(Fresco Nights Saga Book Four) – Deborah L. Cannon

An explosion in the tunnel of the Palmyra museum has collapsed on top of Lucy Racine's new love Norman Depardieu after he rescues a kidnapped Syrian girl doomed to be a terrorist's bride. To make matters worse, Lucy's pregnant sister learns of Lucy's new job saving antiquities from war zones. Horrified by the news, she arrives in Syria to bring Lucy home. Lucy must avoid her sister at all costs. There is hope that Norman survived the blast. A man meeting Norman's description is sighted among the militants in the desert. Why doesn't he return to the ISORE base? Lucy's love for the brave rescuer has her desperate to find him. But before the team can infiltrate the terrorist stronghold, Lucy is inside their camp. She faces a terrifying reality. Has Norman turned to the enemy side? Is he working for them? He doesn't recognize her. But one thing she does learn—all is not as it seems. Norman has a private agenda. It has to do with the Winged Bulls of Nineveh, which is in a stolen truck on its way to Baghdad. The greatest test of Lucy's strength comes in the thrilling fourth installment of the Fresco Nights series.

Acknowledgements

They say you never forget your first love. The same can be said of your first writing teacher. A warm thank-you to author Carolyn Niethammer. Carolyn was my first fiction instructor and was always constructive and encouraging in her comments on my work. I am so pleased that we reconnected on Facebook and that she continues to follow my writing career as I do hers. When I did a writing course with her, oh so many years ago, little did I know where it would lead me! Thanks, also, to Goodreads fans of *Fresco Nights* who have made writing this sequel a joy. And as always, my never-ending gratitude to my husband for eagerly accompanying me on my adventures in my books *and* in real life.

About the Author

Deborah L. Cannon is a novelist and short story writer. She writes under three names: Deborah L. Cannon under which the Fresco Nights novels are written, Deborah Cannon under which are published The Raven Chronicles series and her Chinese epic fantasy, *The Pirate Empress*, and Daphne Lynn Stewart who writes a series of Christmas romances for pet lovers. She is also a contributor to the *Chicken Soup for the Soul* franchise. She lives in Hamilton, Ontario with her archaeologist husband near the Royal Botanical gardens lakeside.

Made in the USA
Middletown, DE
18 February 2023